Norma
Ever After

a novel

Nancy Baxter

BALLANTINE BOOKS
NEW YORK

A Ballantine Books Trade Paperback Original

Published in the United States by Ballantine Books, an imprint of The Random House Publishing Group, a division of Random House, Inc., New York.

BALLANTINE and colophon are registered trademarks of Random House, Inc.

Library of Congress Cataloging-in-Publication Data
Baxter, Nancy.
    Norma ever after / Nancy Baxter.
        p.   cm.
    "A Ballantine Books trade paperback original"—T.p. verso.
    ISBN 0-345-47914-9
    1. Americans—Scotland—Fiction.   2. Orkney (Scotland)—
Fiction.   3. Single women—Fiction.   I. Title.
PS3602.A983N67 2005
813'.6—dc22   2004060878

Printed in the United States of America

www.ballantinebooks.com

9 8 7 6 5 4 3 2 1

First Edition

Book design by Mercedes Everett

To my Venus Circle

Norma
Ever After

CHAPTER 1

Once upon a time, specifically *our* time, there lived an ordinary commoner named Norma Dale. Norma Dale, hovering near thirty, had not given up on finding passion, or even romance. She had never *expected* passion, or even romance. Not since puberty and the retirement of her single Ken doll and his harem of Barbies.

First, it was the name thing. For this, she blamed her mother. There was simply no excuse. Her mother had come up with Madeline for her first girl, and Norma's younger sister was named a perfectly decent Bethany, so why had her mother dried up so thoroughly in the middle?

Mrs. Dale, herself named Elizabeth, had never acknowledged her choice as bland.

"Norma is a fine name, Norma," she would say. Oblivious. Compounding.

"Norma is an *aunt* name," Norma would counter. "Like smelly lavender and rotten old lace. Why didn't you name me Myrtle and be done with it?"

"Myrtle *is* lovely," her mother would say, "I believe your

father had a great-aunt Myrtle." (At this point Norma's father would look over and wink.) Then her mother would drift off for a moment and resurface with, "Marilyn Monroe was named Norma, wasn't she, Norma? She was such a beautiful girl."

Norma had neither the luxury of a movieland fantasy machine nor the fallback of a decent middle name, being seconded with the imageless "Lynn." In middle school she had made the inevitable attempt to change her persona—in this case she simply dropped the *m* from her name and tried for a while to be "Nora."

Ah, glamorous Nora. She of the emerald green eyes and chestnut hair. The slender ankle and cocky little hat, she of snappy banter and the devastating flirt.

We *were* talking middle school, however. Poor Nora was suffered her *m* back in short and humiliated order.

Norma's hair *was* chestnut, by the way—when freshly washed and highlighted by a bright overhead sun. Her eyes *were* green, or at least there were green flecks in the brown when viewed in the same bright sun on the days that she wore her one green blouse. A blouse that didn't look too good with her skin, which couldn't take too much of that sunlight, which was okay, because the cute guy was never going to be standing there in the first place to gaze upon her undiscovered beauty. The cute guy would always be off with Ashley or Jessica or one of the other girls whose mothers had not cursed them with a bad name or used up all the good genes on their popular and happy sisters.

There. The second cause of nonexpectations of passion. Or even romance.

Norma was not ugly, she wasn't even plain. She had sometimes wished for plain, this during hours gazing into the bathroom mirror of scrutiny and shame. Plain you could work with. Plain was a blank canvas on which to build—blue hair, nose ring for the Goth, perfect makeup for the prep, even scrubbed and healthy for the jock.

No, Norma's problem was that she was pretty, but pretty from another time.

She'd had that epiphany one night during a sleepover. She and her non-Ashley, non-Jessica friends were up at two in the morning in their powder pink and pony purple sleeping bags watching late-night cable TV. The movie was black-and-white, an old musical with that rubbery-faced guy with the popped-out eyes, who sang and danced and dressed in embarrassing black-guy drag. Set in ancient Hollywood Rome, one of the big dance numbers involved hundreds of naked slave-babes concealed only by their chains and long blond wigs.

Norma's friends were making hilarious fun of the corny old erotica, but Norma had sat there, stunned. That was *her* body, under the wigs and chains. *Her* face. Heart-shaped, with Cupid's-bow lips, big round eyes, and a little beak of a nose. Like Betty Boop. But on Betty it looked good. Betty could *do* the chunky little thighs and tiny feet. Short waist, custard-cup breasts. And she was "Betty," right? She wasn't Norma Boop.

Norma's decline of self-esteem had been slow but thorough throughout the tortured trail of her teens. The night of the sleepover had marked the bottoming out of her expectations. So she had settled. She'd dated the geeks and the dweebs who'd settled with and dated her.

But her virginity had not been lost to a dweeb, but to the king of her high school prom.

Trey Bliss. He was the boy of her dreams. Every night. Attainable until the radio clock shattered the gossamer screen. So cute it hurt. So blond. Such blue eyes. A body to die for. Captain of the soccer team, lead in the school play, president of the senior class, all that jazz—but cool—got into trouble, even. Cute trouble. He and Ashley had been going together since middle school. Ashley, who was the queen, wore Trey's promise ring on her tanned and slender finger.

Norma went to the prom with Ricky Pierce. King of the chess club. Greasy glasses. Sweaty palms. Hair too curly. Shaped like a Bosc pear. His rented tuxedo didn't improve on that.

Norma thought she was looking good. (Though her father had been the only one to say so.) Not "Nora" good, but close. She'd found a shade of green satin for her gown that worked (almost) for her skin and her eyes, and her hair had been done in a soft wave, offsetting (almost) the roundness of face. She was having a good time at the prom. (Almost.)

She and Ricky had shuffled around a bit on the dance floor and then he had mercifully gone off to join the pocket of other dweebs. Norma stood for a while on the edge of things, hoping for a miracle, then gave up. At least this phase of the torture was almost over and she could go away to college. A thousand miles away from here, a thousand miles away from these people.

The music stopped and the spotlights circled and landed on the stage. Trey and Ashley were about to be crowned into their cheesy but oh-so-coveted high school royalty. Norma couldn't take it. She left the rented ballroom with its rented glitter and its rented lights. Magical lights and magical glitter that would never fall on a girl named Norma with her prettiness out of time.

Consequently she missed the big fight.

She never found out what had started it, and later it didn't matter, but the newly crowned king and queen of the prom had a royal falling-out. Words—bad words—were exchanged on the dance floor. A crown was hurled, a designer dress was ripped. There were tears and screams, accusations, and one delicious slap, all played out in front of the extreme appreciation of the entire student body.

Except the Betty Boop body of Norma Dale.

Norma had left the hotel ballroom by then. The town was too small for a fleet of taxis to accommodate her dramatic (though unwitnessed) exit. It was also safe, so she decided to walk home. Her heels were too high, of course, but she didn't really care. Pain would be a welcome thing on which to concentrate. Halfway home, when the pain had gone way past its welcome, she heard the roar of a combustion engine and then the screech of braking tires.

It was him. Trey Bliss. In his throbbing muscle car of iridescent ultramarine.

He'd popped the door, flashed his killer smile, and said to hop in.

She'd hopped.

Yes, she'd hopped. How could she not? Here he was—her knight on four shiny new Michelins.

His custom-cut tuxedo jacket was gone. His tastefully ruffled white shirt was torn, a portion of his hard and smooth perfectly formed Trey Blissian chest exposed, and across it ran three bloody red trails of Ashleyesque claws. He was drunk. His handsome hand clutched a half-empty bottle of Herradura Silver, the remaining half of which was graciously offered.

She took it.

Yes, she took it. How could she not? Here it was—her dream incarnate—Trey Bliss in the slightly damaged flesh, all for herself.

Norma had never tasted tequila before. She took a sip. It was good. Kind of salty. She lifted the bottle to her Cupid's-bow lips and took a big manly slug.

Trey Bliss had said, "Atta girl," and then laughed. He'd thrown back his head and howled. He'd gunned the engine and taken the bottle back for a big manly slug himself and they had roared off into the night.

Years later, on the very few occasions of sharing the story of her "first," Norma would always say, "The rest was a blur—I woke up in the motel room the next morning and I was no longer a virgin." She would then give what she hoped was a knowing and sophisticated smile. But it was a lie. There was no blur. Despite the tequila, despite the hot hormonal rush and fervor of their teenage coupling, she remembered every detail. Every word. Every touch. Every sensation. Everything.

He'd taken her there without asking. It wasn't a cheap motel. It was nice. With carpeting in the lobby and nice potted palms. The room number was 323. The big double bed had cream-colored sheets, and the bedspread was a pleasant stripe of taupe and gold. There were two pictures on the walls. Matched. Botanical prints of ferns with close-ups of the seed pods and unreadable cursive script. Two chairs, prints of taupe and gold, and a round dark wood table between them. (The tequila bottle had been on that table in the morning, on its side, sticky and hollow.)

Trey had kissed her then. A long, drunken, tongue-thrusting kiss, with his arms tight around her and his hard-on pressed up between her legs.

Norma tried to kiss back—but he was doing enough kissing for the both of them, so she just melted into his arms. He stripped her. Not expecting a steamy encounter with Ricky, the king of chess, her underwear was woefully unsexy, but it didn't stay on long enough to matter. Trey gathered her, melted and trembling, and lay her on the bed. He ripped his shirt open all the way, exposing the full glory of his wound, ripped off his cummerbund with one hand, and with the other zipped open his pants.

Norma's virginity didn't put up much of a struggle. Later, she would wonder whether he even knew what he had taken. But that evening, all she knew was the wonder of Trey Blissian manhood. He was good, and it was years and many disappointments before she understood to what extent. The first thirty seconds, though, were pretty much about the Trey, for the Trey, and nothing but the Trey. Norma had barely gotten started when he grunted—manfully—and collapsed on top of her. For the next thirty seconds she lay gasping under his cologne-drenched bulk—bewildered and beginning on the bothered part. And then Trey did what eighteen-year-old boys do best—he retumefied—rather splendidly and right inside her.

Norma let out a soft cry of surprise. Trey lifted up on muscled arms and flashed her his grin.

"This one's for you, baby," he said, and began to move.

Until then she hadn't been really sure what an orgasm was. The next ten minutes thoroughly honed the definition.

The third time was for Trey again—but that was okay, she was getting the hang of things by then. After that they took a short break while they finished off the tequila, and there was a wonderful few minutes of breast-fondling, drunken nuzzling, and sweet talk. Well, one sweet sentence, anyway. He had his mouth full at the time, and Norma wasn't sure if he said, "You're so pretty," or "They're so pretty," but she wasn't going to quibble. Then he flipped her over and she discovered, intensely, the thrill of coming from behind.

But halfway through fourthsies Trey slowed way down, then stopped moving altogether—which was just as well. By then she was getting a tad sore, and the fern prints on the wall above her hands had begun the Herradura swirl. Trey fell off of her and onto his pillow—he had passed clean out. Norma let go of the wall and sat back, knees folded to the side like the White Rock girl, and watched him. Watched Trey Bliss as he snored—beautifully—next to her on the bed. The bed where she, Norma Dale, had made love—repeatedly—with him—Trey Bliss—the boy of her dreams.

Eventually she lay down, too, and finally fell asleep, wondering what the hell she would say to the boy of her dreams in the morning.

That problem never arose.

In the morning—mid-morning, it was—the rattle of the maid's cart two doors down woke Trey up first. His movement woke Norma. She opened her eyes to the wonder of his Trey Blissian back and the edge of his Trey Blissian butt. His blond hair was sticking out all over and his head was bent to his handsome hands.

Norma rose to one elbow, acutely aware of her nakedness and the out-of-reach sheets twisted at the foot of the bed. Her movement stirred him to turn slowly around. Bleary blue eyes widened and he spoke the words that would haunt her for the next dozen years.

"Oh, no," Trey Bliss had said, *"not you."*

To his credit, he was instantly sorry, which only made it worse. He apologized and said he hadn't meant it like that, but Norma knew. She wasn't Ashley, she wasn't even Jessica. She was Norma, the oh-no, not-you girl. In the naked light of dawn—well, mid-morning—it was all so perfectly clear.

She scrambled from the bed, a dried smear of blood down her thigh, and scrambled in horrid awkwardness for her unsexy panties and her unsexy bra. Her prom dress was hellish. The texture and color of generic canned peas. Ricky's browning pink carnations crouched on the bodice like a knot of dying tooth fairies. Norma struggled into the dress, hearing but not hearing Trey's pitying words. There was something about breakfast—something about a ride—something about "don't be ridiculous of course I'll take you home." Then her too-high heels were on her bare feet—panty hose abandoned for the giggles of the maids—and she was out and away from him, the door closed on the worst moment of her life.

There were, however, many more and much worse to come. Fate had taken notice of Norma Lynn Dale.

CHAPTER 2

A thousand miles away actually helped a lot. Norma found a college in a fairly big city. Her mother, with an implied "something to fall back on since you won't find a decent husband like Madeline did and Bethany is bound to," advised her to get an MBA, so she chose Liberal Arts. This, of course, was a complete waste of her tuition. After graduation she shared tiny apartments with others of her ilk for a couple of years and then managed to find herself a well-paying job. This bit of luck came out of left field—she found herself doing research for a firm of professional genealogists. It was nothing for which she had prepared herself, or even anything in which she was interested, but she was good at it, and the position had excellent health coverage, plus dental.

Norma spent most of her days hunched in front of microfiche machines or library computers, and occasionally turning the giant pages of dusty old record books in dusty old courthouses, deciphering undecipherable script of long-dead clerks.

Her love life during college hadn't been all that bleak.

Her slate was shiny clean (almost), and college people, being a few steps closer to the great real world, are a lot more forgiving. Or perhaps there was just a wider range of geeks and dweebs from which she had to choose.

After college—well, after college the fun part of bleak pretty much dried up.

Norma had herself another epiphany about four years down the road. She was spending a lot of time researching a large and extremely dull clan, who seemed to have thought the name Edward to be serviceable unto the hundreds. There was a man—a reasonably handsome man—who always occupied the library computer three computers down.

He was youngish, with gold-red hair. His eyes, just a bit squinty, were an interesting coyote shade of brown, and he always had an attractive blush of red across his cheeks. He was tall, but not stooped, and hours of sitting—Norma observed on his treks to the bathroom—had not yet turned his butt to mush.

Unlike the usual example of the male species of genealogists, who were generally old, balding, half blind, stoopshouldered, flat-assed, and invariably colored gray, the man was a hunk.

Glances were exchanged several times a day for a week. Norma started taking a little more time with her makeup and clothes. On the eighth day (and the 237th Edward) Norma got up to go to the stacks. These were on the third floor, shelves and shelves and more shelves of microfiche boxes in a maze both dark and secluded. She had a box of microfiche to return, and on the way a long glance was exchanged with the redheaded man.

Several steps past him, Norma heard the scrape of a chair, and her heart quickened. She didn't turn, but she knew he was going to follow. She climbed the wide staircase to the third floor. There were return carts about but she passed these by and entered the maze of shelves. She could hear footsteps behind her.

Norma felt a quiver of excitement and then felt silly. Who was she trying to kid? But she carried her box past the shelf where it belonged and made two distinct turns to the most ancient of boxes in the darkest of corners. When she turned, he was standing there.

He looked down at his box and she looked at hers. The blush of red across his cheeks had turned to a blaze. When their eyes met, they both knew. They both put their boxes quietly on the floor and went for it.

They kissed; he tasted of wintergreen Tic Tacs. They kissed again, more hungrily this time. He nibbled around to the back of her ear and she felt the quiver again. The silliness was gone. Except, of course, for the setting. Forbidden sex in the driest of places. She wasn't dry, though. The redheaded man reached under her skirt and discovered this for himself. He looked at her again, seriously, with a coyote yearning in his gold-brown eyes. There was a brief fumbling of clothes, the jingle of his pants hitting the floor, then they froze at the sound of an echoey footstep—they didn't care, let them be discovered. He entered her and she clutched his neck, wrapping her legs around his back. He kissed her as he made love; she liked that. It had been a long time between dweebs, and this guy was definitely a step up. She was lost in the pleasure of the moment, the gentle thrusting, the danger, the hot forbidden wetness with the ancient dead, reduced to data bits, silently looking on.

She cried out as she came—a short, whispery cry—and then he came, too, silently, with his head on her breast. The sex was good—not Trey Bliss good, but enough that she could easily do this again.

They held each other a moment, not so eager to be discovered now, then he lowered her again to her feet.

Norma was never good with after talk, but somebody had to say something.

"That was, well, it was just lovely," she ventured, and hoped her library hush was sultry.

She reached forward to straighten a lock of his hair, but he bent down to pull up his pants and she found herself, instead, straightening a lock of air. So she pulled up her own panties and smoothed her skirt, and then smoothed her own hair as he went about buckling his belt.

"I'm Norma," she tried again.

"I'm married," said the redheaded man. And then, "I'm sorry."

"No," said Norma. "Don't be. It's okay. It was nice. It's fine, really. I don't mind." Had she finally run out of stupid little things to say? No, she had one more. "But I'd like to know your name."

"Edward," he said.

"Ah," said Norma, "that would be two hundred and thirty-eight."

He looked at her, puzzled. Then he stooped to pick up his box.

Norma saw a bald spot on the top of his head and then he looked at her.

"I—We—I mean we can't—" He stopped and then started again. "I don't usually do this sort of thing."

That was horseshit, but she let it pass.

"It's really okay," she said. "I wasn't expecting anything."

That was horseshit, too, and it was the beginning of her new epiphany.

He smiled, but he really looked like a coyote now, one who'd just stolen a pork chop off the barbecue grill. He stood and, with one hand holding the box, straightened his own lock of hair, gave a little cough, then walked away.

There was another echoey footstep, and Norma wondered

if whoever it was had been standing there all this time, one foot raised waiting for them to finish. And then the epiphany arrived. That was her. Norma Dale. Standing in the stacks of life, one foot raised in expectation. But in expectation of what?

In three short minutes—the time it took for the redheaded man to spend himself in guilty pleasure—she had already pictured them in love, married, picket fence, a flock of redheaded children at her knee. And now she was standing alone in soggy underwear.

Almost *too* pathetic, right?

She had to face it. It wasn't going to happen. She was the oh-no, not-you girl, till death do her part. If she wanted marriage, children, then fine, there was a sea of Ricky Pierces from whom to choose. But she had to lower that foot and accept it. She had to settle.

∞

And so she did. She married the brother of one of the partners of the firm. He wasn't so awful. He was a pharmacist, so they had a nice house, nice clothes, nice cars. Norma quit work after a while and became a full-time suburban housewife. She picked up a few plots of the soap operas, got into clipping coupons and the pros and cons of various cleaning products, did Meals-on-Wheels, joined a quilting club, watched Martha Stewart, but had no expectations about that, either.

Sex was okay. It was regular and at least he kept himself clean. Babies were avoided for a while, and then, when decided upon, never came. Five years went by. They seemed like twenty. Norma forced herself to keep both feet on the floor. Dweebs were smart, and her dweeb was a hard worker, too, and loyal—or so she thought.

Norma had caught them. In her own bed. On her first

hand-stitched quilt. Log cabin, in rectangles of red and black velvet. The shock was not so much that he was cheating on her, but that the woman was so good-looking. How did *her* dweeb become someone else's prize?

She could have forgiven him. He certainly begged her enough. Begged and wheedled. She almost stayed, but then she was given somewhere else to go. Fate had glanced over and sent Norma Dale spinning with one dainty lift of her stern little brow.

Norma's father, gentle and kind but always a mouse of a man in a house full of women, had had a stroke. Her mother needed help to care for him at home, and since Madeline and Bethany both had thriving families . . .

The thousand miles closed up again, and Norma, twenty-nine and counting, found herself once again with both feet firmly planted in the middle of square one.

CHAPTER 3

*L*ife back in Norma's little hometown was challenging and rewarding in every way.

Okay, that wasn't true. It sucked.

Norma's mother dithered her way through her fog of perception, another decade of practiced obliviousness under her belt. She was easy enough to control. With a few bumps and tugs here and there, she pinged from one daily task to another like a well-coiffed pinball in Dearfoams.

The town had grown. It had a three-screen multiplex now and a big ol' Wal-Mart where a useless grove of trees used to stand. The old high school crowd was represented fairly well. Her old pals in unpopularity were still there, one married with a drinking problem, one divorced (her pills were no problem at all). Ricky Pierce had gone to California and started his own dot-com company—made a fortune, so they said. Norma's pang of regret lasted only until she pictured him cheating with dweeblike precision on poor Mrs. Pierce.

Several months passed before Norma ran into Ashley, downtown, coming out of her father's jewelry store.

"Norma?" Ashley had said. And she looked just great—mint green Prada suit, hair cut in expensive layers, tiny mint-green purse, alligator shoes in the perfect shade of brown. "Norma Dale—is that really you?"

Norma was wearing sweats that she'd purchased at the Wal-Mart. Her unwashed, scraggly long hair concealed with a navy blue bandana.

"Yes, it's me," Norma said. "And is that really Ashley? Ashley Cunningham?" She tried to mock, but was promptly topped.

"Ashley *Bliss,* silly girl, haven't you heard? Trey and I have been married for *ages.*"

The flashing of the diamond was overkill.

Norma knew this, of course. Trey and Ashley had reconciled not twenty-four hours after she had limped home bare-legged in her crumpled prom dress. Ashley never knew about her and Trey. Nobody did. Ashley merely had the instincts to be naturally cruel. Trey was now a partner in his father's law firm. They had two children—an adorable blond boy and an adorable blond girl.

Yes, life back at home pretty much sucked. Norma had the image of caring for her ailing parents for several eons, claiming her scant inheritance, and then living out her life in her shabby childhood home, alone—or perhaps with some cats. Yes, that would be the ticket, lots and lots of cats.

Fate, however, had a different plan.

∞

Norma's father spent his days in a rented hospital bed, cable TV his last remaining link to the world. He could barely talk, though this hardly mattered, as he had never talked that much in health. Norma loved him and knew he was fading away. Being able to tend to him gave her the tiny bit of solace she needed to not simply fade away herself.

One morning she went in with his breakfast tray, set it on the arm table next to his bed, and went to turn on the TV. She heard him grunt and was surprised to see him looking at her with a clarity in his eyes that she didn't think she'd ever seen, even in the days before his illness.

He signaled to her to leave the television off and then patted the bed to his side.

She went to him, concern rising.

He smiled the half smile that he could manage and shook his head, like, not to worry. Then he spoke.

"You were always my favorite," he said.

His voice was a whisper but there was no slur.

"Oh, Daddy—" Norma started, but he signaled her to silence.

"Sometimes," he continued, "I thought all you women would drive me crazy. Especially your mother. And your sisters—empty-headed, vain—not a lick of sense between them. But you—you were my little jewel."

Tears welled up in Norma's eyes.

"I wanted to name you that," he said. " 'Jewel.' You never knew. I told your mother at the hospital after seeing your sweet little face looking out of that blanket in the nurse's arms. I said, 'Elizabeth, let's name her Jewel.' But your mother would have none of it. 'We can't name her that,' " he said in a perfect imitation, " 'Jewel Dale? Why, that's absurd.' So she plastered you with Norma Lynn. *Phaa*. I should've just left her. Taken you and left her right then and there."

Norma couldn't believe what she was hearing.

"But I didn't," her father went on. "I didn't, 'cause I didn't have the balls."

"Daddy, don't say—"

He hushed her again.

"It wouldn't have been right," he said. "I knew that. I'd made my bed, and by God, I've slept in it. But I did do this . . ."

He signaled to the dresser with a wavering hand.

"Bring me my keys over there."

Her father, like most men his age, kept a ridiculous number of keys on his key ring. Norma, wondering, went and got the jangling bunch and brought it to him.

"Camouflage," he said, then gave a whispery cackle. "Elizabeth couldn't see the tree for the forest."

With trembling fingers, he held up one of the keys.

"It was my escape plan," he said. "Never used it. Didn't have to, just havin' it did the trick." He looked her in the eye. "Now I'm passing it on to you. My jewel. Come on, take it offa there."

Norma took the ring of keys. She struggled opening the ancient ring. The key was in the middle of the bunch and she had to take half off to get it. They fell to the bed in a clatter of brass and iron.

Her father had fallen back to the pillow and closed his eyes, his breathing shallow. Norma looked up in alarm.

"Daddy?" she said. "Daddy?"

He opened one eye—the clarity was gone. And he said one final word.

"Basement."

∞

The funeral and all took up the next two weeks. First, Norma's mother fell completely apart—enjoying every minute of it. Then Madeline and Bethany came to town, their husbands and kids in tow. But they got her father buried, everyone left, all the casserole dishes were returned to their proper owners, and it was just Norma and her mother again.

Norma finally allowed herself some grief. And guilt. She had never—well, not for a long time—really appreciated him. She, like the rest of them, had just taken him for granted. And now he was gone and there was a great gaping hole where once her father had been. Always there. For her. His understanding smiles, his winks of solidarity—the gentle touch of his hand. So first Norma wept for her father and then she wept for herself for a while and then, finally, allowed herself to consider his dying words.

Jewel. It was wonderful. Her secret name—her secret identity, which she never got to live.

If only, she thought. If only.

Jewel never would have settled.

Norma stood in her old bedroom and looked at her father's key. She had kept it all these days in a soapstone jar on her dresser. The same little jar where she had kept her sacred button. Trey Bliss's button. It had fallen off his shirt in algebra class, tenth grade. Rolled first in a circle, then, wobbling slightly, rolled right to a stop at the tip of her shoe. The button had been her talisman. Her voodoo. Her link to Trey and all the promises of his world. The button had been pale blue from his pale blue shirt that had set off his pale blue eyes.

The morning after the prom, she had flushed the button down the toilet.

Jewel would have flushed Ashley down the toilet.

Norma sighed.

The key was small, made of black iron and with a rounded head. Four letters were embossed in the metal: USMM. United States Merchant Marines. Her father had been in the Merchant Marines before he married her mother. His old sea chest. Black iron. In the basement.

Norma's mother called out from downstairs.

"I'm goin' to the Chat 'n' Curl! I've put out the roast to thaw. Can you chop the vegetables, Norma? And put it all in the stockpot? I've put it all out on the counter."

"Sure, Mom," Norma said. She waited a few minutes with practiced patience and then her mother called up the stairs.

"Norma, I'm goin' to the Chat 'n' Curl! Can you chop the vegetables for the pot roast? I've put the meat out to thaw."

"Yes, Mother, I will."

Pause.

"And the stockpot's out on the counter."

∞

The old iron chest was back in the corner of the basement behind Bethany's rusted Schwinn and an old black-and-white television. The television had its antenna extended in an obsolete V, an old red rag hanging from one ear. Norma shoved the set to one side and wheeled the bicycle with rotating squeaks across the floor. She knelt at the chest, her knees on cold cement, took a long deep breath, and lowered her expectations.

Chances were very, very good that her father had no idea what he was saying. This possibility had kept Norma from coming here before. She had wanted to postpone the crushing moment of finding nothing but a stack of *Reader's Digest*s and a moldy old Merchant Marine uniform. She had wanted to prolong the feeling—the rare and precious feeling of hope.

She put the key in the lock and turned it. She heard a click. The lid was a little rusty, but a good tug freed it and she opened it wide.

A little plush puffin looked up at her with its beady stare. Head and neck, back and wings, were black, like a little hooded overcoat to cover its puffy white shirt and pants. Enormous orange feet with three orange toes. The beady button eye set in a big circle of white with a slash of black, like makeup on a mime. Little spot of orange blusher on the cheek. Beak, half again as big as its head, was striped yellow, black, and orange, like a circus tent. And beneath the puffin— Norma's eyes went big.

Money.

Stacks and stacks of crisp, clean, and very, very green money.

CHAPTER 4

Norma held the stuffed puffin to her chest. Now it was time for a few more tears. She had done quite a bit of laughing while flinging green leaves of freedom about and dancing and screaming and punching her fist in the air, but now it was time again to cry.

The puffin had been hers, its white breast grubby with the grubbiness of *her* own childhood. The memories came rushing like a winter's rain down the summer-parched gullies of her mind.

Her father—her dear dead daddy—had given her the puffin. She was four. He had dark hair then. It was weird to remember him with dark hair. He had been for so long so quiet, so old, and so gray.

Norma remembered that her father had been in his forties when he married, ten—no, sixteen—years older than her mother. He'd already had a life, a long full life, before he'd become the mouse in the house full of women.

She remembered sitting on his knee, just the two of them—Madeline and Mother in the kitchen—and he'd tell her wonderful stories of fabulous places—palaces and jungles, lands of ice and snow, elephant rides and chasing whales, dark and beautiful maidens doing dances in the sun.

Tears rolled down Norma's cheeks. She'd thought they were stories, but he'd been there, hadn't he? He'd been all around the world. He'd seen these things—lived them—and nobody cared but a wide-eyed four-year-old girl.

Norma stroked the little bird. She looked at the scattered hundred-dollar bills and let out one long aching sigh for the unknown man who was her father and all that she had never been.

Tammie Nories.

The named popped into her head.

Tammie Nories. That's what her dad had called the little stuffed puffin. Tammie Nories. And he'd had a wonderful story to go along with the name.

Tammie Nories hatched on a great rock cliff—

Norma sat up.

Tammie Nories hatched on a great rock cliff—in the enchanted Isles of Orkney—

She wiped her eyes with her hand.

Tammie Nories hatched on a great rock cliff in the enchanted Isles of Orkney and lived with her mother and father and her thousands and thousands of cousins and cousins and her thousands and thousands of aunts and aunts and uncles and uncles high above us all, high above the great blue Northern Sea.

Norma remembered. And now she understood. It was real. He had been there. He had seen this fabulous sight with his own brown eyes. They had been young eyes then. Young eyes watching thousands of puffins at the top of the world, the sunlight catching his flecks of green.

She gathered up a handful of hundred-dollar bills and clutched them in her fist.

"Thank you, Daddy," she whispered fiercely. "Thank you. I'll escape *for* you—no, I'll escape for *me*! That was what you were trying to tell me, wasn't it? I'll go see the world that you saw, and at the very least I'll find some goddamn wonder before I die."

Then she laughed a big laugh of relief and, like Scarlett cursing her turnips, held the stuffed puffin in the air.

"I swear," said Norma Dale. "I swear. Though I don't know where the hell they are—I'll find these enchanted Isles of Orkney and I'll go there, by God, and set Tammie Nories free!"

CHAPTER 5

*T*he Orkney Islands weren't all that hard to find. Finding an Internet connection was the toughest part, since her parents hadn't updated beyond their IBM Selectric. The public library came to her aid, as did Google, and then Orosius, from the fifth century A.D., who pinpointed for her:

"Beyond Britannia, where the endless ocean opens, lies Orkney."

The handy Orkney online Enchanted Tourist Board narrowed that down for her even further, and Norma learned that Orkney was a cluster of about seventy islands, sixteen big ones, just off the tip of the northern Scottish coast. The mainland, known cunningly to the locals as "Mainland," was extremely civilized, open-armed toward tourists, and boasted of scenic walks, prehistoric sites, fine knitwear, an ancient circle of standing stones, picturesque hotels, and all the puffin souvenirs one cared to tote home.

But Norma wasn't planning exactly on coming home. She whipped out her credit card on the spot and made a one-way reservation on a plane bound for London in two days time. *There.*

Her mother, on hearing of her plans, didn't seem all that concerned.

"London? Well, that's nice, Norma, you do need to get out more. You know your father and I had a lovely trip to Cleveland not long ago."

Actually, the trip to Cleveland had been in 1977, but who was counting?

Then there was the little logistical matter of $480,000 in cash. The manager of the bank downtown was now Grayson Mitchell, also known to his former chess club fellows at the high school as "Sponge." Norma decided on straightforward honesty. The money, she told him, as she opened an account, was her inheritance from her father. Grayson didn't even blink as he filled out the proper paperwork, though he did push up his slightly greasy glasses with his characteristic and unfortunate middle finger. Then he took her bulky duffel bag and handed her a big stack of traveler's checks.

"Have a good time," he said. And he even managed to carry off an undweebish wink.

∽

A good time was definitely on the itinerary. Norma packed light. When she got to London, she planned on going shopping for a whole new wardrobe. Then she planned on going shopping some more. After that, a little sightseeing—the Tower, Buckingham Palace, Carnaby Street, Big Ben—then she would go shopping. And she would get her hair done—that's right—at the fanciest salon she could find. After that, more shopping and perhaps she'd take in a show.

Norma figured a week or two in London, just to acclimatize herself, then she would take the train to Edinburgh. A few days there, then she'd rent a car—why the hell not?—get used to driving on the wrong side of the road, then motor across the Highlands to Scrabster.

Scrabster—there was a lovely name. But Scrabster, at the tippy-top tip of Scotland, was where you caught the ferry. From there, with the Atlantic on her left and the North Sea on her right, Norma would ride the ocean waves to Orkney.

And that's exactly what she did.

CHAPTER 6

She stood at the upper deck railing of the ferry ship *Hamnavoe*. The North Sea sprayed its salty mist on her face, and she shook her new hairdo in triumph. She was here. She was doing it. Tammie Nories was tucked deep and snug in the stylish pocket of her charcoal Prada jacket.

Norma had never felt better in her life. The Dramamine had helped, and set her apart from the poor green-gilled tourists down below. She liked being set apart. In her new London drag, basically clad in black, her hair still long, but volumized and perfectly shaped, she'd been mistaken for a native three times. On the third occasion, quite smug by then, she'd affected an accent and actually given the poor sod directions. To where, she'd had no idea.

In another hour they'd be docking in Stromness, Mainland's south-shore port and second-biggest town. Hamnavoe was the old Norse name for Stromness. Norma was learning all sorts of useful tidbits like that. She'd also learned that Orkney was not really a Scottish place at all. Though now a part of Great Britain, in its early history it had been settled by Norsemen (and one presumed a few Norsewomen) for something like five hundred years. So—Vikings. Norma was looking forward to big brawny Viking-type men.

She grinned to herself. And why not?

And suddenly one was right there.

He didn't have the helmet with the horns or a big furry beard, but he was brawny and blue-eyed with a big thatch of yellow hair blowing fetchingly in the wind. He was lighting a cigarette and he looked up, catching her eye, like, "You don't mind, do you?"

Norma smiled. She'd been away from smoke-free America long enough that it didn't even shock her anymore.

Then he smiled back.

Dang good-looking he was. Norma wondered what he did for a living. Fisherman? Sheepherder? Maybe a little pillaging on the weekends? Her smile turned into a grin, and then she blushed because he'd started grinning back. She hoped he'd think the blush was from sea breeze rather than from his charm. No such luck, he was coming over.

"We're coming up soon to the Old Man of Hoy," he said.

Weird, Norma thought. Orkney accents sounded just like—

"I'm from Houston," he continued to drawl, ". . . you know, Texas? We grow our women pretty back home, but you Scottish babes sure give 'em a run for their money."

Norma burst out laughing.

"My God," she said, "that just may be the worst line I've ever heard."

His eyes got big, then he registered what had just happened and burst out laughing, too.

"All right. Too-shay. I apologize," he said. "But that doesn't mean I take back the pass, okay?"

"Pass accepted," Norma said, still smiling. "Who's the Old Man of Hoy?"

The Texan pulled a guidebook out of his back pocket and showed her. A rock formation, a sandstone chimney 480 feet high.

"The captain said we'd be passing it here in about fifteen minutes. I'd—"

"Russell?"

The voice came from behind them. Norma turned. Female. Red hair of no color found in nature. Long legs. Big boobs. Tiny waist. Big frown on her expertly made-up and highly attractive face.

"You through with that yet?"

The tone implied that she wasn't talking about the cigarette.

The Texan said quietly as he turned, "She's not my wife, we're not even engaged. I'm really falling for you, sugar." Then he winked with the eye that the redhead couldn't see and tossed the cigarette into the sea.

"Yeah," he said to his nonwife, nonfiancée, "I'm coming."

Then he sauntered across the deck. *They must teach that in the Texas school system,* she thought. Sauntering.

Norma turned back. A gray mass appeared in the fog, presumably the aforementioned Hoy. Her eyes searched for the Old Man but her mind still lingered on the Young Man from Houston. She was trying not to be flattered by his ridiculous attention, but she wasn't trying very hard. And why should she? Was this or was this not the twenty-third day of standing on the new leaf she had just turned on the brand-new page of her life?

The Old Man was coming into view. He was impressive, though more rock than old man. This whole place was impressive. The ocean was rolling and cold and slate green, with the power of life itself roiling in the sheer vastness of its deep. The sky was gray and huge and everywhere, like the Pentecostal dome of a temple perched in the heavens. The island of Hoy looming ahead of her, with it great and terrible rock face standing grim through the ages of time.

She gripped the railing with both hands. *Yes,* Norma thought fiercely, *I'm here and I'm doing it and it's great.*

∽

Stromness, described by someone as "draped like gray lace on an emerald shore," was almost like that. Little boxes of stone set in order, not too straight and the stacks not too high, up against a moderately green hillside—but pleasing, very pleasing to the eye. Then Norma went through the antipostcard moments of disembarking from the ferry. This meant about forty minutes of breathing car fumes and waiting in a metal line, rather than tripping down the gangplank like Audrey Hepburn with a floating handkerchief and a smile. But after that she drove up the flagstone street and wound her way through the town. She had rented a maroonish-purple Escort back in Edinburgh, they had become old friends by then, and she put Tammie Nories on the dash next to a sprig of hand-picked Highland heather.

Her plan was to eat lunch in Stromness, then drive the thirty or so miles on to Kirkwall, the largest town in the islands and, rightly so, their capital. As far as plans went, that was it. She'd decided, back in the States, to wing it.

Norma spotted a likely fish 'n' chips place far enough away from the touristy center and pulled over. She got out of the car, took off her jacket, and lay it over the backseat. It was summertime in the Orkneys. The sun, which would never quite manage to set, was bright and warm. She wore a cotton knit pullover, black, with three-quarter sleeves, black jeans, and a pair of walking shoes, broken-in nicely courtesy of the moors. She grabbed up the stuffed puffin and put it in her purse and walked to the door.

The windows of the place were authentically greasy, and as Norma went inside her mouth watered at the lovely smell of decidedly unhealthy and deliciously fried fish.

She went to the counter and ordered the haddock, chips, and a Coke.

Norma looked around. Nearing noontime, the place had what she took to be about a dozen actual Orcadians. At first glance they were not that much different than Londoners, or even the Scots. But there was something—were they all just a tad bit better-looking? Or was it the brightness in their eyes?

"You from the States?" asked the girl behind the counter. She had light brown hair and a very nice smile.

"Yes," Norma said.

"First time to Orkney?"

"Yes."

And then they both laughed—of course it was.

Norma was reaching for her money, and on a whim pulled out the puffin instead.

"I'm here to see these."

"Ah," said the girl, "Tammie Nories."

Norma stared. How on earth did she know?

"Don't confuse the poor lady, Janny."

Norma turned. This came from a gray-haired man sitting near the counter. Then a younger fellow from another table piped up.

"Tammie Nories is what we call the puffin birds 'round here," he said.

Norma's ears were adjusting to the singsong quality of their voices. Like the Scots, but soft, more feathery. And then she twigged to what they were saying. And was delighted.

"Tammie Nories!" she said, holding up the puffin. "*This*

is Tammie Nories. My father named her that—he came here, see, a long time ago, and then he brought me this and I thought—I thought that he'd made the name up!"

Everyone had stopped eating and was listening, chips raised to mouths and eyebrows up, not quite getting the joke but not wanting to offend the wacky Yank.

"So that's why I've come," Norma said, winding down, "to see the thousands of puffins—to see the thousands of Tammie Nories."

"Oh, dear," said the older man. "Thousands?"

Janet, from behind the counter, looked sympathetic and shook her head. "You won't be finding a thousand puffins on Orkney, I'm afraid. Not even during the nesting season."

Season? Puffins had seasons?

"That would be the Shetland Islands you're looking for, dear." This from a woman in the corner. "But not this time of year."

"Puffin season's just about over," said the young fellow. "Early May to the middle of August—that right, Ed?"

"Aye, that would be it," said the older man, and the woman in the corner nodded.

"Oh," Norma said. "Then I guess I've missed them. I guess I should have—well, planned it a little better. I—I've been, kinda winging things."

There was a moment of silence and everyone in the shop tried to look suitably sad.

Then the old man broke out in a grin. "Looks like them Tammie Nories's been winging it, too!"

Everyone, including Norma, burst into appreciative laughter and the sadness was dispelled.

The cook put a white plate of fresh fried haddock and potatoes on the counter with a satisfying thump.

"Two walkers from Japan were in t'other day," he said gruffly. "They seen a bunch of them birds out on Rackwick. Hoy. A couple o' dozen do you?"

Norma smiled. A couple o' dozen puffins would do her fine.

CHAPTER 7

After much discussion and advice from the patrons at the fish 'n' chips, Norma had a plan to view the puffins. She drove halfway to Kirkwall, to Houton, a little coastal settlement that boasted both the car ferry to Hoy and an accommodating hotel. Norma checked in and treated herself to an afternoon soak in the communal bathtub just down the hall from her sweetly decorated room. She had high tea in the just as sweetly decorated conservatory with two (also sweetly decorated) little old ladies from Dublin and then retired to her room. Sleeping in the odd twilight of the endless summer day proved to be no problem. Norma had a dream, slightly weird, involving ten-foot-tall puffins and the Old Man of Hoy in a Stetson hat.

In the morning she had breakfast—she was developing a fondness for wide meaty bacon, beans on toast, grilled tomatoes and mushrooms, and even the ubiquitous little glass of tinny orange juice—and then she drove her car to the ferry.

The ride was twenty-five minutes of pleasantness and

views. Hoy, in sight the entire trip, was the second largest of Orkney's islands, and shaped like a rectangle—roughly ten miles long and five miles wide. To the northwest was the high and craggy red sandstone cliffside with the Old Man that the ferry had passed yesterday on the way to Stromness. Now, to the northeast, Norma could see the other highest parts of the Orkneys, the mounds—no, one would have to call them summits—of Ward Hill and the Cuilags. The rest of the island was the more typical Orcadian geography of flat lowlands, rolling hills, bogs, and moors. Development, such as it was, ran mainly along the eastern coast. Norma had been told not to miss Moness and the Hoy Inn, basically the only place on the island to eat and, most important, the old fellow had stressed, to get a decent pint to drink.

They docked in Lyness, on the eastern coast and on the southern end of Hoy's one and only highway. Norma put Tammie Nories on the dashboard and headed north.

Less than ten miles wasn't that far to go, but with the sea on her right and the rolling green hills on her left, Norma lost track of both distance and time. She was looking for a road to the west, the only other big road on the island and one that would take her across to the western coast and the crofting (whatever that was) community of Rackwick, population: nine.

So here was a road to the west, but it was a very vague sort of road at best. Norma slowed the car and then took the turn—if it wasn't the right turn west, she would find out soon enough.

It wasn't the right turn. Soon enough the road petered out to little more than a walking path. Norma stopped the car. The road was too narrow and the ground on either side looked boggy. And what the heck was that?

Norma got out of the car. It wasn't her imagination. There

was nothing around but acres and acres of peat bog, flat and windswept, but out in the middle of all that nowhere— Norma squinted. An object. White. It looked . . . it looked like a tiny Taj Mahal.

Norma tested the ground with her walking shoe. It was sturdy enough. And then she saw a distinct pathway going straight there. She followed it. Within a few dozen yards she understood. Like the Taj Mahal, this, too was somebody's final place of rest. She was looking at a grave—a graveyard for but a single grave out in the middle of the godforsaken bog.

Norma kept walking, though a gust of wind made her wish for her jacket. The sky had become overcast in perfect gloomy complement to her mysterious quest.

The solitary tombstone was stark white and shaped like the tip of a spade. The grave itself was surrounded by stones and the rickety rectangle of a whitewashed picket fence.

Norma stopped. It was the most forlorn thing she had ever seen. In agreement, the wind picked up again and gave a sad little howl.

She walked a few steps closer. On the headstone, in very small plain black letters she read:

HERE LIES

and then, after a large space:

BETTY CORRIGALL

That was it. No dates. Nothing else. Just an embossed trim of white flowers and, at the peak of the spade, a tiny black cross.

The grave was fairly well tended. Planted with long, wind-swept grass. Across the mound lay a scattering of hothouse flowers—dried carnations, a withered bunch of lilies, and one single, fresh white rose.

Norma stood for a moment, wondering, and then felt a sudden pang of strange and terrible kinship. Whoever she was and however she had died there was one thing Norma knew. Betty Corrigall was Orkney Island's own "oh-no, not-you" girl. Tears came, instantly dried on her cheeks by a chilly buss of the boggy air.

Norma reached out across the white picket fence and touched the tombstone with her hand.

Good lord. She gave it a tap with her knuckles. It was made out of fiberglass. She looked around her then, stupidly, like the peat bog was going to explain.

And then she saw the bicycle. It was an old bicycle lying on its side down a slope about twenty feet away. Next to it, a knapsack. She felt a small I'm-not-alone chill and then she saw him.

He was farther down the slope. Far away but close enough to see that he was glaring.

He was an artist. She could see that. He had his portable easel and his palette, brushes—everything but the beret. He wore no hat and his mass of long dark hair tossed angrily in the wind.

Norma's heart gave a decided thump. Was he glaring at— why so angry?—was he glaring at her? Then she twigged. Oblivious as her mother, she'd been standing, like an idiot, right in the middle of his scene. How long had she been there, completely unaware? For heaven's sake, she'd probably used up his artistically gloomy light.

As if on cue, a cloud zipped away and the entire landscape was flooded with the bright cheery sun.

Norma held up her hands, like, I'm sorry, then gave a goofy apologetic grin, but the man had turned away, was kneeling to his paint box, his body language speaking loud and clear. Thanks to you, stupid tourist, my artistic solitude is ruined.

Great.

Norma turned and hurried back up the pathway to her car. The mystery of Betty Corrigall would have to wait until a less humiliating time.

CHAPTER 8

They were colorful. They were comic. They were, indeed, puffy. But Norma refused to think of them as "clowns of the sea."

To her they had dignity. Beauty. Even elegance.

She grinned. But they were awfully cute.

She sat, at the top of the world, high above the great blue Northern Sea. A two-hour hike, north of Rackwick, had gotten her there. (*Croft* turned out to be the British word for farm.) From her perch on a red, rocky sandstone crag, she could see not only the Old Man of Hoy but the pebbled beach far below and the grand crashing ocean.

She felt triumphant.

Counting the stuffed one, Norma was in the company of seven Tammie Nories. Two families of them, she was pretty sure. Two moms, two dads, and two almost-grown chicks. The last of the mating puffins on Hoy. They didn't have nests. Among the rocks were areas of ground where they had dug out little burrows. Or she assumed they had. Their big orange feet seemed capable of the job. Or maybe the holes had already been there. There were dozens of the burrows, most of them empty now except for white dots of puffin crap and feathers.

The nice barkeep back at the Hoy Inn had packed her a lunch. Norma sat munching happily on cold kidney pie, vinegar crisps, and warm bitter beer. It was heaven.

After this, she thought, *I ain't settling for nothing.*

∞

Norma downed the last bit of her beer and carefully gathered all her paper wrappings. Now there was only one more thing to do.

Tammie Nories—the plushy—was sitting on a nearby rock facing out to the sea. Norma picked it up. It was time for this puffin to go home. Norma had already picked out the burrow, it was only a matter of getting there. Carefully, mindful of the beer she had just consumed, she walked down a slanted ledge to a lower level of the cliffside. There were burrows more accessible but she didn't want to get too close to the live puffins. All she had to do was lay down flat on her stomach, scoot to the edge of the cliff, and, holding on to a nice solid-looking rock with her right arm, reach her left arm over the side.

She attempted the maneuver, and only at the last moment did it occur to her how silly she must look from behind. *Thank goodness,* she thought, *it's just me, the puffins, and the sea.*

"What the hell do you think you're doin'?"

Norma's life would have been greatly simplified had she, at that point, tumbled off the cliffside and down to the beach below. Instead, she let out a startled yelp and scuttled clumsily sideways like a guilty crab. She turned, her hair promptly flopping over her face. She shoved it back, smearing her forehead with dirt and puffin crap.

"I—I—" she said, then stopped. What she was doing could not be summed up in a nutshell.

Her accuser stood above her on the cliffside, the sun behind his head like a nimbus of righteousness.

"Are you daft? You'll get yourself killed. Stay there," he said, "I'm comin' down."

Norma stayed there.

The man was tall and slender, his dark hair pulled back in a ponytail. He didn't bother with the path she had taken. He came right over the rocks, nimble as a cat.

Norma was still holding the puffin, and like a naughty child, put it quickly behind her back.

"This is a reserve, you know," he said. His voice was deep, but softly graveled. "Not a playground for outlanders. Whatcha got there in your hands?"

"It's—"

His hands were on his hips. Stern. Dark. Dark pants, dark shirt, dark Windbreaker, dark hair—dark, dark eyes—and pale, pale skin.

Norma took a breath. The man was beautiful and he had no right to be. His features were all wrong. His face was square, his lips too thin, his nose crooked, his brows thick, his eyes like hot black ball bearings set deep and far away, yet burning close as he stared into hers—and his skin, his strange white skin, nearly luminescent in the pale of the Orkney sun.

"That better not be what I think it is—there's a very stiff penalty for killin' birds—"

"Oh, no!" Norma said. "I'd never—I'd never—" and she thrust the stuffed puffin toward him. "It's not a real one. I'd never, *ever* . . ."

The man took the puffin.

He laughed. The beautiful man laughed at her, and Norma started to cry.

"Hey, hey," the man said, "no, don't start that, now. For mercy's sake, woman."

But Norma couldn't help it. She put her hands to her face and sobbed.

And then he was patting her back and actually saying, "There, there."

Cool gentle hands were pulling hers down. A soft white cloth was wiping at her tears. It was a handkerchief—an actual handkerchief was being put to her nose and he was actually saying, "Now, give us a blow."

Norma blew. She looked up at him with her, no doubt at all, red swollen eyes.

He smiled. It was a crooked smile with one long dimple to the side.

With a clean part of the no-kidding handkerchief he dabbed at her forehead and hair.

"Might as well get the birdshit, while I'm at it," he said, and her humiliation was complete.

"I'm not—not usually—this stupid," Norma said. Then she sighed. "Yes—Yes, I am. I am usually this stupid. Sometimes I'm even stupider."

He didn't argue. He lifted the stuffed puffin along with his dark black brows.

"It's—" she said. "It was from my father, okay? I was four. He gave it to me and called her Tammie Nories. He told me this wonderful story about all the puffins on the Islands of Orkney and I thought it was all made up. My whole life, and I thought he'd made it up. I never knew that he had been here. I never knew what he had seen. And then he died. I was there when he died and he gave me a key. It was his escape key, and he gave it to me. It opened a sea chest full of money and the old stuffed puffin that I hadn't seen—I hadn't thought of—in years. All those years and he gave *me* the key. And so I came here. I came here for him and I came here for me and—and this was supposed to be—it was symbolic, okay? It was a ceremony for my dead father, *okay*? I promised myself I would come to Orkney and see them—the thousands of puffins—but I screwed it all up because I didn't check about the seasons and they're all in the Shetlands anyway—wherever the hell they are—and I just wanted to put the goddamn bird in a goddamn puffin nest, okay? It's not a crime. It's a—a—"

The man was pointing over Norma's shoulder.

"What?"

She looked over her shoulder and then looked back at him.

"What?"

"The Shetlands," the man said. "They're northeast of Orkney. Hundred or so kilometers—as the puffin flies."

Norma sniffed and he dabbed her nose one more time with his handkerchief.

"And, no, it's not a crime," he said. "It's a gesture. A lovely gesture. I'm sorry I interfered. I've gone and spoiled your little ceremony. May I make it up to you?"

He put the handkerchief in his pocket and lifted the puffin.

"The burrow that you've picked, it's way too shallow. Little birdie'd get washed out with the first good rain. I know a spot—may I?"

Norma nodded.

The man went to his knees and was over the side of the cliff in one fluid movement.

Jeez. Norma leaned forward, carefully, and looked over the edge. He was scaling down the wall of the cliff, the puffin clutched in his teeth. About twenty feet down, he plucked it with his hand and signaled up to her, like, here's a good spot.

She grinned and made an okay sign with her thumb and forefinger.

His entire hand and arm and the puffin disappeared into the side of the cliff, and then he pulled back his arm, hand puffin-free. He scaled back up the wall and was standing next to her, dusting the red cliff dirt from his pants.

"Am I forgiven?" he said.

"I can't believe you did that," Norma said. "Who's the daft one here?"

"Ah," he said, "I know these cliffs. Been doin' that since I was a boy."

"Well, yes then," Norma said, "you're forgiven. And thank you. Thank you very much."

"Little birdie'll be there come next spring," he said with that crooked smile, "and won't she give the new tenants a surprise?"

Norma smiled, too, and then laughed and threw out both of her arms and closed her eyes and drew in a giant breath of fresh sea air out on the cliffside with this crazy beautiful man. Her heart was beating very, very fast.

Too fast. She opened her eyes and the cold blue Orkney sky was doing a crazy beautiful spin.

He caught her. He held her with his strong and slender arms and led her up the path to the top of the cliff.

She had fallen anyway, of course. For this sexy, strange man. How could she not? The heights were wuthering, nearby moors—it was getting pretty Heathcliff outside.

He was saying something—something about sitting down. So she did. Then he was asking something—something about if she was all right.

No, she wasn't all right. What was wrong with this picture? There was no Cathy here. Just Norma with her birdshit hair and big red nose.

"Yes, I'm all right—thank you—God, I'm such a dork."

She was trying to get her breath; just a tiny bit of dignity would be nice, too.

"A very pretty dork. Is that an American term?"

What had he said?

"I'm Brian."

He was holding out his hand.

"Brian Burroughs."

What had he said?

The hand was still there. Right. She should take it. Shake it. Tell him *her* name.

"Norma," she said. "I'm Norma. Norma Dale." And there really was no question—what the man named Brian had said was "pretty."

And what neither of them heard, coming from that cold blue Orkney sky above, was laughter.

CHAPTER 9

*L*ater, running it over and over in her mind as she drove back to Lyness, she clarified—what the man, what Brian Burroughs had said, was "*very* pretty." Then she allowed herself to revel.

So they had introduced themselves, there at the top of the cliff, and, just as Brian had pulled the band from his hair and shaken loose his long black locks, Norma saw the bicycle and the paint box and the easel.

"You're him," she said. "The artist on the peat bog."

He looked at her, puzzled.

"I'm her," Norma confessed, though she didn't know why, "the idiot standing in your view."

"My lucky day," said Brian Burroughs.

She wasn't quite sure how he meant that, but on she forged.

"I'm really sorry—I mean, interrupting you like that."

"Then I guess we're even."

He didn't smile, and Norma became even more confused.

"Were you—were you painting the grave?"

Good one, Norma, state the obvious.

"No," he said, "I was waitin' for a tourist so I could paint her."

This time he did smile—oh, that long lone dimple—and she smiled back, with an inward wince at the "tourist" label.

"What is that place?" Norma said. "I mean, who was Betty Corrigall and why—well, what was the deal?"

Brian looked at her. "You really don't know?"

"No," said Norma.

"You're not much of a tourist, then, are ya?"

Norma felt a hot rush of blood flush her cheeks, and she turned to the wind, hoping for cover. Why was she blushing? But she knew. This man confused her and he turned her on—big-time. His black hair—blue-black, it was, and glossy, to his shoulders—blue-black, glossy long hair framing that face. That face—with its contrast of paleness and black burning eyes. His nose—she wanted to run her finger down the narrow and straight—right to the charming little bump. And why stop there? That dimple was mighty touchable— For God's sake, get a grip!

"Are you tellin' me you just happened onto the place?"

"I was lost," Norma said, still facing away. "I made the wrong turn and then I saw the grave. I—"

"That's lovely," he said.

Norma felt his hand on her shoulder.

"The perfect way. Not knowin'—then seein' her there. I wish I *had* painted you."

Norma turned and looked at him. She felt another hot flush of blood, but lower this time.

"That's what you do?" she said, chalking up another under Obvious. "You paint?"

"I paint."

"I mean, you know, like, for a living?" Norma wanted to thump her own forehead. Just how clumsy could she go?

"Aye," Brian said, "it does rather resemble a livin' from time to time."

He dropped his hand and made a move toward his bicycle.

She was going to lose him and she had just found him. Panic sent her last two brain cells into total stupid mode.

"You ride your bike here?"

He showed mercy and matched her obviousness. "You hike?"

She nodded.

"Long hike back," he said. "Park at the head of the Rackwick trail?"

She nodded again.

"Tell you what," he said. "I'll show you a shortcut, walk you to your car, and tell you the tale of Betty Corrigall."

Norma nodded a third time while inside she was thanking the gods.

∞

"Betty Corrigall," Brian Burroughs said, "was a lass born on Hoy about two hundred and fifty years ago."

"Hold it," Norma said, "I'm doing the math."

"Seventeen forty-eight. But the story starts twenty-seven years later."

"And the Orkneys were part of Scotland by then, right?" said Norma. "So she wasn't, like, a Viking."

Brian looked at her.

"You really aren't a tourist, are you?" he said. "You came to Orkney with your little stuffed puffin and are in total ignorance otherwise?"

"I think of it as winging it," Norma said. "And don't make the bird pun, I've already heard it."

He grinned as he pushed his bike along.

"Well, you are correct, Ms. Dale. Orkney has been ruled by Scotland since just a bit past 1468. We were part of a dowry—in Margaret of Denmark's hope chest right next to her table linens. So no, Betty Corrigall was not a fair Viking maid. She was fair of skin, though, so it is said, her hair dark—the color of yours."

Norma reached up by reflex and smoothed what the wind had tattered.

"And as long."

"Oh?" Norma said. "There are pictures—I guess a portrait, right?"

"No portrait," Brian said. "Betty was the daughter of crofters—she lived in Greengairs Cottage near Rysa, south of here. The stories never say why, but she was not married and she was twenty-seven. In those days that was gettin' on in years."

Norma sneaked a look at him, wondering if he was wondering how on in years *she* was. He looked enough on in years to be a few years on past her.

"She had a lover, though. A sailin' man, more's the pity. The story says he came to the islands on a whalin' ship. I've often wondered if it was just that once, or whether she at least had the joy of waitin' for him to be returned to her from the sea."

"Just that once?"

"Miss Corrigall turned up with child," Brian said, "and we're not talkin' happy endin'. I always like to think that he loved her, that he would have married her had he known."

"But he didn't?"

"The story goes that he deserted her. But I wonder if he even ever knew. The whalin' ships would be out to sea for months at a time, even years."

"So she had the baby out of wedlock?"

Brian stopped pushing the bike.

"No," he said. "She didn't have the baby. She killed herself."

"Oh, dear," Norma said. "Oh, my goodness—the grave? That's why—"

"Aye," Brian said. "The Lairds of Hoy were very much holier than thou. No suicides in the kirkyard. Church land was preserved for a better class of sinner."

"But that's awful," Norma said.

"It's a very awful story."

"How did she—"

"First by drownin'."

"First?"

"She waded out into the cold dark ocean. My heart just breaks thinkin' about it. How she must have yearned for him. Thought maybe he was dead—why he'd never come back, you know?—that he was on the bottom of the sea and that she could join him with their little bairn. But some villagers saw her. Saved her, they did. Dragged her poor self out of the ocean. And saved her for what? The poor wretch felt so guilty, so shunned by her good neighbors, she hanged herself two days later. Hanged herself and her poor unborn child from the rafters in a barn."

Norma watched him. She watched Brian Burroughs. His black hair tossed about in the wind and he stared off across the moors, lost in time. Then tears came to his eyes. One spilled to his pale skin and he wiped it away with the heel of his hand.

That did it.

Norma felt a surge of pure I-want-this-man. And not just lust. Seeing him react like that—she felt something stir that hadn't stirred in a very, very long time. Maybe she was even feeling something that had never stirred. She felt it deep inside her, and she felt it hard. So deep and hard she had trouble taking her next breath.

He had started pushing the bicycle again.

She continued to watch him. His long fingers wrapped around the handlebars. The muscles of his thighs straining beneath the dark denim of his jeans with each sexy graceful stride. Norma took her breath. A jagged one with just enough oxygen to the brain to get her walking.

"They wouldn't bury her proper," he said after a moment. She had caught up to him, oxygen flowing better now. "The sanctimonious bastards took her out to the bog and dumped her in a godforsaken hole."

"But the little fence—"

"No fence," Brian said. "No nothing. The grave was just the other side of the parish boundary—unmarked, unholy, and forgotten for the next one hundred and fifty-five years."

"Uh," Norma said, "okay, hold on—I'm doing the math again."

"Nineteen thirty-six. Two men cutting peat uncovered the corner of a box. Gits thought it was a treasure. They dug it up and opened the coffin."

"Jesus."

"Jesus was nowhere around," Brian said. "What they found was poor Betty—fair skin turned a bit brown, but other than that the lass was perfectly preserved—lovely as the day they buried her—long dark tresses curled to her poor dead shoulders. Peat does that to a corpse, you know—preserves them. And here is the kicker . . ."

Brian paused again and looked at Norma with his burning black eyes.

"The rope she had hung herself with was lyin' there in the coffin coiled by her head, you know, keep tauntin' the poor woman for what she had done on beyond death itself."

Norma shivered, caught up in a terrible blend of desire and dread.

"The rope," he said, "upon its encounter with the sunlight and the fresh Hoy air, was said to have turned to dust right before their unbelievin' eyes."

Norma shuddered this time—visibly—and Brian noticed. He let the bicycle drop to the ground, took off his Windbreaker, and draped it over her shoulders.

"Look at this," he said, "frightenin' the poor tourist with my scary tale. Forgive me—we painter types, you know, we take this dark stuff pretty seriously."

His arm was around her, holding her. Her eyes locked with his. Norma knew then that she loved him. Irrational, sudden, and fathoms deep. Love. Ridiculous love. She wanted him to kiss her. So badly that it hurt. Painful love, that's what it was—the kind that had struck her—an unrequited arrow straight through the heart. There were two, no, it was three long delicious seconds when she thought that he *would* kiss her, and then he dropped his eyes, dropped his arm from her shoulders, and picked up the damn bike.

At least she didn't say something utterly stupid.

"I will forgive you," is what she said, "as often as you wish to trespass."

She said it softly, softly enough that he could pretend he hadn't heard.

He gave her another look. Tantalizingly close to a lingering look, and Norma felt two big ol' unrequited tears making their embarrassing way straight to her eyes. No. Crying wasn't going to do. Not at all. Norma got out her mental whip and gave a good snap over the near-spooked herd of her emotions.

"Uh," she said, and managed a smile, "so what happened then?"

Brian's eyes got in another few seconds of lingering, then he seemed to realize what she had just said. The burning eyes dropped from hers, thank God—he grabbed the handlebars.

"All right," he said. He cleared his throat. "Let's see."

He began to walk, and Norma did, too.

"The fellows buried her again. Isaac Moar, the postmaster, had been consulted during all the excitement of the treasure. They realized it was Betty Corrigall, the long-dead sinner of Hoy. This time they marked the grave with a little stick. Decent of them, eh?"

Norma nodded, but he didn't see. His eyes were now to the ground.

"A few years passed by with Betty's ghost left to rest, then, with the war, there was no peace for anybody."

"The war?"

"That's right. You wouldn't know about that, either, never having let a guidebook cross your path. World War Two, I'm talkin'. Orkney was home to thousands of British troops, naval base at Lyness during the anchorage of Scapa Flow. The war was all over Orkney—" He gave the slightest pause. "—we even had our own prison camp."

"Really?" Norma said. "Germans?"

"Actually, no."

"Japanese?"

"Italians."

"From Italy?" Norma knew she'd scored another in the stupid box. "Right, right, Mussolini and stuff, you forget about that part."

"Aye," Brian said. " 'Tis easy to forget about the Italians." His look turned into a scowl.

They walked in silence for a while. Norma kept sneaking glances. She couldn't help herself—the man was like chocolate, dark and sweet and tempting and mysterious and—well, chocolate wasn't mysterious, but it was certainly delicious and she loved it, didn't she?—and that's what she was feeling now—right? *Oh, my God, was there a grip to get* anywhere *in the friggin' moor?*

He looked at her, puzzled, but the scowl was gone.

"So Betty—" Norma said, "during the war?"

"Aye," he said. "Betty. During the war." Another clearing of the throat. "It seemed that Betty's grave was in the direct line of sight for the antiaircraft guns they were settin' up. This wouldn't do, so they sent some soldiers out to the bog to move her. Fifty meters is all it would take, just a little shift for God, King, and country. The soldiers did their duty, but one morbid sod couldn't resist a little peek at the corpse. There was Betty, beautiful as ever. Quite a story it made back at the barracks. There were nightly sorties to view her for a few weeks, then one group of wags decided to sneak out to the grave site, dig up the coffin, and steal poor Betty's corpse."

"You're kidding," Norma said. "That's just terrible. What a terrible thing to do."

"Grave robbin'? Aye, grave robbin' is terrible. What's worse is puttin' the unloved remains of a long-lost girl at the head of the table at the officers' mess."

"Oh, no—they didn't."

"They did. I'm sure it seemed right jolly at the time. Hell, I forgive the bastards, even. Seen in the light of war, the darkness of war . . ."

"But still. How awful."

"Aye, awful," Brian said. "The repeated exposure to the air finally brought on decay; our Betty was beautiful no more."

"What did they—you know—do with—"

"Well, they buried her again. The soldiers got some wrist-slappin'—mind you, the grave robbin' part of the tale you won't find in the guidebooks—and this time they put a slab of stone over the coffin, you know, to stop any more mischief. And then they put back her stick."

"Gee."

"It was one of you Yanks who finally brought her some dignity. After the war. A minister, Reverend Kenwood Byrant, was visiting the islands in 1949. He was moved by Betty's plight and sad little marker. He's the one who made that little picket fence. He also gave her a cross and made the customs officer of Hoy—Harry Berry, if you can believe the name—promise to erect her a proper headstone."

"Ah," said Norma. "A happy ending."

"Not quite," said Brian. "It took Mr. Berry twenty-seven years to get around to fulfillin' the deed. I'll do the math for you. Nineteen seventy-six. And it turns out a head*stone* was too heavy for the boggy ground. That's why—"

"It's fiberglass!" Norma said. "They made the headstone out of fiberglass so it wouldn't sink in the bog. I get it now. Wow, what a story."

"It was a *life,*" Brian said fiercely.

Norma looked at him, but his eyes were off into the distance again.

"It was a life made *into* a story—made into a *tourist* stop."

She watched those beautiful black eyes watch the dark sea and then lift to the pale blue sky above their heads. Then he looked at her. Glared at her, breathing hard.

"I've *tried* to paint it," he said. "Again and again I've painted her, but all I can do is just pigment on canvas—do you understand that? It's crap—sentiment—shallow exploitation of her tragedy—like I was diggin' up dead beauty myself just to gawk and paw."

Whoa.

Brian wiped at his eyes and started pushing the bike again.

"That's what I was tryin' to do today—out there. And it's so damn—she just doesn't—" A quick burning look and he said, "You, though—" And that was all. He shook his head like the mane of an angry black lion, gave one fierce sigh, and said, "Shit."

Norma didn't say anything.

They walked in silence. She tried to think of something

supportive, something soothing—something not stupid. The man was gorgeous, intriguing—hell, beguiling is what he was. Yup, he'd pretty much beguiled her ass good. But maybe his painting *was* crap. Maybe he did crap art like the guy with the fuzzy hair and the happy trees. She sneaked one more glance at him—and he looked *so sad*. They walked on for an uncomfortable ten silent minutes.

"Then *don't* show me," she finally blurted.

"Show you what?"

"The painting. I mean, what if it *is* crappy? How embarrassing that would be."

He stopped the bike and flipped open his art box. He showed her the painting.

Unfinished. But good. Really good.

"It's good," she said. "Really good."

"I know," said Brian Burroughs.

∞

And then they were at the car. It went fast. The parting. Way too fast. She returned his Windbreaker, thanked him for walking her, thanked him for the story, thanked him for the puffin, and he said you're welcome, you're welcome, my pleasure, and then got on his bicycle and pedaled away. A small backward glance, his crooked smile, a wave, and that was it.

Norma had replayed the walk a dozen times in her head by the time she pulled into the line of cars waiting for the ferry. She'd laughed, she'd cried—she'd pressed the pause button again and again on that wonderful terrible near-kiss.

"Near-kiss, my ass," she finally said to the sprig of heather on the dashboard. "He *didn't* kiss me. *Did* he? No. It was all in my head. My stupid, stupid head. When am I ever going to—"

There was a tap at the window, and Norma reached for

her return ticket stuck behind the visor. She pushed the window button down and turned.

"Here you go—"

It was Brian.

On his bike. Breathing hard. With a grin.

"Oh—" she said. Norma's blood drained, with a slight delay at the bend where she was sitting, to the tips of her toes.

"Oh," she repeated with eloquence.

"Took another shortcut," he said. Then he sat back and with both hands swept his black hair from his face. "Whew."

"What?" Norma said. "Why?"

He grinned again, and at the sight of that dimple, Norma's heart restarted her circulation with one great pumping thud.

"I don't know," he said. "I—"

Their eyes met. His grin slowly faded and he cocked his head. The puzzled look returned to his eyes.

"What I—what I told you out there. I don't do that. Talk. About my paintin'—"

Norma couldn't speak—the cat of astonishment had firm hold of her tongue.

"And then—what you said—"

He was doing the burning thing again. Norma knew she had to say something—anything—or just sizzle away to nothingness.

"That it wasn't crappy?"

Oh, jeez. But at least he smiled again.

"Aye, that."

He leaned over then and placed his long-fingered hands on the open window of her car door.

"But—I don't know, luv—I'm thinkin'—I'm feelin' . . ." His voice had gone all soft-gravelly low, and Norma felt her very bones dissolving. Then he reached one hand in through the window and touched her. Two fingers—the slightest of caresses down one cheek and then a gentle stroke of her hair and he leaned back, hands to the handlebars, and laughed. He laughed and shook his head.

"Mother of mercy," he said. "What an ego, eh? Chase a poor tourist across the island 'cause she said his fuckin' daubin' was nice. I *am* daft, don'tcha know—daft and desperate."

"I am *not* a *tourist!*"

Of all the things to come out of her mouth—

Brian looked at her.

"No," he said, "I guess you aren't. But that is the question, now innit—what, Norma Dale, exactly are you?"

Then there was a blast from the horn of the arriving ferryboat and the roar of a dozen car engines coming to life.

Norma looked at the boat and then back to Brian again.

He lifted a foot to one pedal of the bike and gave a little shrug.

Well, shit.

The car in front of her started to move. The car behind her gave a little toot, and Norma fumbled at her car keys, started up her engine, and slammed it with a terrible grinding into first gear. She looked out her window again. Opened her mouth to say something—anything—but Brian had circled his bike. Leaving. He mouthed something—"Thank you?" "See you?"—and then gave a little good-bye salute and pedaled out of her life again.

CHAPTER 10

Nightfall found Norma back on Mainland and heading into Kirkwall. Well, night didn't really fall, it just meandered around in the pale light.

Norma's thoughts meandered around with it. That was slightly better than the frantic racing her thoughts had been doing on the ferryboat ride. They'd gone from jumbled confusion and self-flagellation for being such a mumble-mouth dimwit to a growing realization that dark and mysterious painters on Orkney apparently *liked* mumble-mouth dimwits. At least the pretty ones. No—check that—the *very* pretty ones. There was hope—there was—dare she think it? There was expectation. Fresh and new and—

How the heck was she going to find him again?

Did he even *want* her to find him again?

Did he want to find *her?*

Norma took a deep breath. *Don't start,* she told herself. *Don't borrow trouble.* The entire population of Orkney was somewhere around twenty thousand. How hard would it be to find him? She had all the time in the world, right? If it came to that, she could always have a little sleepover with Betty Corrigall. Norma smiled.

Allow yourself some happy, girl. Enjoy this, for Pete's sake. The man bicycled five miles across a peat bog to see you again. Okay?

Okay.

Norma followed the main road into the southwest corner of Kirkwall and up through the middle of town. Kirkwall was lovely. Cluttered with modern bits, of course, but she'd learned by now to edit that stuff out and concentrate on the picturesque and historic. It was a harbor town on the northeast side of the island tucked into the southern end of the Bay of—what else?—Kirkwall. She wound her way through the town, past Saint Magnus, the big-deal cathedral, and on up to the harbor itself, where she found the—what else?—Kirkwall Hotel. Red and yellow sandstone, several stories in classic squarish Orkney architecture, overlooking the water—seemed perfect.

She booked herself a room on the third floor. It was pleasant, with a nice view of the bay, a clean white bedspread, and an *en suite* bath, though the bathtub was one of those odd European sitters. She took a bath, realized how hungry she was, and went downstairs to eat.

What she wasn't expecting was to find Russell, the good ol' Houston boy. He was sitting at the bar, alone, with a drink and a cigarette. He saw her and broke into a big ol' Texan grin.

"Sugar!" he said, which, with the handsome grin, didn't sound at all irritating. "You staying here, too? Come on over, I'll buy you a drink."

Norma went. Happiness apparently loved company, too.

"Hello again," she said. "Where's the woman to whom you aren't engaged?"

He chuckled but didn't answer. He lifted his glass and signaled the bartender. "Hit the pretty lady with another one of these."

"Oh, gosh," said Norma, "I shouldn't. I haven't even eaten."

"Oh, sure you should, sugar."

"And I hate scotch. That's scotch, right?"

The bartender put a glass with clear golden liquid in front of her.

"Yes, ma'am," he said.

"You won't hate this," said Russell. "It's Highland Park—single malt, distilled right here in Kirkwall, right, Teddy?"

The bartender smiled and went to another customer.

"They brew it with heather—no kidding, give it a try."

Norma took a sip. It was pretty smooth. She took another and felt the warmth go down and, sure enough, a heady little aftertaste of heather presented itself with a pleasant little Scottish fling.

She smiled.

"See?" Russell grinned again, this time with a wink. "So you been sightseeing all day?"

"I went to Hoy," Norma said. "To see the puffins."

"Cute. Linda wants to do that. But today she dragged me to all the prehistoric crap."

So. Linda.

"And there's a buttload of that ancient stuff around here, I tell ya. Today, Scara Brae, tomorrow them covered mounds, and then the Stones of Stenness or some such shit. I mean, it's interesting and all, but rocks is rocks even if some Scottish caveman dragged 'em into a bleeding circle."

Norma was laughing and shaking her head.

"Notice how I stuck 'bleeding' in there? I'm picking up English real good, ain't I?"

"God," Norma said, "you're awful. No wonder Linda dumped you in a bar."

"Good one," Russell said. "Real subtle. Okay, I'll level with you, seeing how we're drinking buddies now. Linda's my girl friend. As in girl—space—friend. She's an anthropologist. No, really, they make 'em that pretty these days. She and I have been on and off each other since our high school days. We like the sex, but we drive each other crazy. This trip came up for me, well, to Aberdeen down there, and Linda just twisted my arm till I said I'd take her up here to Orkney, which is some kind of anthropologist's wet dream. She didn't dump me here—this is my 'time-out before I strangle her' time. She's up there, on the Internet, e-mailing all her cronies, and I'm down here talking up the pretty lady I met on the boat. Clear 'nough?"

Norma took another sip of scotch. No wonder the Texans were taking over the world. It was outrageous, but some grade-A flirting. Or was it the single malt on an empty stomach? Okay, there was a good comeback.

"I can't tell if I like you," she said, "or if it's this single malt on an empty stomach."

"Then I'll feed ya. They say the grub here is pretty good."

And he did. And it was. And she did like him, but then, she told herself, in the afterglow of her day with Brian Burroughs, she'd like the devil himself, even in cowboy boots with a Marlboro hanging from his lip.

∞

"So what was in Aberdeen?" she asked him. They were well into their after-dinner Highland Parks.

"Right," he said. "My profession. What does Russell do? You ever hear of Red Adair?"

"Red Adair?" Yes, she'd heard of him. "You put out oil well fires?"

He grinned.

"Man," Norma said, impressed. "Oil well fires in the North Sea? You *are* a crazy sonofabitch."

"I ought to let you think that till I get in your pants," Russell said, "but that would hardly be sporting. I don't put out oil well fires. I insure against them."

It took a moment for it to register. She was still trying to get past the remark about her pants.

"You're—you sell insurance?"

"Hey, it's a dirty job . . ." he said, putting up his hands, "but—tell the truth—now you're really hot for me, right?"

Norma laughed. To tell the truth, another scotch or two and she would be. So she shook her head and put down her drink. It was time for bed.

"It's time for bed, Mr. Salesman," she said. "Me to mine, and you to Linda's—where you obviously belong."

"We'll see about that," he grinned. "We'll bloody see."

∞

Morning found her, thankfully alone, still happy and strangely satisfied. It was an odd feeling, but a good one, so she lay there awhile wallowing. Then it was a bath in the little tub and breakfast à la room service, a pretty good way to avoid Linda and Russell at their breakfast.

There were guidebooks in the room and Norma finally gave in to them and planned out her day. There was a "butt-load" of stuff to see and do right here in town. There was Saint Magnus and the Earl's Palace, maybe a tour of the Highland Park distillery would be fun. And shopping. She'd gotten to be pretty good at that little skill. Shopping for sure.

Norma smiled. Maybe she could find a little art gallery somewhere.

∞

No luck on the art gallery. But she'd found a really nice knitwear shop where she'd dropped a satisfying bundle. Sheep were big on the islands. Sheep and wool. Everything in the shop was local. Locally grown, locally designed, locally knitted. Norma bought herself two sweaters, a hat, big thick socks, and, to her delight, a sheepskin. Not an ordinary sheepskin. This was the fluffy wonderful pelt of a North Ronaldsay sheep. It was a creamy light gray, thick and woolly and, down the center, long wonderful woolly strands streaked in black. The shop clerk, a lovely, sweet woman (Norma was beginning to suspect that the entire population of Orkney was lovely and sweet) explained to her that the pelt had come from a prehistoric line of sheep carefully culled from the semiferal, seaweed-munching flock maintained on the far northern island of—where else?—North Ronaldsay.

After her long day, she was hungry enough to eat seaweed herself. She thanked the clerk, got directions to the village of Saint Margaret's Hope and The Creel, which was Orkney's only four-star restaurant. Then she gathered up her big woolly-stuffed shopping bags and went back to the hotel to change. She walked gingerly through the hallway, not wanting to run into Russell and Linda, but then she thought, *Why the heck not?*

On the twenty-minute drive down the coast to Saint Margaret's Hope, Norma thought this out a bit more. She wasn't seriously considering letting Russell get into her pants. She didn't think he was all that serious, either. Russell was a big attractive hunk of Texan who must have flirted his way through his whole life. She was flattered by his attention. That sort of attention—the hunk sort—was new to her, and it was nice. And yes, exciting and sexy and a grand indication that she was emanating, for the first time in her life, I'm-worth-it vibes.

The truth, the real truth, which she had busily filled her day touring and shopping to avoid confronting, was that she quite possibly loved Brian Burroughs. Tortured artist. Handsome, black-haired, wind-tossed Brian Burroughs.

Her window was open, and, as she had learned like a good tourist from her guidebooks, she was crossing the famous Churchill Barriers, created during the war and creating what she understood now was the famous body of water known as Scapa Flow.

She leaned her head out the window and yelled, startling a seagull to flight. "Brian Burroughs makes Trey Bliss look like a week-old bag of haggis!"

Oh, yeah. That felt good. Damn good.

She'd actually had haggis back in Scotland, and for minced guts and oatmeal boiled in a sheep's stomach, it hadn't been half bad. A woman brave enough to eat haggis was brave enough to hunt down and get whatever man she chose. Norma honked the horn for emphasis, sending yet another seabird into panic. It was meant to be. She was beginning to see that. To believe it. She had come to Orkney to find Brian Burroughs. Okay then, that was settled. Even Saint Margaret didn't have such hope.

The little seaside town was adorable. The Creel was squeezed into a line of quaint sandstone buildings standing shoulder-to-shoulder along the waterfront. Norma parked with her two left wheels on the curb behind a little red sports car. The restaurant was adorable, too. Cozy and homelike with low ceilings, watercolors on the walls, and mismatched candlelit tables with cream-colored tablecloths. The place was crowded, and Norma realized she was the only single diner, which caused her momentary chagrin, until the sweet and lovely staff made her feel totally welcome and seated her at a prime windowside table without batting an eye.

Next to her was a big round table seated with a large and happy family. Norma eavesdropped while waiting for her waitress, enjoying the singsong sound of happy Orkney chatter.

For starters she had the Parton salad, which was fresh crab with lemon mayonnaise, then she had the North Ronaldsay mutton terrine, with homemade rhubarb chutney, and then the trio of steamed fish, which consisted of seared sea trout, steamed wolffish, and lemon sole, with a cherry tomato and basil salsa. This was served with island-grown new potatoes and a vegetable medley and home-baked bannocks, which were oatmeal griddlecakes, and to die for. Then the waitress suggested dessert, The Creel's famous strawberry shortcake, and Norma begged to be allowed to breathe first, and could she have a palate-cleansing Highland Park scotch?

At this point the large and happy family rose up en masse and prepared to depart, clearing Norma's view to the far corner of the next room.

Brian Burroughs, *her* Brian Burroughs, was sitting right there.

For the first half of the second split by time her heart rose in a wonderful bounding leap to the stars, only to come crashing down broken into the pit of despair when her brain caught up with her eyes.

Next to him, practically nose-to-nose, in the sweet golden flicker of candlelight, sat what had to be the most beautiful girl in the seventy Orkney Isles. She was young, fresh, dewy, sparkling—blond, oh yes, she was blond—practically screaming Norse goddess descended from Valhalla come to drive a big fat fucking spear through all of her dreams.

Shit.

The waitress set down her glass of scotch on a little paper napkin.

Norma drank it in three swallows.

"Goodness," said the waitress. "You ready for your short-cake now?"

Maybe the blonde was his sister.

Right.

"Bring me another one of these," Norma said, and lifted the empty. "No, wait. Tell me something. Do you know that couple in the corner over there?"

The waitress turned and looked.

"Oh, aye," she said. "They come here every Friday just about. The fellow is the famous artist, Brian Burroughs, and that's his girlfriend." She leaned down in confidence. "They say she's the most beautiful woman in all of Orkney. She's from one of the oldest families on Stronsay, and her name is—"

In that tiniest pause between words, Norma realized if the waitress said "Ashley," she would pick up the butter knife and commit seppuku right there on the spot.

"—Fiona Rousay."

So there was a God. But obviously a cruel, beautiful, blond female kind, and probably laughing her goddess ass off at the mortified mortal down below.

"Ma'am," said the waitress, "are you all right?"

"Yes," said Norma. "I'm fine. And the dinner was fine. I'm just too full for that shortcake, so, do I pay you?"

"Yes, ma'am—and would you like to . . ."

Norma realized she was offering to get Brian and Fiona's attention.

"Oh, God, no," Norma said. "I mean, no, God, no."

The one bit of luck in the whole travesty was that the couple was so intent on each other that she could have danced unnoticed on her tabletop nude. She gave the waitress a wad of pounds, thanked her again for the wonderful meal, then made a break for the door.

The drive back to Kirkwall left the seagulls in peace.

"Well, of course he has a girlfriend," Norma told herself about two dozen times. "Of *course* he does. Good-looking man like that, an artist, for chrissake, of course he has a girl-friend. Of *course* he does."

About three-quarters of the way she had to pull the car over to the side of the road in order to cry. There was a big bump, then a screech along the underside of the car and Norma realized there *was* no side of the road. She had driven the car partway into a gully, cleverly disguised as level solid land by a big thick twisted patch of flowerless heather. Now she sat with the motor running and the horizon at thirty degrees. This was just marvelous. She gave the engine a little gas, and the engine returned in kind with a powerless whine and propelled the car exactly nowhere.

Fine and dandy. She would just sit here until she died. They could find her skeleton years later—no, her mummi-fied corpse—but that was peat, wasn't it? Not the goddamn heather. Norma put her head on the steering wheel and began to sob. After a few minutes of that she heard the roar of an approaching car coming from the south.

Norma dried her face on her sleeve and made a half-hearted attempt to fix her hair. In the rearview mirror she saw the little red sports car convertible. Yes, indeedy. Driving, was the blond and beautiful Fiona Rousay, at her side the devoted Brian.

Kill me now, O Lord. Please kill me now.

No such mercy was forthcoming. Instead, the red car pulled over and Brian jumped out over the unopened door.

Norma gave one last wipe at her snot and faced the music.

"Havin' a bit of trouble?" he said, oh so helpfully. He

smiled the crooked smile, but Norma saw that he was smiling it back to Fiona.

"It *is* her," he said.

Fiona was opening her door and she smiled back.

"The puffin lady?" Fiona said.

The puffin lady. Great. And Norma realized that he'd told his girlfriend all about their secret, wonderful day.

Brian turned his smile back to Norma.

"I thought this was your rental."

"I ran off the road," Norma said. Obviously.

"Don't feel stupid," Brian said. "Happens all the time. Why they don't put up markers is beyond me."

"Heh heh." She felt very, very stupid.

Fiona had approached, and Brian took her slender little hand.

"Fiona," he said, "this is Norma. Norma—"

"Dale," said Norma. Like it mattered.

"So nice to meet you," said Fiona in her sylphlike voice. "Brian told me all about you and your little puffin. That was just so charming, such a sweet story. Welcome to Orkney, and I'm so sorry our silly road has let you down. You aren't hurt, are you? Brian, take my car and go get Peter Flett."

"Right, luv," Brian said, and to Norma, "Peter's farm is right over the ridge. He's got a winch."

And so—so sadly so—did Brian.

CHAPTER 11

The really hideous thing was how nice Fiona was. Norma had a nice long stretch of time to find that out. They sat on the crooked "bonnet," as Fiona charmingly called it, of Norma's purple car and had themselves a nice long girl chat.

"I'm so sorry about the death of your father," Fiona had graciously started out, "but such a touching tribute that brought you to our shores."

Yes, she actually said that, "brought you to our shores." But from her lips it sounded kind and natural. Lovely and sweet, you bet. Fiona was the Orkney embodiment of lovely and sweet.

"Thank you," said Norma. That was it. It was all she could utter when what she wanted to do was scream. With a sidelong glance she checked out Fiona's bod. No flaws there, of course, Norse goddess all the way.

"And where are you from in the States? I don't believe Brian mentioned it."

Brian hadn't asked, that's why.

"I'm from the Midwest," Norma said. "A little town you wouldn't have heard of. A little dump of a place."

Fiona giggled—a sweet, silvery fairy bell of a giggle.

"Brian said you were funny."

Yes, she was a real laugh riot.

"I've been to the States," Fiona said. "But only the East Coast. My college had an exchange program with Bryn Mawr, so I was there a year."

"Oh?" Norma said. Bryn Mawr. Bryn friggin' Mawr. But she had to say something. "What college?"

"Cambridge."

Norma wanted to punch her. She couldn't be a *dumb* blonde, no.

"You and Brian—" Norma said, then stopped. "Where did Brian go to college?"

Fiona was looking at her. Her eyes were deep blue, like lapis lazuli—beautiful lapis lazuli eyes.

"Brian didn't go to college," Fiona said. "At least I don't think he did."

Aha! Was that a chink in the relationship?

"How long have you been—" Norma stopped again. "How long have you known him?"

"Two years," Fiona said, and smiled. She had two cute little dimples. "I came home from Cambridge and all the girls were on about him. The mysterious painter stalking the megaliths. Of course, I had to see for myself. Strange and dark and brooding they said. No one knew where he came from, but all of them had a good idea where they wanted him to go!"

The silvery laugh again.

"But I thought—" Norma said. "Isn't Brian from Orkney?"

I know these cliffs. Been doin' that since I was a boy.

Norma remembered every word Brian had said.

The question brought the first unlovely thing to Fiona's face. A tiny pucker, the smallest wrinklette between her finely arched brows.

"Well," Fiona said, and the tiny pucker wrinkled a fraction more, "he was born on Orkney. On Hoy. But he was raised in Scotland. I think. He's only been back these few years, now."

"I see," Norma said, though she didn't. Time to take the plunge.

"And are you two—are you guys engaged?"

The dimples again and Fiona said, "Well, we're engaged to be engaged, you could say. I love him with all my heart and there could be no other man for me, that's for sure."

Well, crap. Big-time crap. Then Norma saw that pucker again and hope sprang eternal.

"But . . ." Norma coaxed.

"It's my family," Fiona said. "They—"

"Don't approve?"

"No, it's not about approval, they just—"

"Think you can do better?"

"No, not that exactly, it's, they just don't understand why I'm—"

"Throwing your life away on an artist?"

Those lapis lazulis were looking Norma's way again. Did she detect a tiny bit of sharpness there?

"My family wants the best for me. They're coming to see that Brian is the best. I know it. Then we will marry."

Norma let a sigh escape, but Fiona was oblivious. The thought of Brian having interest in the puffin lady was non-existent.

"How about you?" Fiona said. "Boyfriend? Husband?"

"Husband," Norma said. "Ex."

"I'm sorry," Fiona said, and actually patted her on the knee.

"Could have been worse," Norma said. "Like Betty Corrigall."

"Oh—so you went there, did you? That's the most unpleasant story—Brian has painted it over and over—I've *told* him that his brighter things are what he should concentrate on—people don't like to buy pictures of graves."

Norma felt her hope surge like the tide. So he *hadn't* told Fiona everything—and better still, *she* was the one who had connected with him about Betty Corrigall and Fiona, *nah nah,* hadn't.

Fiona's other-woman sixth sense finally stirred. "How long will you be here?" she asked, not quite so sweetly.

"I'm not really on any kind of schedule," Norma said.

This time she got the lapis lazulis *and* the wrinklette, then a white Land Rover appeared up the road.

"Ah," said Fiona, "there's Brian and Peter."

The girl chat mercifully came to an end.

CHAPTER 12

Norma's third night on the islands did not pass blissfully, and there was not a lot of happiness in the morning in which to wallow.

The men had pulled her car from the ditch with a minimum of grunting and cursing. There was no damage, and Norma thanked everyone thoroughly and there were dumb tourist jokes bandied about and then Peter Flett drove away and Brian and Fiona wished her well and said that they should get together sometime, but nobody made any move to arrange that, and then the happy couple got in the little red sports car and sported merrily away.

Norma took her odd little morning bath, then sat by the windowside watching the boats and the gentle morning bustle of Orcadians. Then she got out her North Ronaldsay sheepskin and brushed the black strands like she'd brushed the long strands from her long-ago Barbie doll's hair.

Brian Burroughs was a lost cause. The tides of hope could surge all they wanted, they were just grinding her chances—grinding her chances into smaller and smaller grains of sand.

Then Norma grabbed herself by the virtual collar and gave herself a good shake.

This was her new life, darn it. Her brand-new freshly turned leaf. She was falling back into the same old rut like a creaky milk cart behind a saggy old dray horse.

She had five thousand years of history in which to wallow, the endless ocean opened right outside her door, and she was surrounded by twenty thousand of the loveliest, sweetest people on the globe.

Shake, shake, shake. Get yourself dressed, fix yourself up, go get your caffeine fix, and then go out there and be a goddamn tourist.

∞

Late afternoon found Norma, in fetching little walking shorts and a sleeveless black T-shirt, on the narrow strip of land between the Loch of Harray and the Loch of Stenness. She had made her way west from Kirkwall deep into the Heart of Neolithic Orkney, as Orcadians were wont to say. First the Unstan Cairn chambered tomb (they'd found a "buttload" of Neolithic pots there), then on to Maeshowe, which was considered the finest chambered tomb in Western Europe, no slouch that, until the Vikings had slouched in around 1150 and plundered the sucker. But the Vikings had left a dandy collection of runic inscriptions on the wall. These were cool "twig runes," called that mainly because they resembled twigs.

After Maeshowe, she stopped by the Barnhouse Stone Age village, which was pretty interesting, and then on to admire the Standing Stones of Stenness. These impressive megaliths were erected somewhere around three thousand years before Christ. The guidebook proudly pointed out that this predated many of the henges on mainland Britain. There were only four stones standing out of an original circle of twelve, unfortunately not including the legendary Odin Stone. This stone, along with a bunch more, was toppled back in 1814 by a farmer tired of plowing around them. (The guidebook sniffily pointed out that he was a tenant farmer and *not* an Orcadian.)

Then up the road to the solitary Watchstone, which, at nineteen feet, really was impressive. This stone was said to dip its "head" and drink from the loch at midnight on New Year's Eve.

Norma felt she could dip her head over a nice glass of Highland Park about then, but she drove northwest about a mile to see the third-largest stone circle in the British Isles. This was Orkney's pride and joy, the Ring o' Brodgar. She parked her car and walked the last bit to the gently sloping plateau, and boy, was she glad she did.

It was huge (104-meter diameter, the guidebook said) and was once composed of sixty stones, of which twenty-seven now remained. They were not as tall as the Stones of Stenness, but there was an eerie magic to the place for sure. For the first time, Norma felt that she was here on Orkney, that she had arrived. People—strange, mysterious Neolithic people—had been here on this ground four thousand years ago, and now here she was—Norma Dale—standing on the very same spot.

She walked to the nearest stone. It was about seven feet tall, surprisingly thin and flat, and wider at the top than the bottom. She touched the cold sandstone and ran her hand over the roughness. Then she walked slowly from stone to stone, touching each one.

Perspective. This was excellent perspective on the whole love thing.

One of the broken stone stumps was supposed to have twig runes carved into it. Norma kept hunting until, on the northeast side, she found the carvings. The guidebook had a little chart with letters and numbers explaining how to interpret the runes. In this case the symbols spelled out the personal name "Bjorn."

What now, Bjorn? Norma thought, getting all heavy.

And then, *What now, Brian? What will happen four thousand years from now?* She knelt and ran her fingers over the runes, sighed, and looked around.

The sun was casting a warm orange glow on the slabs of stone. Behind each one, a long soft shadow ribboned out. The last of her fellow tourists were wandering back up the path toward the car park. Norma mused about spending the night here. Bet that some convincing Orkney magic would rise up somewhere around three in the morning. She smiled. Maybe with a sleeping bag, granola with M&Ms, and a flashlight.

She stood and walked to the center of the circle. One story said this had been called the Temple of the Sun; the Stenness circle was the Temple of the Moon. The Watchstone, the Odin Stone, all the stones broken and plowed under. They had all been part of a greater system of circles stretching for miles along the great henge between the lakes formed from the natural earthen bowl of hills, sky, water, and the years of labor of man.

Or not.

The oldest legends told of a race of giants who came to dance in the light of the moon. They danced and danced, losing track of time until the sun rose, turning them all to stone. It was said they danced to the tune of the giant fiddler, who stood and played his fiddle outside of the circle. He, too, was turned to stone. Norma looked to the east and saw it. What they called the Comet Stone. About 150 meters down a little valley, then up a little hill. She walked in that direction. The stone wasn't very tall—about six feet. It was fatter than the others, the top shaped like a sandstone Gumby head. Norma thought, *I'll go touch the fiddler, then I'll go back to Kirkwall and hunt up some fish, chips, and a beer.*

Then she saw the cowboy boot. It was sticking out from behind the other side of the stone and kind of tapping its toe to an unsung tune. A very familiar boot. Norma walked around the stone and stood there shaking her head with her hands on her hips.

Russell. He was sitting on the ground with his back leaning against the fiddler, cigarette on his lip and a silver flask in his hand.

He gave Norma a squint and a grin.

"Sugar!" he said. "I was just thinking about you."

He held up the flask.

"Slug of this damn fine heather juice?"

Suddenly she was very, very glad to see this big lug of a man. So she grinned back and said, "You're darn tootin'."

She took the flask, wiped the lip with the palm of her hand, and took a couple of big swigs.

" 'At's my girl," said Russell.

"No," Norma said, "that would be Linda, I believe. Where is she?"

Russell waved his hand vaguely in the air.

"She found a bunch of PhDs. They dragged her off to see the Ring of Bookan."

Norma looked in the vague direction.

"There's *more* standing stones?"

"Naw," Russell said, "Bookan is the shitty ring. No megaliths, just rubble. Really boring rubble. That's why I'm sitting here." He gave Norma an unmistakably suggestive leer. "They'll be gone for hours."

He patted the ground next to him.

"Pull up some dirt, why don't you?"

Norma sat down, took another slug, and passed him the flask.

"It shore is pretty out here," he said, "I'll give 'em that.

I'm mean, for mostly being rocks and sheep—this place has its ginny say qua."

Norma smiled.

"You know what I find really attractive about you?" he said.

She lifted her brows in his direction, but he wasn't looking. He took a drink of whiskey and a drag off his Marlboro. Then he did look at her.

"That little spot." And he touched the corner of her mouth with the little finger of his cigarette hand. "When you smile like that. You used that on me on the *Hamnavoe,* you little vixen. It works damn good."

Norma laughed out loud, and he joined her and handed her back the whiskey.

She took a big swallow and then realized she was considering his leer—seriously. She looked at him—with his sparkly blue eyes and thick blond hair—and her eyes traveled down to his kissable lips and then farther south to his broad shoulders and the muscles on his arms, and then before getting to Troubleville, Norma pushed away from the stone at her back and got to her feet. She took a couple of wise steps away from Russell and the fiddler and then, unwisely, put the flask to her lips again. One more gulp of heather-flavored lubrication and an inarguable logic presented itself. If you can't be with the one you love—love the lug you're with.

Norma turned back around and vixened.

"You still interested in my pants, Russell? I got a fire needs putting out."

She couldn't believe she'd actually said that, but there was no retreat now. Russell was already on his feet stubbing out his Marlboro on the petrified giant.

"Hot damn," he said, then reeled her in with one strong arm.

The kiss tasted of whiskey and tobacco and was sexy as hell. Russell's big hands were already groping up her T-shirt and pushing aside her bra. He spun her up against the megalith and pressed her with his Texas-sized hard-on. Norma groaned. Another big ol' sloppy kiss. Then she turned her face to gasp for breath.

"Jesus, Russell," she said. "Right here?"

"Right here," Russell said, "just like the goddamn Druids."

He pulled her shirt over the top of her head.

"I want to see you naked, sugar, up against this rock."

Norma stripped away her bra and let her walking shorts fall to the ground. She kicked off her shoes and socks. Russell gave her his grin, then went for her pants as promised. They came off with a tug, and she stretched her arms against the rock, slave-girl style above her head.

∞

Afterward, they put their clothes back on and sat, backs against the stone, elbows on their knees, and finished off the flask of Highland Park.

"You know," Norma said, "I don't think the Druids probably did that kind of stuff."

Russell chuckled. "Sure they did. You think all these big rocks are about astronomy? Hell, look at 'em standing there. Just a bunch of big ol' Neolithic dicks, you ask me."

Norma thumped him.

They passed the flask back and forth. A moment of comfortable silence.

"You really love her, don't you?" Norma said.

"Linda?" Russell said. "Yeah, I really do." Pause. "The woman's making noises about babies now. We'll do it, you know, get married, all that stuff. I'm ready," grin, "despite, you know, appearances."

Norma smiled.

"In fact," Russell said, lifting up the flask and showing it all around, "I should make this my illicit sex, wild monkey-love swan song." He drank to his own toast and passed the flask to Norma. "You know, I think I really mean it." He shook his head. "Besides, it's going to be pretty hard to top this. And you, sugar."

Norma looked at him. "You really mean *that*?"

Russell gave her his squint-eye consideration. "I know you," he said. "I know who you are."

"Who I am?"

"That's right. You're one of the shy girls. The awkwards. The unpopulars hanging on the fringe. Tight little unblossomed buds with ugly glasses and the wrong clothes. Y'all think life has passed you by even in goddamn high school, and though you go out in the great wide world, you blossom finally, you finally figure how to fill that sexy underwear, it never leaves you, does it? That first rejection—that shoving from the circle. You never really learn to give yourselves some credit. Never believe someone will love you."

Norma let two big tears roll from her eyes. She was pretty much pegged, wasn't she?

"Oh, shit," Russell said, "me and my big mouth."

"No," said Norma, holding up one hand, "you're absolutely right. Absolutely fair bleedin' cop."

Russell took her hand and kissed it. "Someone will, sugar, trust me. And he'll be lucky."

Norma looked at him, sniffed, and smiled. "I guess I should trust you," she said. "If it were pure bull, it'd be coming *before* the sex, right?"

"Darn tootin'," he said. "Now, tell Russell, there's some

guy out there, ain't that true? Some dumbass don't know what he's missing?"

"Yeah," Norma said, "there's a guy. But he's not dumb, he's—well, he's in love with another woman."

"Back in the States? That's why you've come to the ends of the earth?"

Norma shook her head. "No, I didn't come here to lose myself—just the opposite. I came here to find myself. And I did. I did find myself. The trouble is, I think, that I found him, too."

"I see," Russell said. "Local boy, eh?"

"Sort of," said Norma. "That's part of it, I think. The attraction. I'm not sure exactly who he is. He's strange—"

"Oh," said Russell, "big mystery man is it? Is he tall? Dark?"

They both laughed, and Norma had to admit that he was, indeed, tall and dark *and* handsome.

"And he's an artist," she said with a sigh. "That's the topper. He paints, and he's engaged to be engaged to the most beautiful fucking girl in Orkney."

Russell raised his brows. "Are you talking about that Burroughs dude? What's his name—Brian Burroughs?"

Norma stared. "You *know* him?" she said.

"It's Linda. In Stromness. She bought a painting he did of the Stones of Stenness—wouldn't shut up about it. The gal at the little gallery was more than happy to dish all the dirt. About Burroughs, the Italian bastard, Fiona, golden princess of Stronsay—whew, girl, you picked yourself a good one . . ."

Russell went on, but Norma's ears were still back at the Italian bastard part. Italian bastard? What the hell was that? Then her ears tuned back in.

". . . so she was just thrilled when she realized it was him. Insisted we climb the damn hill so she could go gush at the poor guy."

"What?" Norma said. "What did you just say?"

"This morning, at Quoyer Viewpoint. Your Burroughs fellow was painting up there on top of that hill."

Russell was pointing to the northeast, across the loch, sparkling gold in the setting sun.

"Oh, jeez," Norma said, "you think he could still be there?"

"Maybe," Russell said. "Won't know until you look."

"You think I should?"

Russell took her by both arms and looked her in both eyes.

"Fucking A, you should," he said. Then he helped her—they were both more than a little drunk—onto her feet.

"Okay, then," Norma said, "okay, then I will."

Three sheets to the wind, you lose a little perspective.

CHAPTER 13

After a bottle of water and a packet of crisps, and with all the windows rolled down, Norma had sobered considerably by the time she got to Quoyer Viewpoint. So much so that after looking in the car mirror she considered going on, to Kirkwall.

She looked, precisely, as if she had been fucking a Texan on the ground.

Fresh lipstick, a brush, dusting the dirt off her butt, and a mint. *Besides, this was fate. Right?*

Norma climbed the hill.

He was still there.

Panoramic landscape on the easel. One of Fiona's "brighter" pieces, nice, but Norma thought the grave one was better.

Brian was cleaning his brushes; the smell of turpentine and linseed oil reached her nostrils.

"Hello," he said.

"Hello."

"Car running all right?"

"Yes. Wow, they're right, the view *is* beautiful up here."

Norma turned to actually view it. She caught her breath. You could clearly see the Ring of Brodgar. Then she let it out. Any human figure—or figures—would be the size of an ant.

"I've been touring the Neolithic heart of Orkney today. See, look, I got a guidebook and everything."

Brian looked but he didn't smile.

"It recommends seeing the sunset from up here," she lied. "Funny, running into you."

Brian set aside his brushes and picked up his sketchbook and a piece of charcoal.

"I'll draw you a picture," he said. He pointed to a flat rock. "Take a seat."

Norma did. Did he mean a picture—of her?

He squatted, sketchbook on one knee, and looked at her, drew some quick fierce lines, then looked at her again. Guess he did.

"Fiona is—she's really nice."

He didn't answer.

Norma studied him. He did, actually, look a bit Italian. But maybe they just called him that, like Michelangelo.

"She said you guys were—engaged to be engaged."

He sketched a minute more without looking, then said, "When we were out there, out there on Hoy—walkin'—I felt something. But you know that. I told you that. I had to tell you—bikin' like a madman, like a loon—just to see you those few more minutes. What I felt—I couldn't identify. What I felt bothered me. Bothered me enough that it stopped me from tellin' you about Fiona, do you understand that? Fiona, the woman that I love."

Sketch, sketch.

"And when I saw you at The Creel, all alone there, with your long dark hair and the green showin' in your eyes in that damn candlelight—then I did know. And then it bothered me plenty."

Norma's heart had stopped beating. Was he really saying this? Was he saying he felt about her the way she felt about him? But he was so dark, so angry—

"And then to see you there, on the roadside, cryin'. Cryin' 'cause you'd seen me with Fiona—I knew that, I knew why you were cryin'—and I had to leave you there, *with* her, for chrissake, knowin' what she'd say."

The charcoal, with his angry strokes, had been worn away to a nub. He tossed it aside, then flung the sketchbook onto the ground.

"Then to see you today—" He stood up and turned away from her.

Oh, no. He couldn't have.

"And now I'm here like a fuckin' fool. I'd been torturin' myself, actually thinkin'—ah, *hell*—and for what?"

Norma stood. She didn't want to, but she stood, trembling, and went to the sketchbook. She didn't pick it up. She just looked at it on the ground and the picture he'd done.

It was her, naked, up against the Comet Stone. And Russell, too, naked, obscene, wearing cowboy boots.

Norma shook her head. He couldn't have seen, there was nobody there. She felt the shame come up from her feet, up through the core of her body, the core still soiled with Russell, up through her heart, feeling those first wrenching pangs of agony and remorse, and on to her brain, registering there, searing the knowledge deep inside, the horrible shocking knowledge of what awful thing she'd done and could not undo—could never, never undo as long as she lived. But he couldn't have seen—he couldn't have.

There, next to the easel on the ground, black and shiny, like two ugly long fornicating bugs, was a pair of binoculars.

"I met his girlfriend," Brian said. "She's *nice,* isn't she?

Like Fiona? Is that what you do? Find nice girls and then play with their men? It's sick, Norma Dale, it's a sick thing to do."

Then he was there, next to her, grabbing her arm.

"You knew," he said low and quiet, "you knew I was up here, didn't you? That was your game, eh? Fuckin' us both?"

"No," Norma cried, "no! I didn't know, not till after—I mean, when—oh, God, I can't think—it's all screwed up!"

And then he kissed her, hard and deep, an angry kiss like a bite. Then he pushed her away and wiped his mouth, his eyes black as cold coal.

"Aye, woman, that it is, all screwed up."

Norma turned and ran from him, stumbling, then going on and on until she reached her car. The tears came then, then the shakes, and that ever-present dark and horrible shame.

CHAPTER 14

Norma's fourth night on the island was bad. She took three baths, the third one cold, but nothing could wash away Russell and what she'd done. She cried and she tried to think, which made her cry again, then she tried pounding her head awhile, then finally ended up all cried out, naked on the floor, curled up on her North Ronaldsay sheepskin.

Morning wasn't much better. She hadn't eaten, and her wet hair had dried with a big bump cockatoo crest, and she wanted to burn her fetching little walking shorts but couldn't find a match and the ashtray was too small.

Around nine she called room service and got a pot of coffee. What she really wanted was something stronger. Maybe heroin, but she didn't think they served it. Around ten she packed up her bags and went down to the front desk.

The clerk, upon hearing she was leaving so soon, was genuinely upset. Norma invented a lie about an emergency at home, then felt doubly bad when he seemed doubly upset.

That done, she drove her purple rental car back to Stromness and took the first ferry leaving for Scrabster.

The drive through the Highlands was a long, dull blur. In Edinburgh, she turned in the car and took a cab to the airport. It was there—hungry, miserable, exhausted, with her hair still like a cockatoo—that she had another epiphany.

The British Airways attendant—polite, but nowhere near lovely *or* sweet—was asking her the place of her destination.

A simple question. But Norma just stood there staring.

"Ma'am?" said the attendant. "Where is it you want to go?"

And that was it. The simple answer was there in her head.

"Brian," Norma answered. "I want to go to Brian."

"Excuse me?" The attendant blinked, like, is this a nutcase? And Norma smiled.

"I need a ticket to Kirkwall, in the Orkney Islands, please. One way."

CHAPTER 15

Norma stayed in Stromness this time. At first isolated in her hotel room. Three days. Then she started getting odd looks from the staff—and any kind of looking was not what she wanted. Where was an elfin cloak of invisibility when you needed it? So then she took to going out during the day, pretending to tour, but just walking up and down the flagstone streets in sunglasses and a scarf—à la Norma Jean. Then she started getting odd looks on the street. Stromness wasn't all that big a town, but by now she had pretty much sussed that here Brian Burroughs did not abide.

She did find the gallery, though. She stared at the big window full of his artwork, but did not go in. That would come later. Later in time, when the shame, she hoped, would have faded—when her thoughts, she hoped, had become coherent again. Yes, that would be nice. Again coherent thoughts and again a tiny, bitty smidgen of self-worth.

Norma found herself, one day, at the greasy-glassed fish 'n' chips place. The smell was wonderful. And they wouldn't remember her, right?

Wrong. Did none of these Orcadians ever leave this place? They were all there: Janny the counter girl, the gruff yet lovable fry-cook, the old man, the young man, even the older woman in the corner. They greeted her like a long-lost cousin. All smiles, puffin inquiries; the old guy even clapped her on the back.

"Did you get your pint at Moness?" he asked.

Norma assured him that she had. Then her haddock and chips were plunked on the counter and she got her plate and a Coke.

The woman in the corner signaled to the empty place at her booth. What else could she do? She joined her.

"I'm so glad you're enjoying your stay," said the woman.

She had a kind face. And pretty, too. Like June Lockhart, Lassie and Timmy's mom. Her hair, blond with attractive dashes of gray, was done up in that lovely old-fashioned style, classy with waves and a bun. She was wearing a fawn twin set and had a half-moon pair of reading glasses perched on her very nice nose. Splayed open beside her plate of fish was a dog-eared paperback of Robert Browning poems.

"I'm Marion," she said, extending her hand, "Marion Dearness."

"Norma," said Norma, "Norma Dale."

"Besides our Tammie Nories, what else have you seen? Been island-hopping like mad?"

Norma had taken her first bite of fried fish, so she shook her head no, then swallowed.

"Not really," she said. "I've concentrated mostly on Mainland—and Hoy, you know—the stones, and stuff."

"So are we losing you now?"

Losing her? Oh, right. The tourist was back in Stromness, must be heading home. But they weren't losing her, were they? She'd turned up again like a bad penny, like a herpes sore, an unwanted—

Marion was looking at her curiously. Waiting for a reply.

"Uh, no, not really," Norma said. "I was—I was thinking of staying, you know, for a while longer."

The curious look remained.

"I really love it here," Norma said. "I love your islands. I'd—I'd like to do them justice."

Marion smiled. "Well, that's lovely, then," she said.

Norma took another bite of fish. Justice. Justice indeed. She had to, somehow, make things right again. To justify her actions. But how could she? She had condemned herself already. A thousand times over. Put on the black cloth and said guilty, guilty, guilty.

"Are you all right?"

Marion came into focus across the table.

Norma had the wild urge to tell her everything. Like Timmy to June Lockhart, with Lassie bounding to the rescue.

"Yes," she said, "I'm fine."

"Where are you staying?"

"The Orca. But I—" A plan suddenly presented itself to Norma. "I'd like, really to, you know, rent somewhere— a place I could, you know—live."

"My, you really do love our islands," said Marion. "Don't you—isn't there a family somewhere?"

"No," Norma said. "No family. I'm divorced. Like, a year ago. Then my father died. I—There's my mother and sisters, but they—I don't really—"

She was going to cry.

"Goodness," Marion said. "Here I go prying, and look what I've done."

"No, really," Norma said. She wiped her eyes with her paper napkin. "I'm—my emotions—I'm—I'm—"

"A basket case?"

Norma laughed. "Yes," she said. "Exactly. I'm a crazy

American basket case. Precisely. You see, I came here—I'm not really here being a tourist. I had the thing with the puffin, for my dad, then I've been, well, you know, psychobabble, right? To find myself. So I'm here to, it's—it's more like—like a—"

"Sabbatical?"

Norma looked at her. She was good, this woman.

"You're good," said Norma. "Yes. A sabbatical. Exactly. A sabbatical from my life."

Marion reached across the table and patted her hand. "I know just the place."

"You do?"

"I do. My sister—her name is Anne—she does real estate, B and Bs, she's just renovated a string of crofting cottages—in the parish of Sandwick, but north of here, lovely countryside—a stone's throw from the Bay of Skaill. You must have been there, dear, to visit Skara Brae?"

"Skara Brae?" That sounded real familiar. "No, I haven't been to Skara Brae."

Suddenly, the room fell silent.

Everyone was looking at her. Then she remembered. Skara Brae—the Neolithic settlement, the most famous place on all of Orkney, two weeks on the island and she'd not seen it yet. Great.

The old man, the wit of the fish 'n' chips, popped up. "And ya be goin' to London be sure and miss Big Ben!"

Everyone laughed good-naturedly.

"Don't mind Ed," said Marion, shaking her head. "Skara Brae's been there for five thousand years, I imagine it still will be when you get to it. And, if you like the cottage, Skaill is biking distance away."

"Oh," Norma said, "I think I will. Like the cottage, I mean. I really think I will."

∞

And she did. It was perfect. It stood on a little hill in the middle of nowhere. Nowhere with a view of the sea. It was squat, rectangular, one story, with a peaked flagstone roof like a hand-drawn sepia checkerboard bent up in the middle and placed atop the stone-brick walls. Four unadorned rectangular windows on each long side and a front door painted blue. Two squat little chimneys wedged on the flagstone roof—one for the kitchen, Norma soon discovered, and one for the living room. The whole cottage wasn't more than eight hundred square feet, the bedrooms about ten by ten. It was freshly painted on the inside, in yellow and peach and blue, furnished with quaint overstuffed chairs, rickety painted tables, and rag rugs on the floor. The kitchen had a little refrigerator, a little two-ring cooker, and a microwave oven. There was also a small TV and a DVD player.

"I'll take it," Norma said.

Anne was as nice as her sister, though younger and with modern hair.

"That's wonderful," Anne said. "Marion said you were thinking of six months?"

"Or longer," Norma said. "But six months to start."

"We can give you a little cut on the terms, then," she said. "How are you on sunshine?"

Norma raised her brows.

"Because in another few months you won't be getting any, you see."

"Are the winters that bad? I was sorta looking forward to the weird sun and all. I really like the, uh, never-ending twilight thing—what's that you call it?"

"Simmer dim," said Anne with a grin. "And the winters aren't that bad for being so far north—average temperature is, let's see in Fahrenheit, around forty degrees. But we get snow most years, and storms, oh, you bet, storms—waves crashing so loud off the Atlantic you can hear them twenty miles inland. And those long nights. Come Solstice, the sun will be rising around nine in the morning and setting six hours later, so you get that light while you can. Are you . . ." She paused. "Well, Marion said you are rather after some privacy?"

Norma hadn't spilled everything to the older woman but had hinted fairly directly that she didn't want all twenty thousand Orcadians knowing her business.

"Yes," she said, "privacy is very important to me."

"I understand," Anne said, her curiosity almost not obvious, "it's just that I'll worry about you all alone out here. Do feel free to call on me or Marion—"

"Of course," Norma said, and she gave her best "really, I'm not such a loon" smile. "When can I move in?"

Anne handed her the key.

∞

Psychobabble or not, Norma's time alone in the cottage was a time of painful introspection, then of great soothing, and eventually a time of healing.

The first few weeks, after the initial numbness wore off, she devoted herself to sulking and depression. In Stromness, she'd gotten a good supply of Highland Park heather juice, and had liberally applied it to herself. Between drinking and crying, there was lots of fitful sleeping in her narrow cottage bed.

This got old pretty quick.

So she sobered up, ate lots of whole grains and vegetables, and started taking long walks along the rocky cliffs of Mainland's western shore. This is where the introspection kicked in.

Norma, basically, had two questions:

What the hell had happened?

and:

What the hell was she doing here?

The answer to the first question became the soothing part. To the second, the beginning of healing. She came to both answers one day in a conversation with a sheep.

It was not a North Ronaldsay sheep, it was the regular kind—dirty white, woolly, and stupid. On one of her long walks, she found the sheep grazing precariously at the edge of a seaside cliff. No shepherd, no rest of the flock, just one dumb ewe on her own little munching-the-grass trip. The metaphor for Norma's own life leapt unbidden to her mind. Metaphors, especially bad ones, weren't quite as exhilarating as epiphanies, but in this case it did the trick.

"Good God, sheep," she said, "look at you there."

The sheep kept munching.

"What the hell happened?" she said, though the ewe hadn't asked. "What the hell happened? I'll tell you what the hell happened. The man was falling in love with me and I was too damn stupid to realize it. Or maybe it wasn't love, but he was interested, okay? He was taken. With me! I attracted a man like Brian Burroughs *despite* a woman like Fiona friggin' Perfectpants and I was too, too—too dense! Too *sheep*-like, okay? I was a total blind moron sheep with my friggin' head in the sand!"

The sheep looked up at this but didn't seem offended.

"So off I went," Norma continued, "off I went off the edge of the cliff. Crash, bam, boom, okay? First Russell, then Brian—I was attracting men like—like—flies to honey, like dogs to a bone, like—like rams to your fine woolly ass!"

The sheep rolled her eyes.

"Well, it's true," Norma said. "And maybe you're okay with that. Used to it even. But not me. Not me. That day on the boat. Coming here. Russell saw it. He felt it. He didn't see a Norma standing there, he saw my first few moments as an Ashley. He witnessed my transformation, he saw me break from the cocoon and he responded."

Norma began to pace.

"That's it, that's *it*," she said.

The sheep had gone back to nibbling the grass.

"Russell wasn't just a big flirt . . . well, he *was* a big flirt, but he was a big flirt practically on his honeymoon."

And then she twigged.

"No. Jesus! He didn't see an Ashley—he saw a better-than-Ashley. Ashley—all the Ashleys, all the Lindas, the Fionas—they *know* they are attractive. Irresistible, all a man desires, they know it and they've *known* it since their babyhood when they made those first irresistible smiles. What Russell saw was *me,* being beautiful, being something he couldn't quite resist, and *me not knowing! Not* knowing. Don't you see?"

Munch. Munch.

"Right," said Norma. "No, you don't. You're a sheep and you're standing there in all your beautiful sheepness, *un*-knowing, and only I can take that in. Only I can know the soft, warm potential of your thick, wonderful wool, the crisp, delicious potential of your juicy leg of lamb."

"Bheeeeehhhh."

Norma laughed. *Now* she'd crossed the line of sheep sensibility, right? And then she took a deep breath of Bay of Skaill air and raised her arms to the wide Orkney sky. She'd crossed a line, all right. She'd crossed the line from self-loathing to see just a glimmer of understanding. To feel, finally, the return of self-acceptance.

She walked to the sheep and gave her a big hug. The sheep, though mildly alarmed, let her.

Norma looked out across the sparkling gray-blue water of the bay. She allowed her mind to consider Brian.

"Brian," she said quietly.

Attracted, too, by her innocence. By her beauty unaware.

Out there, on Hoy, on their Betty Corrigall walk, when they had stopped, when he put his arm around her—when she had wanted so badly for him to kiss her—Brian *had* wanted to kiss her. That's what the moment had been. Mutual, intense desire. Had she but known, had she been Ashley-aware, she could have had her kiss.

"Well, crap," she said.

To undergo the most romantic moment of your life and yet not get to enjoy it—not fair. Not damn fair.

"If only I had had a clue," Norma said. "Just a clue."

But—no. No!

A light of insight clicked on. A tiny one, the size of a night-light bulb.

If she *had* been an Ashley, if she had sent the right signal—the "yes yes kiss me you fool" sign—she would have gotten her kiss, right? Right. And it would have been absolutely great—the best kiss of her life, right? Right. But it wouldn't have stopped there, now would it? No. They would have kissed, and then kissed deeply, then they would have fallen to the ground and fucked like weasels. Wouldn't they have?

"Yes, we would have," Norma whispered. "Everything would have been different, but maybe not different *good*."

The feelings, Brian's feelings, were *because* she was Norma. The real Norma. Her. Norma, human being. She of the swollen eyes, big red nose, and puffin-shit hair. Unaware Norma. There was something precious there. Something created that day between them. Something fragile and perfect like a freshly opened flower that no one had seen.

And what had she done? She had crushed it. She'd had her weasel sex with Russell instead and bruise the blossom way beyond redemption. But she had acted with innocence, not cruelty. The sex with the Texan had not been a bad thing. She'd been *sad,* okay? She'd had a disappointed heart. Russell had been there and he had responded. Russell had seen the real Norma. He'd said so, right there. *I know you,* he'd said. And he had. And in that moment of truth between them— in whiskey *veritas*—right?—Russell had seen who she was.

"Not a slut," she whispered.

And the night-light switched to full spot—

"For Pete's sake," Norma said loudly. "I'm *not* a slut—I'm *not* a nasty femme fatale who plays with nice girls' men. Jesus."

What had happened between her and Russell had been a good thing, an innocent thing. If not for a crazy bit of luck, things could have been all right. They *would* have been all right. If only Brian could know that, if only he could see what had really happened out there. Norma knew she'd blown it. She didn't expect a relationship—not now—but, somehow, *somehow,* she had to make him understand.

"Brian has to know the truth," she said. She clutched her fingers deep into the ewe's wool. "For both of us."

And thus, along with irritating the sheep, did Norma throw the ol' gauntlet right at Fate's feet.

CHAPTER 16

October came to Orkney, and with it came the darkness, the damp, and the cold. The cottage became less her cozy little refuge and more an isolated stone shoe box on the edge of the goddamn world. But she kept both her hearth fires burning and rented lots of DVDs.

Her healing was just about complete.

Time, she came to know as her friend.

Tim*ing,* she came to understand, was everything. Luck was the cruel goddess who ruled and mocked from above. You had to watch out for Luck. Timing was her power. You couldn't blithely go about tempting Luck to stick out her foot for a good, laughable stumble. Luck couldn't resist sticking out her foot. You had to understand that. You had to watch where you put your feet. You had to plan.

Norma had a plan. Sort of.

Phase one was renting an isolated cottage and getting her shit together.

Check.

Phase two was reconnaissance.

Just what *was* the deal about Brian Burroughs? What was the deal with Fiona? And what was the deal now with Brian *and* Fiona? Norma had to know before she could even think of approaching him.

She had been regularly scanning the island's weekly newspaper, *The Orcadian,* which had come out every Thursday since 1798. She'd hoped to find tidbits, anything—like, God forbid, a wedding announcement—but other than a few mentions of Fiona's extended family, and all the fishing, weather, and Orkney political news she could use, nothing.

There was the art gallery woman. The gossip, the disher of dirt. A good source of data, obviously, but dangerous ground to tread. Gossip was a two-way path, and the last thing she wanted was for Brian to know she was here.

Then there was the scant information she already had. Brian had lived on Hoy as a child, then somehow didn't live in Orkney, since he returned two years ago as the mysterious artist, "stalking the megaliths," as Fiona had put it.

And the Italian thing. The "Italian bastard." What was that all about? Brian himself had made cryptic Italian references. Something about World War Two . . .

Norma found her crumpled Orkney guidebook. After a few pages she saw it. The Italian Chapel. Built by prisoners of war. *Hmmm.*

∞

Though Norma was indeed in bicycling distance of many things on the island, she had wisely purchased for herself a little green motorbike. She had also wisely purchased a warm woolen cloak. A wonderful cloak. Dark blue, with lighter blue designs of twig runes knitted in, and a hood worthy of Meryl Streep as the French lieutenant's woman.

The Italian Chapel, she discovered, was on Lamb Holm

Island, linked between East Mainland and South Ronaldsay by the Churchill Barriers. She had passed it without noticing on her ill-fated happy drive to Saint Margaret's Hope and The Creel.

The day was a mild one and she *putt-putted* up to the landmark on her scooter, just mildly chapped of face, by midafternoon.

The chapel was like a sweet little confection out in the middle of nowhere. On a desolate strip of sand it stood, snowy white with dark pink trim. A bold little false front with columned portico and arched windows, perky little decorative doodads, and fancy little crosses. Behind the false front extended the half-cylinder form of a Nissen hut.

Norma parked her scooter and walked up the cement steps to the entranceway. She opened the door and went in. Her eyes adjusted to the dark, and there she stood, like a telescoped Alice inside a Fabergé egg.

"My God," she said.

"Amazing, eh?"

She jumped. She hadn't realized anyone was there.

"That's why they call it the 'Miracle of Camp 60.' "

The speaker was a plump gray-haired lady. She was dressed in a bright pink coverall, had her hair done up in a kerchief, and was holding a fluffy blue dust mop.

"Camp 60?" Norma said.

"Camp 60," said the lady, "the Italian prison camp."

"I—I haven't done my homework very well," said Norma. She wondered if the island had a Worst Tourist award. "Is there—is there some kind of guide?"

"Nope," said the lady cheerfully. "We get ten thousand people a year to the chapel, and no one guards the place. People come, they look, they say a little prayer." She cocked an eyebrow. "Most know the story beforehand. . . ."

Norma gave a little well-sorry shrug and the plump lady smiled.

"No bother. I'll tell you, if you care to listen. My name is Isabella—"

"Norma," said Norma, extending her hand. "And you . . ." she signaled the mop.

"We island ladies take turns," said Isabella, "keeping our little chapel clean."

"Wow," said Norma, "cool."

"When the Italians came here it wasn't so 'cool,' " said Isabella. She gave a little wink. "Thought I'd start at the beginning."

Norma grinned.

"It was January, 1942. You know much about the war?"

"Well, you know," said Norma, "school."

"It was a grim time. I was nine years old back then. A grim time to be nine years old."

Norma nodded.

"The Italians who came here as prisoners of war—over a thousand of them—they'd been fighting for Mussolini in South Africa. You know who Mussolini was?"

"Oh, yes."

"So they brought them to Orkney to help build the barriers . . ." She lifted that quizzical brow.

"Right," said Norma, "the Churchill Barriers, like to, ah, block the, uh—Scapa Flow."

Isabella nodded approvingly.

"German U-boat had sneaked in, sunk the *Royal Oak,* back in thirty-nine, killed eight hundred and thirty-three of our boys. Winston Churchill could have none of that, so he ordered the anchorage sealed. Only way to do that was to build the barriers. Tons of rock and concrete sunk to the seabeds, built up to link the islands and block the entranceways. Over a mile and a half long—took them over two years. Men couldn't be spared's why they brought in the Italians."

Isabella apparently knew her stuff.

"We hated them, of course, when they first arrived, and they hated us. When they found out what they'd been brought here for they started up a strike. It was bad. Had them on bread and water. Five hundred had been brought here to Lamb Holm. Thirteen huts, mud, wind, and fog. Camp 60. My uncle had seen them, miserable souls, big red targets sewn on the backs of their shirts. He heard them chanting, *'Viva il Duce! Viva il Duce!'* Who knows what would have happened, but someone had the wisdom to appoint Major T. P. Buckland as the camp commander. Major Buckland was a kind man and he spoke Italian. After the major took over everything was fine—as fine as a prison camp could be, of course. The Italians, they were good Christian men. Roman Catholic, but Christians nonetheless. They started work on the barriers, and in return the major made sure their lives were good. They were fed well, paid even, with camp money, and treated with respect, treated like soldiers. To lift their spirits, the men were allowed to have sports, music, and even theater. Several camps put on operettas complete with painted scenery and props. They had football and they even made a concrete bowling alley with concrete bowling balls."

Norma laughed.

"And a concrete billiard table. Used an army blanket for the cushions! Concrete is what they had around here—lots and lots of concrete—and that's where the miracle comes in. The soldiers, they were content—I mean, relatively content, they were thousands of miles from their homes and their families, and prisoners—but what they needed, spiritually, was a

church. Major Buckland gave them permission to build one.
He had a Nissen hut set up especially for that purpose, and
this"—she held out her arms, one hand still holding the fluffy
blue dust mop—"is what they created."

"It's beautiful," Norma said. "Really beautiful."

And it was. The ceiling was scrolled in archways, golden
and red. Carved marble lined the walls. Light at the end from
two windows lit the little altar, like a priceless trinket in God's
pocket. Lacy ironwork protected, and a fresco adorned, a very
sweet Madonna with her very sweet Child. Very sweet cheru-
bim and clouds. On the ceiling before the altar, the scroll-
work had been filled with a rich, heavenly shade of blue. In
its center on a field of sunshine yellow was a dove.

"It's all trompe l'oeil, you see," said Isabella. "Trick of the
eye."

"You mean it's not really—" Norma stepped close to one
of the walls. "—not really marble?"

"Now, where would they get marble out here? Go ahead,
touch it—everybody has to."

Norma did.

"It's all painted wallboard and cement. Not the ironwork,
though. That's real. And these lanterns."

Norma looked at the ornate square fixtures hanging from
the ceiling.

"They made those from Bullybeef tin cans!"

"Wow," Norma said, "wow."

"In the end, we Orcadians loved them. The Italians loved
us. It was God's doing, of course. And we've never forgotten.
The descendants of the prisoners still come here to visit. They
stay as our honored guests."

At this, Norma turned around. "Really?" she said, maybe
a tad too eagerly. "Are there—did any Italians—settle here in
Orkney?"

Isabella gave her the cocked eyebrow.

"Just curious," Norma answered, though a question had not been posed.

"No Italians."

There was a chilly silence. The tour had apparently come to an end.

"Thank you so much for, you know, being my guide."

"Not at all," said Isabella.

"Is there a—may I make a donation?"

"Right over there."

Norma stuffed a ten-pound note through the slot of the iron donation box. This brought a slight reprieve from the sudden coldness, but there was still no smile. Norma felt sure she had tapped into something. Italian bastard indeed. Isabella was not, however, going to be the font of information that she needed.

It was time, Norma decided, to do a little gallery browsing.

∞

The pale white disc of sun was beginning to slide behind the distant gray mound of Hoy by the time Norma motored into Stromness. She took the Ferry Road, which soon turned into Victoria Street and took her to the center of town. Her scooter went *thunka thunka* as she crept along the flagstones, avoiding pedestrians. The gallery was on a narrow lane on the Brinkles Brae side of town, Brinkles Brae being the three-hundred-foot slab of granite ridge that sheltered the little port. But first Norma pulled over to the Bank of Scotland and the automatic teller machine.

She had opened an account there with her big bundle of traveler's checks. Norma had a couple of hundred pounds with her already, and withdrew three hundred more. She had thought about her strategy on the way over. The gallery owner, Ms. Looselips, would likely be loosest having her hinges oiled. Norma figured she could spring for some artwork, not even necessarily Brian's.

She wondered how much an original Burroughs usually went for. She wouldn't kid herself—she'd love to have one, but discretion was the word of the day, anonymity the goal.

She drove the two blocks to the foot of the lane and parked her scooter. The climb was steep, and besides, she wanted to look "on foot"—as touristy as possible. She pulled back the hood of her cape and got her shoulder bag out of the motorbike's basket.

"Norma?"

Well, there flew away anonymity.

Norma turned. It was Marion Dearness across the street with a wave and big happy smile.

"Marion!" Norma said. A big happy smile had popped up on Norma's face, too.

They crossed the flagstones together and met in the middle with a hug.

"It's so good to see you, dear," said Marion. "How *are* you?"

"I'm fine," said Norma, and she meant it. "I'm really doing well."

Marion held her at arm's length and took a good look.

"Yes, I think you are," she said. "Sabbaticals must suit you."

"What suits me is my crofting cottage," Norma said. "I really can't thank you enough for that. And Anne. It's just perfect, and I've been so—it's just the perfect place to—"

"Mend one's basket?"

They laughed, and Norma said, "Exactly."

"Well, this is so fortuitous," said Marion. "I was going to give you a ring, but then Anne said you'd never had the phone service started."

"I know," said Norma. "I'm terrible. I have a cell phone, but—"

"If you don't give out the number?"

"Right," said Norma. "I'm sorry, I—"

"Oh, don't be sorry," said Marion. "We were a bit worried, but look at you. You really do look good. In fact—have you lost weight, dear?"

Norma smiled. "I think about fifteen pounds—there's no scale at the cottage, but either that or my waistbands are stretching. I've been, you know, walking—taking care of myself."

"Well, it certainly shows. Anyway, I wanted to reach you, you see. I'm having a little dinner party on Saturday. We would love to have you join us—do you think you might come?"

Norma was touched. What was this feeling again? Oh, right—human contact. And it felt pretty nice, so before really thinking, she said, "Why, I'd love to."

"That's wonderful," Marion said. She took Norma's elbow and gave it a little squeeze.

Then ol' paranoia raised his shadowy head. To what had she agreed? A dinner party? What if—but that was silly— what would be the chances? But what about Luck, eh? Luck and her malicious sense of fun?

"Sevenish," Marion was saying, "at my place. Let me give you directions. It's above my dress shop on Grieveship Road. Do you know where that is?"

"You own a dress shop?"

"Yes, I do," said Marion. "Dowdy English-lady clothes, nothing you'd fancy."

Norma would have come up with a polite protest but she could see the twinkle in Marion's eye, so she smiled and twinkled back. Here was a woman with whom she could level. So she did.

"Marion? I need to ask you—I need to be rude."

"Go right ahead, dear."

"Who will be there? At the dinner. I—I just need to know."

Marion looked her in the eye for a moment. "All right," she said, "I'll confess."

Oh, jeez.

"It's a setup. Anne and I have been plotting against you."

Norma felt herself go pale. Oh, God. They knew. Everyone on the island knew. How could she think she could have kept it a secret? And now what? A dinner with Fiona and Brian? How about Russell and Linda? Were they invited, too? Let's throw in Trey Bliss and—

"Norma?"

Marion was looking at her with concern.

"He's not that bad, really—"

"Who?" said Norma stupidly.

"Our nephew."

Their nephew.

"Colin. He's our brother Andrew's son. Andrew and his family live in Glasgow now and Colin teaches at the university. The poor darling's just gotten out of a bad relationship, he's come to visit his aunties back home and, well, we thought—there's just old ones will be there, Anne and her husband, the Sinclairs—she works at the library here in town, a very nice couple, and then Agnes, who co-owns the dress shop—and we thought, poor Colin! Surrounded by the ancients. Then we thought of you!"

Norma felt a flood of relief, with more than a flotsam of silliness to go along. Colin—their nephew.

"But, if you'd rather not, we'd certainly—"

"No," Norma said. "No, don't mind me—I've just—just

gone a little feral out there by the sea. I'd love to meet your nephew. I'd love to meet all of your friends, really, I'll come."

"Well, then good," Marion said. "We'll look forward to seeing you. Now, I'll let you get on with your shopping before we lose all light."

They hugged again and parted.

Norma watched her go before she started uphill to the gallery. That had been nice. Real nice. There might be hope for her yet. Colin, the Glaswegian professor. Norma shook her head with a grin.

Brian's paintings were still in the window. A landscape featuring the Dwarfie Stone was front and center. (She hadn't been there, either.) Next to that, a really quite good picture of Stromness itself, and, on the left—Norma's grin faded—it was the panorama from Quoyer Viewpoint. The painting Brian had been working on when—oh, good gravy. He had painted it. The Ring o' Brodgar. She looked closer and her heart stood still. No one would recognize what it was, not by just looking, right? You would have to know—you would have to be in on the sick little joke.

He'd painted them. Her and Russell. Having sex. Up against the fiddler, up against the Comet Stone. Tiny black shadows, tiny and vile. Norma didn't know whether to laugh or to cry. A little sound escaped her, kind of a combination of both. A giggling whimper that she stifled with one hand to her mouth.

Well. She certainly wouldn't be purchasing *that* one.

She waited for the shame to rise, but, surprisingly, it didn't. Instead, a weird sort of triumph had taken its place. Gad, she couldn't wait to analyze that. Her heartbeat had kicked back in again. Norma took a breath, squared her shoulders, and went inside.

∞

The presumed Looselips, a petite blonde, impeccably tailored and coiffed, was waiting on a couple of actual touristy types. Cameras around the neck—dead giveaway touristywise. They were considering a rather cheesy-looking Old Man of Hoy. Acrylic. You could always tell. Looselips gave Norma an "I'll be with you in a minute" one-finger lift, and Norma gave her a smile and a finger twirl back—no hurry, just looking around.

Norma walked through the gallery with her hands behind her back, eavesdropping with all her might. No gossiping about Brian, alas, they were talking about shipping costs to Portugal.

A dozen Burroughs lined the walls. Excellent execution but . . . Norma realized that the Quoyer Viewpoint was by far the best of the lot. She squinted up at the little embossed white cards with titles and prices.

Zowie.

View from Ward Hill—£1,500. *Graemsay Sunset*—£2,000.

Here was a little puffin, surely that would be *Puffin*—£1,500.

Dang. Norma wondered what they would charge for the paintings he had actually felt. She saw that there was a distinct lack of Betty Corrigalls.

Looselips was walking the Portuguese couple to the door, everyone was all smiles. She let them out, then turned to her.

"Now then, may I help you?"

Norma, to her complete surprise, answered back in a British accent.

"Yes, thankyouverymuch, I was just admiring these land-scapes."

At least she hoped it was a British accent. Affecting an

accent back in London had been for fun. Now, it suddenly seemed prudent. There was a bit of a look of the shark in Looselips's eyes.

"Ah," said Looselips, not batting either of them, "our Mr. Burroughs. Quite talented, wouldn't you say?"

"Oh?" said Norma. "Is he local?"

"All of our artists are local." She smiled with a great many teeth and extended her well-manicured hand. "Helen Spence."

Norma took it, briefly, and then out came a big whopper. "Penelope Smythe."

"Manchester, am I right?"

Okay. Sure. Norma nodded brightly.

"Staying long?"

What was this, the Spanish Inquisition?

Helen added a few more teeth.

"I've noticed you around town on your motorbike," she said. "Aren't you the one staying in Anne Skathamore's place?"

Oh, well, golly. Would you like a DNA sample?

"That's me," said Norma merrily. Ha ha ha! She had to get out of there. Quick.

But Helen, the shark, had her by the arm.

"Did you see Mr. Burroughs's latest? It's quite breath-taking. I think he's achieved a new emotional depth."

Norma was being steered toward the window. Helen Spence snatched the painting from its stand and whipped it right in Norma's face.

"Such detail. Don't you think?"

"Y-Yes, it's striking," said Norma. Not the details, please. "I noticed it coming in. His latest, did you say?"

"Uh-huh." The woman held it for a moment more, looking at it herself. "He sent it in just last week. Brian Burroughs—such an *interesting* man."

Oh, yeah, come on, Helen, loosen those lips.

"To tell the truth, I was a bit worried about him."

Norma held her breath, not wanting to break the spell.

"He's quite the prolific boy—I wouldn't be giving anything away to say he's quite the best we have. Works just fly off the walls—and then, from the end of August it was almost six weeks—"

Oh, no, don't stop now.

Helen looked up from the painting. Her shark eyes were slivers of silver in the waning light. She slid them toward Norma.

"Woman trouble," Helen confided in a bitchy whisper.

Bingo. Bingo. Bingo.

"Do tell," said Norma in her best British bitchy whisper back.

Then a customer came in.

Jangle jangle went the doorbells, and Helen Spence went instantly professional again.

It was a fat guy, and Norma could have easily shot him. Helen replaced the Quoyer Viewpoint painting and, to Norma, held up her one-minute finger again.

"Mr. Wexelblatt, how delightful to see you again!"

Bloody hell. The moment was blown. Totally blown.

She'd probably have to buy something now. Something cheap. Or come back tomorrow with a bigger wad. But how suspicious would that be? Two thousand pounds in cash? Penelope Smythe. What had she been thinking? Discretion— righto! Jolly good, eh what? Crap.

Norma looked around desperately. Something cheap— something today. Norma circled the store twice. In the back of the shop the door to Helen Spence's office had been left ajar. Against the door, a stack of paintings in their frames, brown paper backing side out. Norma saw, scrawled in pencil, a BUR. She went to them and knelt. Flipped them, one,

two, three, and there it was. Burroughs. She turned the painting around.

Dark. Strange. Unreachable. The painting was *beautiful*.
Like Brian. It was in blackness. A place. Mounds with doors,
the sea in the distance, the black sky, and thousands and thousands of stars. How had he done that? Captured the stars in
his net of paint and canvas? And the people. Were they people? Or shadows, or ghosts, or places in time where people
had once been? Norma wanted to weep. It was just so absolutely stunning—this painting turned to the wall. And Brian.
Who was this man—and what had she lost?

Norma heard the jangle of the shop bells. The fat guy was
going. She stood, holding the painting, shutting her eyes, and
took a deep breath.

The woman was tap-tapping back across the floor.

"What have you got there?"

She had to have this. She didn't care if she looked like a
fool, or what the hell Helen Spence thought.

"Oh," Helen said, "that. Poor Brian. He insists every now
and then. His dreary work. It never sells. That one has been
around for months and months. My, my—you *like* it?"

Norma nodded.

"Three hundred pounds?"

"I'll take it."

"It's yours. Brian will be thrilled." She laughed. If sharks
could laugh, that would be the sound. "Of course, it will just
encourage him. Would you like to charge it?"

"No," Norma said. "Cash."

"Let me wrap it for you—or would you like it delivered?"

"No," Norma said. "It will fit. In my basket."

If it didn't, she'd walk it back to the cottage.

Helen pulled a giant square of brown paper from a roll.
She laughed again and said something as she tore it. Something that sounded like "Fiona."

"What?"

"Oh, nothing."

"No," said Norma. "What did you say?" Oops, the fake Manchester slipped a little that time.

Helen looked at her. Shark eyes again.

Norma looked back. *I've paid for my gossip, woman, now spill it.*

"I said, 'Fiona is going to kill me.' "

"And who," she said as lightly as she could, "pray tell, is Fiona?"

"Fiona Rousay," said Helen, "is Brian Burroughs's fiancée."

"Ah," said Norma. Then she leaned forward in bitchy conspiracy again. "The 'woman trouble'?"

Helen had wrapped the painting and was now pulling out several yards from a ball of string.

"Technically speaking, no."

Dramatic pause, and then the floodgates opened.

"You see, Brian and Fiona, they'd been an item for quite some time. Engaged to be engaged, don't you know. It would have been official, ages ago, but there was some sort of trouble with her family. Fiona, the princess of Stronsay, she's a dish, a beautiful girl—is just mad about him. Anyway, this summer it seems there was some other woman—not from the islands, but my goodness, the rumors flew—and Brian up and broke off the engagement. He left Orkney and went back to Edinburgh—that's where he's from—well, he's from Hoy, but he'd been living his adult life in Edinburgh. And Fiona, well, Fiona was inconsolable, totally inconsolable—we all thought she'd fling herself into the sea—but instead, she flung herself onto an airplane and flew to Edinburgh, used all her golden-girl charms and brought Brian home again." Helen glanced up and smiled wickedly. "Just between you, me, and the teapot, Fiona's histrionics were more about Fiona than

Brian—that girl has never played second violin even once in her life and, trust me, once she seals the deal she'll never forget that Brian fiddled around. The deal is very close to sealing, too. The engagement is official—Fiona said her family be damned, and, frankly, I couldn't be happier—I've got my handsome painter producing again. And, if Fiona has her way—and Fiona *does* have her way—there won't be too many more of these." Helen had deftly tied the package up in four knots. She gave it to Norma. "There you go."

Norma handed her two hundred-pound notes and two fifties.

"Very good." Helen Spence showed all her shark's teeth again. "And between you and me, Ms. Smythe, maybe I just won't tell either of them right away that I sold this."

"Mum's the word," said Norma. *Please, oh, please, let mum be the word*. Norma could see the Thursday's headline in *The Orcadian*:

PENELOPE SMYTHE, FAKE MANCHESTER TOURIST, BUYS DREARY PAINTING BY LOVERBOY BURROUGHS, THE ITALIAN BASTARD OF—

Oh, shit. She hadn't found out a thing about the Italian connection. Was it too late? *Uh-uh, and thank you for that fascinating story. You must know everything around here—no, no wrong thing to say. Come on, think. . . .*

Helen had handed her the package and was ushering her toward the door. Thank-yous were exchanged and good-byes and such a pleasure meeting you and enjoy your little painting, then Norma was outside in the cold.

Right. The sun was completely gone. Norma clutched her painting to her chest and trudged down the hill to her scooter. It did fit in the basket, sort of. She drove back to the cottage rather wobbly, one hand on the painting, one on the handlebars.

Half frozen, she lit both her fires and started up all the

space heaters. She poured herself a couple of fingers of Highland Park—it really was very good whiskey—and then opened up her package in front of the living room hearth.

It was still beautiful. She got all weepy again. A little white card fell out—on it: *Skara Brae.*

CHAPTER 17

Okay, then. So—reconnaissance.

Check.

Sorta. If Helen Spence could be trusted—and she certainly seemed a grade-A gossip—then Norma knew she had a very big part of her "what was the deal with Brian and Fiona?" answer. Brian, out of guilt, probably, or—sunniest scenario—feelings for her, man-player that she was, had left Fiona. But Fiona didn't take this lightly. Whatever Brian had told her about "the other woman"—and really, what was there to tell?—Fiona still wanted him. Maybe for selfish reasons, yes—or maybe there really was "no other man for her." Whatever it was, Fiona apparently forgave him and made the big gesture—telling her family to shove it—and with that, won him back. Or not. Norma reached her conclusion. Fiona probably just went to Edinburgh and fucked him.

Norma sighed. She was out near the Bay of Skaill. She'd been brooding for two days, drinking whiskey, mooning over Brian's painting, and feeling sorry for herself. This morning she'd done the ol' collar-shaking routine and decided on caffeine and an outing. She motored to the Skaill House. Two hundred yards inland from Skara Brae, it was a hard-to-miss Orkney landmark. Norma knew all about it. This time she had done her homework.

Skaill House was a huge stark rambling white mansion, the site dating back to the 1500s. *Skaill* was the old Norse word meaning hall, and there had been one here when the Vikings ruled Orkney. The core of the present-day house had been built in 1615 by Earl Patrick Stewart, but after his "trial and execution," the guidebook intriguingly said, the ownership passed to a bishop. The bishop must have been a bad boy himself—there were cryptic guidebook references to "being too lenient on adulterers and incest." He was unseated in 1628, but the house managed to remain in his family all the way down to the present. It was one of those family members, the Laird of Breckness, who, in 1850, had discovered Skara Brae.

Skaill House was no longer occupied. It was now a pretty spectacular museum, or so the guidebook teased. Tours were available only through the end of September. Norma parked her motorbike and started the leisurely hike toward the bay. The day was pretty. Mild. The sun had struggled up from the southeast and was now making a halfhearted attempt to dominate the cloudless sky.

As she walked, Norma mused on the ancient history lesson the guidebook had provided. Mesolithic man had been the first human to see Orkney's view of the halfhearted sun. Almost ten thousand years ago. The great ice sheets were melting, the sea level still low, Stone Age hunter-gatherers had crossed from Stone Age Scotland to hunt and gather on the emerging green hills. They'd left nothing behind them. Five thousand years, and just a few stone flakes to show that they'd even been there. Then Neolithic man had crossed the now-wider Pentland Firth, bringing with him more tangible evidence of existence. Neolithic man brought with him sheep and cows, pottery and tools, religion, and the Neolithic garbage—*very tangible stuff, that*—and the ever-important Neolithic women and Neolithic bairn. He came, settled, lived, and died on Orkney for the next six thousand years.

Norma could see it now: Skara Brae. The tourist center first, clean and white and round, with a cute overturned pan roof, then the site. There were walkways with ropes around lumps of green grass, surprisingly green, but then, Mainland had yet to have its first freeze. And the beach and the sea beyond that, the shores of the bay very close now to Skara Brae. But not four thousand years ago. Four thousand years ago the little community had been surrounded on all sides by fertile green farmland for their grains, and grazeland for their sheep and cows. The sea had been there for them, too, walking distance to the north. They could go and fish, gather limpets and hunt for seals. Find the occasional prize—like a washed-up whale—that was good eating. But the people of Skara Brae had been mainly farmers, and for seven generations they had lived, worked, loved, and wondered at the stars, and reproduced and perished right here. Right here.

And then something had happened. No one was quite sure what, maybe something terrible—but from what Norma knew of life, probably something ordinary—and the people of Skara Brae had gone away. They'd forsaken their little community, and nature had come and claimed it back. And the sea had come ever closer, the grinding sands of the sea, and buried Skara Brae, lost to the collective memory of man for more than forty centuries.

Norma did the obligatory tour of the tourist center and then wandered to the settlement itself. She was practically alone. One group of winter tourists—maybe Korean?—and their fair-haired Orcadian youth guide.

In 1850 one of those winter storms had come to Orkney.

The great storm tore away at the grassy dunes, exposing the outlines of rock buildings. Over the next eighteen years the initial four dwellings were uncovered, with the typical Victorian excitement over that sort of thing, then the site was all but abandoned until 1925, when another big storm caused some damage and the discovery of the remaining four dwellings after the more archeologically savvy citizenry decided to build a protective seawall.

Norma was standing on that seawall with the Bay of Skaill crashing its foamy waves behind her.

The entire site, all eight dwellings and the passageways that connected them, were beneath ground level. It was not unlike the layout of a miniature golf course, only the rounded fairways were sunk deep in the ground between strips of grassy tufts. The Victorian archeologists assumed that the original village had been underground, but this was not so. The people of Skara Brae had built their spacious huts above the ground and surrounded and then eventually buried them under midden. Midden, Norma had learned, was great big piles of domestic waste. Animal bones and scraps, broken pottery, food waste, and even dung. It sounded fairly disgusting to her, but not only did it provide for a snug homestead for those long-ago Orkney winters, it helped support the sandstone slabs of rock built, mortarless, for their walls. Orkney had been nearly treeless then, as it was now. If you didn't have wood, you used stone and anything else you had.

Norma walked east. Twenty yards to her left the surf continued to curl up across wet, white sand.

The next big hollow below was known as Building 1. Norma looked down upon the first true dwelling, roofless now, exposed to the sky.

And there she saw them. Skara Brae's famous beds of stone.

If you didn't have wood, right? All seven of the dwellings were furnished and laid out in exactly the same manner. Buried to the rooftops in midden (you could collect a lot of waste in seven hundred years), the huts were connected ingeniously with undermidden stone-lined passageways. Two of the "roadways" had survived the passage of time and still had their sandstone ceiling slabs.

Norma tried to imagine how it had been.

∞

A visitor, coming across the grasslands, through the herds of hairy-headed Neolithic cows, through the fields of ripe barley and wheat, sees only the rounded mounds of thatched heather or straw that make up the roofs. You cross the patio of stone, called the Marketplace, and then, after being greeted by and passing muster, the tough and wiry Skara Brae elder pushes back the sandstone rock guarding the main door and allows you to stoop and enter the darkened tunnel. The first room, called the Workplace, is just that. The men, a few boys, are hard at work chipping with their flint, carving fish stickers from rocks and red deer bones. Over there, a female sits working the grooves into the rounded base of her unfired clay bowl. It is hazy, peat and dung burning in the center of the room. Smoke rises through a hole in the center of the smoke-darkened thatched ceiling. But you don't mind. It's deliciously warm in here. And somewhere, someone is cooking mouthwatering lamb.

You greet them in your Neolithic way—not a grunt, but a well-mannered prehistoric "Hi, there"—and pass on through down the main tunnelway. The elder has told you—perhaps he's drawn a little sketch in the dirt—go past the next doorway, and so you do. Your destination is the next room, the largest in the village. There are two children here in the tunnel, naked and warm and playing with a ball. The ball is made of stone, of course, carved all around with knobby projections. Five thousand years from now these balls will puzzle so-

phisticated people. Religious icons, very significant, they will just about all conclude. But you smile now, for you know it is just a ball.

And then you enter, a little afraid, the sandstone slab is pulled aside. And you see it, lit from the central hearth fire, across the thirty steps of the room. A stone "dresser," they will call it, five thousand years from now. But it is more than that, this shelfwork of rock across the room. Here sit the gods. All powerful. Givers and takers of life. Feathers, bones, long scary strands of wool, precious pearls for eyes—those omnipotent eyes—humble you in their presence, and you bow low to the ground.

You have worked hard all the long summer days to please these gods, you and twelve others, many strides from here between the great brother waters—hauled the giant stone slab to join the others in the sacred Circle of the Moon.

And then, the ceremony over, you turn your attention to more worldly things. You try not to look, but you can't help it, there she is, your intended mate. She is on the woman's side of the room, sitting on the woman's-side stone bed. Filled with heather, you can smell its fragrance. She's sitting on the curled wool of a brown sheepskin, her hair done all beautiful in red ocher beads. Your eyes flicker to her briefly, then you get control of yourself. There's her father. Head of the village, sitting on his big stone chair. Big man. Big frown on his face. But you know it will go well, her mother and her sisters pulling fresh shellfish from the water tank, all smiles and hand-covered giggles.

∞

The young guide's voice broke into Norma's prehistoric reverie.

"And one of the most remarkable things," he explained to the rapt Koreans, "is the underground, stone-lined, drainage pipes. Aye." He pointed and they all craned their necks. "You can see it there, and over there. Hard to believe, but we think these ancient people actually had their own sewage system."

The Neolithic visitor sits on the stone potty. The roast lamb wedding feast has been delicious, and now—

Norma grinned to herself—no, story over. The spell had been broken. But it was truly amazing, this Skara Brae. She wandered across the wooden walkway and gazed down into Building 4. They *were* all laid out exactly the same. The central hearth, the stone dresser, and, to each side, the three stone slabs that formed the remarkable stone beds against the wall.

The guide's voice drifted over again. "We believe that, even in its heyday, the village was home to perhaps fifty and certainly no more than a hundred people. The life span of these people, if you survived childhood, on average was thirty years, fifty if you were lucky."

Norma looked to the southeast. Rolling hills, and then down to the great earthen bowl between lochs and the Ring of Brodgar, the Stones of Stenness, the great underground burial cairns. It was all happening here. Really happening. Time was slow and life was brief and hard. But it was good, wasn't it? Then later, the scratch of twig language: Was that what they were trying to say across millennia? "We were here. We lived, goddamnit. We lived."

Norma looked down at the dresser, the beds, the round stones that lined the hearth. She wanted, like with the megaliths, to touch them. She sighed. She was getting some of that darned ol' perspective again. That was good—really. It was why she had come. To shake herself loose from the brooding, from desire.

Oh, gad. She'd used it. The D word.

Norma wandered slowly around the walkways, looking down into each of the rooms. Was that why she had stayed on Orkney? A secret desire, a hope—to win Brian? *Win Brian—*

jeez. She hit her forehead with the heel of her hand. Win Brian. Like he was a Kewpie doll in a huckster's stall. Across the sunken room a Korean man looked at her, sideways, from the corner of his eye. *Right. Public spectacle. Always a good idea.*

Leaving Skara Brae, she walked back to her scooter and drove back to her cottage. Plenty of daylight left. Lunchtime. She nibbled at some Stilton cheese and sawed herself a hunk of bread. The bottle of Highland Park sat temptingly on the counter. Great. Should she drink herself to a nice heathery death?

She went to the living room and flopped down in the blue chintz comfy chair. With the toe of her shoe she sorted through the DVDs scattered on the floor. *Seen it, seen it—too depressing, seen it—not in the mood. Oh, hell,* she thought, *I'll watch* The Matrix *again.*

"There's always a chance," she said to herself, "I'm in a tank somewhere dreaming all of this."

The rest of the day went pretty much like that until, mercifully, she finally went to bed.

∾

At three in the morning Norma woke up. She lay there a minute. What had she been dreaming? Too late. It was gone. She rolled over. Nope, she wasn't drifting off again. She turned her pillow to the cool side. No, that wasn't working. Oh, boy. Wide-awake. She could feel it coming—a bad case of the witching-hour thinks. She sat up. Well, this is what she deserved, right? After her day of denial?

Norma rubbed her eyes and ran her fingers through her hair. She put her legs over the side of the bed. Across the room, propped on a little table, was the painting. Moonlight was shining through her curtainless window. She could see the outline of people he had painted glowing in their ghostly white. She understood the painting now, having been to Skara Brae.

She wondered if he'd been there—been there in the night.

Norma got out of bed. She dressed. Warmly. Then she put on her woolen cloak, her muffler and gloves. She went into the front room and got her North Ronaldsay sheepskin from the back of one of the chairs where she'd draped it, rolled it up and went outside. It was cold. But not that cold, right? Not freezing cold. She mounted her motorbike and turned the key. It roared, horribly loud, of course, and she drove off into the night.

Skara Brae was in total darkness. Except for the moon. Almost full, the moon watched her in lunatic camaraderie.

She'd parked her scooter in the lot behind a large TOURIST CENTRE sign. Taking her woolly bundle, Norma walked along the path, the pathway, of course, crunching horribly loud. She reached the northern area of the site and walked along the edge of the grassy seawall. She was now standing above Building 1. Where her fantasy Neolithic man had come to meet his bride. There was a moment of guilt—it was, after all, a national treasure—and then she went over the side.

She grinned. Okay, so she was crazy, and a vandal, but this felt really, really good. She stood for a moment taking it all in. Then she went to the dresser, took off her glove, and touched it. Like a little Stonehenge it was, standing on its side. Stacked there like a college boy's cinder-block and wood-plank four-thousand-year-old stereo shelf. Was it for the gods? Or just a place to put their clay pots, their stone tools, their best Sunday skins? Norma looked across the room to the low entranceway. It was the placement that made the scholars think the former. The stone shelves, in every room, straight across from the door.

She knelt next to the limpet tank. Now these were really cool. Stone-lined tanks sunken into the floor. *Caulked waterproof, ta-dah!—fresh fish for supper.* She ran her bare hand along the sandstone and shivered. She looked at the hearth, could almost see them. The prehistoric family gathered around the fire. She pictured them as dark, hairy cavemen types, then thought, *No, they must have been fair. Generations up there at the top of the earth living with their pale disc of a sun.* She stood and went to the bed. It was the larger one, to the right of the door. The men's side, or so they'd figured, the scholars. To the left, the women's. They'd found beads and paint in the smaller beds, right? So they had to have been for the women.

Norma chose the bigger one anyway. She unrolled her sheepskin and carefully laid it between the stone slabs. Then she climbed in and lay down. She smiled. She replaced her glove and wrapped her cloak snugly across her legs and arms. She pulled up her muffler and under it tucked in her nose.

The stars. Even with the moonshine she could see thousands of stars. Brian *had* seen them like this. *Well,* she giggled to herself. *Not like* this. *Not daft.*

She could hear the waters of the bay breaking on the shore. She let the sound rock her, rock her gently beneath her blanket of stars, and she drifted off, quite happy now, to sleep.

CHAPTER 18

Norma woke in the morning very cold and as stiff as a board—no, strike that, she thought—as stiff as a slab of sandstone bed.

And then she thought: *I must be out of my ever-loving mind.*

And then: *What is that whistling sound?*

She could see, in the sky above, the rosy-tipped fingers— three of them with pretty pink cloud-rings—of dawn.

Dawn.

In the northern climes.

So that would mean, what? Around 8:45.

Christ on a cracker! When *was opening time?*

The whistling got louder. It was a U2 song. And footsteps. Getting closer.

Norma sat up. *This would not do. No sirree Bob.*

She not so carefully began to scramble from her sandstone crib. She rolled out with a thud. *Man. Think. Quietly, okay? And try not to break four thousand years of history.*

The whistling, ever closer, turned to off-key lyrics. It was the one with all the "follows" in it.

She quickly rolled up the sheepskin and tucked it under her arm. Then she gathered up her cloak and tucked it under her other arm. Then, on all fours, she began to creep toward the entranceway.

Bono was wailing now. Badly.

Right, fellow—don't quit your day job. Norma had reached the head of the tunnel. She crept into the darkness.

He was right overhead. He stopped. Norma held her breath. Then he started up his wailing again and the footsteps receded.

She duckwalked down the rest of the tunnel. She came out in what she remembered as Building 4 and popped her head up over the grassy edge. Bono was just opening the door to the Tourist Center. He disappeared inside, and Norma leapt, ninjalike, up onto a wooden walkway. She walked quickly, quietly, and as casually as possible toward the car park. She only had to push the motorbike a quarter of a mile or so up the road. Then on she hopped, started it up, and headed for home.

Once out of risk of horribly embarrassing discovery range, her actions became quite the grand adventure instead of one of the stupidest things she'd ever done. Funny how that worked out.

Norma sang as she drove. The U2 song. Unlike Bono back there, she was practically in tune.

She pulled up to the cottage with a grand spray of gravel, got her sheepskin bedroll, and went inside.

∞

Norma fixed a generous breakfast with kippers, grilled tomatoes, and thick slices of buttery fire-toasted bread. She kept breaking out in big grins. That was really the best sleep, stiffness aside, she'd ever had in her life. Afterward, she took a shower and plucked her nice warm towel from the nice warm towel warmer. Great invention that. She wrapped up and walked barefoot into the living room.

Ah, she thought, *what to do today?* When were those DVDs due? She could rent a big ol' stack of new ones, make some cocoa, pop some corn—then she remembered. It was Saturday. Marion's dinner party.

∞

The sidewalks of Stromness were pretty much rolled up for the night by the time Norma motored into town. She puttered up Back Road (nice name), past Saint Peter, and turned left onto Grieveship Road. Marion's shop, like the gallery, was high up on the Brinkles Brae side. She would park her scooter at the bottom and hoof it. She turned off the engine and dismounted.

The weather had grown colder, with mist turning to drips, and Norma wrapped her cloak tightly around her. She'd gone a bit skimpy on her dress length tonight. A little black cocktail number, she'd bought it in London. Versace. Probably a bit much for the Stromness set, she thought. She got a pair of red stiletto heels from the scooter's basket and switched them with her running shoes. She smiled. Might as well go over the top.

Speaking of which . . . she looked up the steep hill. Yeah, she could make it. She smoothed back her hair. She'd done it up in a neat little French twist. Red drop earrings to match the heels. Red lipstick to match the earrings. Then she saw him. A single man. He was crossing the street and heading for the covered stairs that went up to Marion's flat.

He had an umbrella, and he stopped and pulled it closed, giving it a shake.

This had to be Colin, right? Oh, boy. He was—well, face

it—he was on the round side and vertically challenged. His bald spot would not have been so bad if not for the contrast of the puffy clown fringe. Thick glasses. A fussy mustache. Yup, *très* professor. The man had taken off his overcoat and was shaking that, too. Elbow patches. He actually had elbow patches on his jacket. He disappeared up the stairs, and Norma followed, shaking her head.

On the way up she practiced her not-disappointed, glad-to-meet-you face. Two stairs from the top, she stopped. But would that have been good? Colin, a professorial hunk? Yes, she decided, it would have been good.

She pushed the buzzer and Anne opened the door.

"Ah, my lovely tenant," she said. "how delightful to see you again."

They hugged and did a little air kiss on the cheek.

Marion, with a tray of cheese and crackers, beamed from across the room.

"Welcome to my home," she said. "You look absolutely beautiful. Anne, will you do introductions?"

Anne took Norma's cloak and then led her to a plump, sharp-eyed woman with short red hair.

"Norma, this is Agnes Caithness."

Norma smiled and said, "How do you do?"

"And these," Anne led her to an elderly couple, like a white-haired walrus and a little gray bird, "are the Sinclairs, Frederick and Alberta."

"Nice to meet you."

"And this," said Anne, leading her over to Colin, "is my husband, Bryce." She kissed him on the lips and brushed at the droplets in his clown fringe hair. "Poor thing, look at you, you've gotten all wet."

"Ah," said Bryce, "at last, I meet the mystery woman."

Norma was still getting over her mistaken-identity fluster.

"You are correct, my darling," he said, "she's a pretty thing, isn't she?" And then with a twinkle, "Too bad I'm already taken."

Anne gave him a little slap on his chest.

"Bryce is the worst sort of flirt," said Marion, coming over.

"Yes, the worst sort," he admitted, "such a sexy brute, yet so unattainable."

Everyone groaned, and Norma, recovered, said, "And I'm utterly heartbroken."

Marion gave her a hug.

"Let me console you with a drink, my dear. Pimm's? I've got Colin mixing in the kitchen."

"Pimm's?" said Norma.

"Good lord," said Frederick, "you Yanks are so deprived. Pimm's Cup number one, girl, practically the British national drink."

"It's really a summer drink," put in Alberta. Then she gave a little chirpy giggle. "But, since we don't get much sun up here, we have to drink it all year round."

"Not me," said Agnes. "It's a sissy drink. Norma, join me. I'm having tequila shots."

"Oh, God," Norma said, "I never drink tequila, not since—not since high school."

"How intriguing," came a masculine voice from behind her, "there must be a story in that."

Norma turned.

Professorial hunk was putting it mildly. Damn.

He was tall, broad-shouldered, with short-clipped sandy blond hair. Dressed in well-fitted black pants and a crisp white cotton shirt. Mustache, but it wasn't the least bit fussy. It went well with his handsome grin. And green eyes. *My, oh my, green eyes.* The color of the first leaf on the first day of spring. He was using them, too. Looking Norma unabashedly up, then down.

"Norma," Marion said, "this is our nephew, Colin Tait. Colin, this is Norma Dale."

Colin stepped forward and took Norma's hand. He sparkled his leaf-green eyes into hers and said, "Charmed."

Like-fucking-wise, Norma was thinking, but she managed to just smile. Acutely aware how much the "ancients" were enjoying this, she prayed that he wouldn't kiss her hand. Oh, she wanted him to, sure, she had taken a good long look at those lips, but if he did, she was going to wet her pants.

He didn't. He let her hand, lingeringly, go and then pointed his thumb over his shoulder.

"Drinks are ready," he said, "though Agnes, I've eaten your worm."

∞

Pimm's, it turned out, was a dark brown herbal cocktail, gin-based, mixed with ginger ale and an assortment of fruit and vegetables, including lemon and a cucumber slice. It was delicious. As was dinner. Enormous homemade ravioli with marinara sauce, crunchy breadsticks, a big crispy salad, and a deep, raisiny Barbara.

The conversation had been delightful and informative. Among other things, Norma had learned that Bryce was Anne's second husband; Marion had been divorced, too, and then widowed; Colin was a professor of mathematics, no less; the Sinclairs had been married in Zanzibar; and Agnes was gay, though celibate for these last twenty years. Also obvious, but not discussed, was that Agnes was in love with Marion, which hardly mattered, really, as the rest of them were, too.

They were settled before the fire, mellow and full, sipping hot lattes and palm-warmed cognacs. Norma, who had been seated next to Colin during dinner, made a point to settle on the sofa next to Alberta Sinclair.

"Marion tells me you run the Stromness library?" Norma said. She had opted for coffee.

Colin was leaning against the mantel with his cognac, watching her, bemused.

"Oh goodness, no," Alberta said. She put her papery hand on Norma's knee. "I just do volunteer work."

"Nonsense," said Frederick. "Bertie runs the whole shebang—kit and caboodle. Set up the whole ancestors department single-handedly."

"Ancestors?" Norma said. "Like genealogy?"

"Yes, indeed," said Marion. "Genealogy has become our third industry. The Orcadian gene pool seems to have populated half the western world. We have several organizations just to handle all the inquiries that come in—thank goodness for the Internet, I must say."

"Alberta is a whiz with computers," said Agnes.

"Wow," Norma said, "I'm impressed."

"Pish-posh," said Alberta, though she was beaming with pleasure, "they make it so simple a pig could do it. Well, a fairly smart pig. And he'd have to have thumbs."

Everyone chuckled, though Norma wasn't sure that Alberta was trying to be funny.

"Freddy was telling me you finished up the Stronsay branch," said Agnes. She turned to Norma. "Stronsay is where my family hails from. The Caithness clan—we go back to the Picts."

"And Agnes," said Bryce, "was the Pict of the litter."

After the laughter and groans died down, Alberta said, "Well, dear, I'm afraid Frederick has misled you a bit, I'm only up to the Rs. Let's see, I finished up Rendall, and now I'm halfway through with Rousay—"

Suddenly the atmosphere in the room took a barometric plunge.

Norma had frozen at the name, and, to her alarm, everyone else seemed to have frozen along with her.

"Oh, my God!" This was from Anne.

Bryce burst into laughter.

"You aren't the only one, Bertie," he said merrily.

"What?" This from Frederick. "What?"

"It's Fiona," said Agnes, "Fiona Rousay. And Brian Burroughs."

"Oh, dear," said Alberta, then gave one of her chirpy little giggles. "I guess I've put my foot in it, haven't I?"

Then from Colin, "I'm with you, Fred—totally in the dark. What's going on with Fiona and Brian?"

"What isn't?" said Anne. She turned to Norma. "I'm afraid we've stumbled over Orkney's juiciest bit of gossip."

Norma felt the blood drain from her face. "Oh?" she managed to croak.

"Fiona Rousay," explained Anne, "is, well—"

"The hottest lass in all of Orkney," said Bryce, "present company excluded, of course."

"She *is* lovely," said Alberta. "And Mr. Burroughs is a *very* striking man."

"And an artist," said Anne, "a very good one, too. They were Orkney's perfect couple."

"Tell that to Archie Rousay."

Bryce had mumbled that under his breath.

"But this summer, there was trouble in Paradise. No one knows for sure what happened, but Brian broke up with Fiona—just like that. Left her, left the island, went back to Scotland—Fiona was devastated."

"I heard it was a woman," said Agnes, her eyes aglitter, "a redheaded tourist—married to an oilman from Texas!"

"Oh, really?" said Alberta.

"Well, that was one story,"said Anne. "Everyone knows it was a tourist—a tourist from the States, but—"

Marion, who had been silently watching Norma, broke in.

"Not really, dear," she said, "I heard she was from Spain." Norma met Marion's eyes. Marion knew.

"And I heard," said Bryce, "that she was British."

"Oh, you did not," said Anne.

"Did so. I heard it today. My secretary had lunch with Helen Spence, and Helen told her that the woman was British—from Manchester—and she was living right here on Mainland."

"Nonsense," said Marion. "Secondhand with Helen Spence as the source? Might as well get your information from these coffee grounds. And look at us, boring poor Norma with all this prattle. I know, let's bore her to death with the mayoral race."

Bless her heart. Norma realized that Marion was trying to divert them.

"Robb!" said Frederick, taking the bait. "If that man wins, I'll go join Burroughs in Scotland."

"Oh, no," said Anne, "Brian came back, don't you see? We have a storybook ending in the works. Brian came back and now he and Fiona are finally going to marry."

"What's wrong with Robb?" said Bryce. "Better than that dunderhead, Flett."

"Flett is twice the man Robb is," said Agnes.

"But Flett is a woman," said Alberta.

"Exactly," said Agnes.

Frederick made the sound of an angry walrus and the argument was on.

Marion was smiling. "Fresh drinks, anyone? Colin, why don't you show Norma the conservatory?"

"My pleasure," said Colin.

The two escaped the escalating clatter of politics.

Marion's conservatory was a small room with six potted ferns, two wicker chairs, and a side table. On the glass of the bay window the moon cast silvery highlights on the cumulative droplets of rain.

"Whew," Colin said.

He could say that again. Norma's legs felt shaky. The high heels weren't helping. She sat down in a wicker chair.

Colin stood at the window. Over his shoulder Norma could see dark clouds rumble across the sky. Marion's tactics had worked, though, all embarrassing potential left safely behind. Norma felt her heart slow and she took a deep breath.

"Poor Brian," Colin said.

Oh, jeez Louise.

"He would just hate all that—the talk, the gossip."

"So," Norma said, because she had to say something, "you know him?"

"I knew him," said Colin. "Years ago. We were mates. In school."

"On Orkney? I thought you came from Glasgow."

"I was raised in Kirkwall. My family didn't move until I was seventeen. Brian—well, Brian . . ."

Here was the moment. She could change the subject or—

"I have to admit," she admitted, "I am rather curious."

Colin turned and sat in the other wicker chair. He had brought his cognac and he gave it a good swirl.

"My family," he said. "We were a happy lot. And big. My dad, Aunt Marion, and Annie—and there are two other brothers as well. I have a brother and a sister, and Aunt Anne has three children. Marion has two. There are fifteen cousins in all." He laughed. "We're part of that spreading gene pool, you see. Only Marion and Annie are still living on Orkney, but back then we were a big crazy clan. But Brian . . . Poor Brian only had himself."

"You mean he was an orphan?"

"Well," Colin said, "not technically, no."

There was a pause, and Colin shook his head. "I'm as bad as the folks in there. The gossip, I mean."

"Hey," Norma said, "you can't stop now."

"Okay," he said. "I give. It *is* rather fascinating. Lord, it's been ages since I thought about it all."

He gave a sigh. The sky, clouds covering all but a sliver of the moon, gave a silvery dragon's-eye stare.

"I always liked him, Brian Burroughs." Colin paused. "Though the other boys . . ." Pause again. "Well, you know kids. . . ."

He looked at her.

"Rotten?" she offered.

He smiled. "And mean. It's instinct. You see the black sheep, you go for it. Brian, you could say, was born on the wrong side of the flock."

Italian bastard, Norma thought. Well, that explained the bastard part.

"As was his mother before him."

Whoa. The plot thickened.

"Have you been to see the Italian Chapel?"

Norma tried for nonchalant, despite her inner *Aha!*

"Uh-huh," she said, "just the other day."

"You know about it? Where it came from and all?"

She nodded.

"That's where Brian's history starts. In that little Italian Chapel."

Norma had discovered her source of the Nile.

"Brian's mother was found there," Colin said. "On the altar. Back in December of 1945. A little newborn baby, I kid you not, wrapped in swaddling clothes."

"You mean she—the baby was abandoned?"

"That's right." Colin took a sip of his drink. "And no-body knew who her mother was."

"Wow," said Norma.

"They still don't. One of the enduring mysteries of Orkney."

"So—the way you said that . . . Did they—I mean, what about the father?"

"Well, that became obvious as the little baby grew into a little girl, and later into a bigger girl. Not that the rumors hadn't always been there. The speculations. After all—why there? Of all places, why there?"

Italian bastard. Norma's brain tumblers clicked into place.

"Oh, goodness," she said. "Are you saying—"

"That's what I'm saying. It seemed rather certain that Brian's grandfather had been an Italian prisoner of war."

Norma hoped Colin couldn't see the beating of her heart through the thin layers of her Versace.

"Brian's mother," he continued, "they named the baby Mary—was obviously of Italian descent. Her skin was fair enough, like an islander's, but—I never saw her, mind you, but Brian's skin is the same. The most peculiar—well, they say 'olive,' don't they? But strange. Like—like olives and ice. And her hair. Blacker than a raven's wing—" Colin stopped, then gave a snort. "Listen to me now—you'd think I taught romantic poetry."

Norma smiled.

"But Brian's story will do that," he said.

The sky, in romantic cooperation, let loose a downpour of rain.

"So, the baby—Mary—who raised her?"

"She was fostered about at first. Sounds harsh, but it wasn't really like that. Right after the war things were chaotic, fami-lies split up anyway and, of course, everyone kept hoping she'd be—well, claimed. But she wasn't. Eventually, she ended up with a woman out on Hoy. The woman had lost both her husband and her only child—a son—to the war."

"Well, that's really sad."

"Aye, it was. Also the woman was Catholic. She had a little farm, near Linksness, that's up in the northern part of Hoy. Poor wee Mary grew up wild out there. Isolated. I think that was the idea all along, more's the pity. Out of sight, out of mind—people just didn't—well, that's the way things were back then. Her adopted mother, though—the way I understand it—the woman really loved that little girl. Totally devoted. She homeschooled her—back when that wasn't done—let her have a menagerie, you know, dogs, ducks, sheep, rabbits—a little pony from Shetland. Little Mary wasn't abused, no, she was just—well, hidden. Then, when Mary was around fourteen years old, the woman up and died."

"Jesus."

"A family in Kirkwall took her in. They were related to the woman, but it was the obligation to the church, really, and they let Mary know it. Poor lass. To her, Kirkwall was a huge city. Scary, must've been. She lost her animals—her freedom—and, of course, the only person who had ever loved her. The Kirkwall family put her into a strict little Catholic school. It was 1960, I should point out, so you can imagine the effect—"

"Rebel with a cause?"

Colin grinned. "Very good and exactly on the nose. Mary, by all accounts I've heard, was one voluptuous babe. On top of that she had no—*conventions,* shall we put it? Not that she was a bad girl—it was just that she was beautiful and she was different. By 1962 she'd conquered the heart of every oxygen-breathing boy on the island."

"Oh, dear," Norma said. "I can see where this is going."

Colin held up one hand. "Hold it," he said, "don't get

ahead of the story. Mary didn't get pregnant then. Remember, Brian's my age—"

Right. That pesky math.

"—and I'm only thirty-five, and like I said, she was a good girl. All the boys were in love with her, but she, so the story goes, had narrowed the field down to two. Let's see, it was Robert Miller—he owns a bakery now—and a lad from Westray, can't remember his name. They both courted her feverishly over the next year, and, finally—on the day she turned seventeen—they both popped the question."

"Really?"

"Back-to-back on the very same night."

"Well, what happened? Who did she pick?"

"Neither of them, actually," Colin said. He took another sip of his cognac. "Both sets of the boys' parents got wind of the thing. Oh, there was an uproar. The whole ugly truth came out. Mary—she'd never known, see—about her parentage, or lack thereof. Never even knew she was adopted."

"Man," Norma said, "that must have been traumatic. But, the boys—they loved her, right? Did it really make a difference?"

"Oh, aye, it made a big difference. You see, somebody was her mum—somebody on the islands. As much as the boys knew, they could have been related to her!"

"But that's—that's just so stupid."

"Not to mention the stigma of being illegitimate, and being, you know, half Italian."

"God, it's horrible. People can be so—we can really suck sometimes, can't we?"

Colin was nodding.

"So, what happened then?"

"She quit school. Went back to the little croft on Hoy. The Kirkwall family, of course, washed their hands of the whole affair. Mary lived out there, all alone, for the better part of a year. When she turned eighteen she came into the bit of money her adopted mother had left her. Then she split."

"She left Orkney?"

"Aye, she did. No one saw or heard from her for the next four years."

"Where did she go?"

"I don't know—nobody does. All we know is that four years later—it was swingin' 1967, mind you—Mary showed up again, hair down her back, fringed jacket, paisley skirt, love beads, an entourage of whacked-out fellow hippies, and about eight months pregnant."

Norma just stared at him.

"I told you it was fascinating."

"Well, I guess," Norma said. "Jeez. I mean, really, that's kind of cool."

"Orkney in 1967 was way, way, *way* less than cool. Luckily for her, the Orkney 'fuzz' couldn't tell pot from parsnips."

Norma laughed, "You mean they—"

"Oh, you bet," Colin said. "Pot. Mushrooms. Lord knows what else. They set up a little commune out on the old Linksness farm. It was something, I'm told. About a dozen of them. No electricity, water from a well. Mary started up her menagerie again. And, of course, before long came Brian."

"My God—was he—did she do the whole birth out there?"

"Aye, that she did."

"Whoa."

Colin had finished his drink. He set the snifter on a side table, sat back, and folded his arms.

"Has anyone ever told you," he said, "that you're beautiful when you're fascinated?"

Norma was caught completely off guard. She'd been so intent, listening, learning about Brian—she'd totally lost track of the boy-meets-girl vibe that had started earlier between them.

"I—I am?" was all she could say.

"Of course, you're beautiful, too, when you eat ravioli."

He grinned, but Norma was blushing.

"And that blush," he said, "I gotta tell you, it's quite irresistible."

Colin leaned from his chair, put his hands on the arms of hers, and gave Norma a kiss right on the lips.

"Colin!"

They both jumped back.

Marion was standing in the doorway.

"Well, you certainly don't waste time. I came in to see how you two were doing. I shouldn't, obviously, have bothered."

She was smiling, and her eyes were laughing along with her smile.

"I was just telling Norma," said Colin, "how irresistible she is."

"Well, can you resist, nephew of mine, long enough to take Norma home? We old folk are past our bedtimes, and with this deluge . . ." She signaled out the window. "You may take my van, if you will, and pop Norma's motorbike in the back."

"Love to," said Colin. "It was a super dinner, Auntie— and a brilliant guest list."

"I'm glad you two have gotten to know one another," she said.

Norma looked at Colin and they both gave a little laugh.

"Well, actually . . ." This from Norma.

"We've, uh . . ." Colin lifted his hands. "I've spent the whole time yammering endlessly about Brian Burroughs."

Marion looked at Norma. Her expression remained unchanged, but Norma could read the concern.

"About his mother," Norma said. "Mostly."

"Ah," Marion said. "Mary Burroughs. A sad, sad story, that."

Sad? Sad? Norma hadn't got to the ending, damn it, but she had to maintain detachment. But sad? The ghost of Betty Corrigall had risen in her mind.

Marion took Colin's arm and propelled him down the hall.

"Go," she said, "get the van and the motorbike. Norma will meet you out front."

She turned to Norma and lowered her voice, "Are you quite all right?"

"You figured it out," Norma said. "Right? I'm her, the tourist fatale—Orkney's notorious other woman."

"Whatever has happened," Marion said, and looked her in the eye, "I refuse to fault you for it. I've loved in my life, too, my dear, and not just my husbands."

Norma felt the tears well up.

"Now, don't start that," Marion said. "Go. See what my handsome nephew has to offer."

∞

"I love your aunts," Norma said. The van was warm and cozy, the wipers went *swish swish* against the rain.

"So do I," said Colin. "So what do you think? Shall we do it?"

Norma gave him a sideways glance.

"Get to know one another," he said.

"Oh," she said, and lowered her brows. "Sure, that would be fine."

He chuckled, then said, "Well, that felt good."

"What?"

"You looked at me askance. It's been a long time, you know, between askance looks. Glad to know I still got it."

Norma was laughing.

"So did they fill you in?" he said. "About the disintegration of my life?"

"Let's see," Norma said. "I believe just one mention of getting out of a bad relationship."

"That's putting it nicely," he said. "Okay. Here goes. Colin Tait in a nutshell. Raised on Orkney, as mentioned previously, in a big happy clan, moved to Glasgow at age seventeen. Was beaten frequently till I picked up the Glaswegian social graces. Did well in school, especially the math. Became quite popular with the bonny young Glaswegian ladies. Got one pregnant. We married, divorced when my adorable daughter turned two, pictures on request. I got my doctorate in the fine craft of number doodling, worked my way, with blood, sweat, and lots of ass-smooching, to the top of my peers, with one of whom—she shall remain nameless—I fell very sorely in love, and I don't use that term lightly—there was a great deal of pain mixed in with all that splendor and grass, but I endured, missing all the obvious outcomes of all the obvious calculations, one of which involved, after seven long tortured years of blind devotion, finding my beloved on her knees administering to the—shall we call it, 'slide rule'?—of my very best friend, also a colleague." He paused. "This was six months ago. I left her. That was getting *out* of the bad relationship part."

Norma sat silently as the rain pattered on.

"Okay," he said, "now it's your turn."

"Been there," Norma said after a moment. "I caught my ex-husband with a woman in our bed." She paused. "Doggy style."

They looked at each other and smiled.

"Though," Norma said, "I can't really say that I loved him. I—I settled for him. That's the truth. The whole thing had a numbness to it, more than pain."

"I can't imagine you ever having to settle for anyone, Norma Dale. I wasn't kidding with that kiss."

"It was a nice kiss," Norma said. "Your wife must be a real dolt."

"I wasn't married to she who will remain nameless," he said. "Though I asked her innumerable times. And, honestly, I don't really blame her. Do you know how rare female mathematicians are? I should have known I'd have to share."

"You're terrible," Norma said.

"Aye," he said, "that I am. But the humor helps. I have to make light of something so—so like a bloody anvil."

Like a bloody anvil. Well put, Norma thought. About the ache of the heart.

There was a comfortable silence, then Colin spoke.

"Your nutshell was a lot smaller than mine," he said. "The mystery woman keeps herself shrouded."

"That's what Bryce called me," Norma said.

"It's what everyone in Stromness calls you."

Uh-oh.

"I'm not a mystery."

"Then how 'bout an enigma? An enigma wrapped in a cape."

Norma looked at him and he looked back.

"I've been bugging Aunt Marion for two weeks to get to meet you. Or at least tell me who you were. She only agreed when I threatened to start drinking again."

"I can't tell if you're joking," Norma said.

"I'm not joking. I was in pretty bad shape. I quit. My position, I mean. At the university. It was either that or impale myself with a sharpened compass."

Silence.

"The part about the compass was joking," he said.

"I did a lot of drinking recently," Norma said. "Highland Park."

"Good stuff."

"I have—I have some anvil stuff, too, you know, going on. Not about my ex. About my whole life." She sighed. "This me—this me that looks beautiful eating ravioli—it's—I'm—I haven't been that person very long. And I—I'm not very good at it. That's why I—it's the reason for the cottage and all. I've just been, well, a disaster around people." Another sigh. "Men people."

Norma stopped. She was about two sentences away from spilling her guts to this man person. This very handsome, very charming man person.

Colin cleared his throat. "Well," he said. "That certainly clears up the mystery. Now what shall we talk about?"

Norma laughed. "This is nice," she said. "To laugh. Be around nice people." Then she let slip a little flirt. "To get to look askance."

She hadn't meant to. She'd pretty much just warned him that she was bad news, hadn't she? It was the darkness outside, the pelting rain, the intimacy of the van, the charm.

"I could arrange for more of that." Colin took his hand from the wheel and with one finger stroked along the line of her hair in the tender little spot behind her ear. "I've been wanting to do that all night."

"Well, it worked," Norma said. Her senses were still reacting. The touch had reached the pleasure centers along her spine.

They had reached the dirt road that led to Norma's cottage.

"This is it, right?"

"Right."

He slowed the van, turned, then drove the few remaining

yards and killed the engine. Then he shifted in his seat, turning toward her.

His leaf-green eyes glistened in the dark.

"Don't worry," he said. "I don't expect you to ask me in."

"Well, I—"

"We'll let the rain slack down a bit, okay? Then I'll pop your scooter out. We don't want poor Colin to get all soaked, right?"

"Right."

"Gad, that was feeble," he said. "I'll say anything to prolong this—" Then he snapped his fingers. "Got it. The continuing saga of Brian Burroughs—would that tempt you to stay with me out here in the rain?"

If only he knew, Norma thought guiltily, but she smiled.

"Good. Now let's see, right before Marion came in—where did I leave off?"

"Well," she said, falling for it, "you were—"

But he had already leaned in for the kiss, her lips parted conveniently mid-word. It was a good kiss, his hand to the back of her head in case she'd planned on going anywhere, and it was long and fairly complicated. Norma had time to contemplate the old adage, "A kiss without a mustache is like an egg without salt." Maybe they were right about that. She was just about to contemplate the phenomenon further when the kiss ended. He let her go and sat back on his side of the van.

"Right," he said, "and before that we'd gotten up to where wee Brian had just been born."

And then he went on talking as if nothing had just happened—about Brian, for God's sake, the man she loved. But her lips were still tingling and hot, and her heart was pounding for the first time in months for someone *besides*

Brian, and God, was she confused. She felt like she'd mixed two colors of Play-Doh together, her emotions all twisted and impossible to part. And she was missing it—what was he saying?—little Brian, baby Brian, raised by hippies on Hoy.

"Wait!"

Colin looked at her.

"Uh," she said, "I'm—confused." Well, she was. But she couldn't tell him the truth, right? "Uh, who was Brian's father?"

"Oh," Colin said, "didn't I say that?"

Great. So she blurted out a partial truth. "I wasn't really listening, okay? I was thinking about your mustache."

Colin grinned and then frowned. "Good thinking or bad?" he said.

Their eyes met.

"Good."

"Thank the gods," he said, and then, "Nobody knew."

"Knew what?"

"Who Brian's father was. It was assumed to be one of the hippies at the commune, but that was far from certain, and when she left, she left alone."

"She left?"

"Yes, I was just getting to that part. Brian was three or four, five—somewhere in there—and she just took off, like before."

"She left him? Her baby?"

"Aye. Disappeared to who knows where—Mary Burroughs was never seen again."

"She left her child—with a bunch of hippies?"

"That's what I'm telling you. There were about four or five of them still around, though the glamour of the commune was wearing thin. Took the authorities a couple of years to catch on, too. Brian had been running free, like a little animal, he was. Someone finally called social services, you know. They came out there, discovered Mary was long gone, mushrooms in the cellar and a nice big patch of killer bog weed."

"Jesus."

"No one got arrested, it was all kind of hushed up, the hippies deported quietly back to England proper. Took 'em a week to find Brian. Little feral fellow knew Hoy like the back of his hand—they never would have caught him, either, till a clever mum suggested tempting him out with a plate of fresh hot scones."

"You're making this up," said Norma.

"God's honest truth."

Norma, in her mind's eye, saw Brian nimbly scaling the rocks.

I know these cliffs. Been doin' that since I was a boy.

"So what happened?"

"It was like his mother all over again. They took him into Kirkwall and fostered him out to a Catholic family."

"Not the same one—"

"No, it was the sexton and his wife who took him in. They were a childless couple. Too old to be raising a boy. Especially one like Brian. I saw him that day, when they brought him in all wild. A bunch of us young ones did. It was just a few days before we all started school for the first time. He was filthy. Wearing ragged blue jeans, bare feet, tattered tie-dyed T-shirt three sizes too big. His hair was black and knotted in a great mass down his back. Eyes like two black marbles on fire. He stood there, two big ol' coppers holding him down by the shoulders. Like the littlest wild hippie from Borneo."

Colin was staring out the windshield.

"I thought he was the most magnificent thing I'd ever seen. The other boys, though, they stared, they pointed, they laughed. Called him names. He heard them. The name he called back so totally topped theirs that they all stopped. Just like that. We'd never heard such a word before, but we knew, you know, on a glandular level, that it was a mighty bad one. When school started, they brought him. He was all clipped and cleaned. Regular little boy clothes. He learned soon enough that the baddest words in the world won't help you against the mob. Especially a mob of six-year-old boys."

"But you were his friend?"

"Aye," Colin said. "I was his friend. Every chance he got, too, Brian would be off to Hoy. He'd sneak himself on the backs of lorries, ride the ferry from Houton, then spend all day running in his beloved hills."

Colin smiled. "When I got brave enough, I went with him. Ah, those were glorious times. When I was ten, one summer we stayed the whole night sleeping on the Dwarfie Stone. I got grounded for a month, but by God, it was worth it!"

Colin laughed, but when he looked at Norma, two big ol' tears were running down her cheeks.

"What is it?" he said, concerned.

"I—I'm just. It's—" She wiped her face with her hands, then sniffled her nose.

"Oh, man," said Colin. "I wish I was one of those guys could whip out a nice white hankie. How 'bout my sleeve? It's clean pretty fair."

Norma gave a sad little laugh. "You're just a darn good storyteller." She sniffed again, and thought, *And I'm a pretty lousy liar.*

"Poor Brian," Colin said. "It is really pretty sad, isn't it? We had some happy times, but they were few and far between. Brian, of course, was never accepted. He was never one of us. The older we got, too, the farther we drifted, I'm ashamed to admit. Puberty just about cinched it. It was 1980, God help us, the Thatcher years. I was going through my hard punk stage—as hard as one could get in Orkney at age thirteen—about the consistency of Brie. Brian was into his art by then. I mean, really in it. He was Gothic, really Gothic, you see—in a Catholic sort of way. He told me once he was thinking about entering the priesthood. It was really weird. Like they'd have him. He all the time wore white, and was always drawing these dark brooding archangels with long bloody swords and Mary Magdalene vampires and, oh, man—I remember one painting he did. It was Betty Corrigall—do you know about her?"

Nod.

"He painted her out on her grave site, but she was resurrected, like a madonna and child, sitting on her tombstone with her baby—she had a halo and wings, you know, dressed in blue, beautiful, a vision, but that awful noose was around her neck, the rope end coiled around the baby, attached like an umbilical cord, and man, there was deep red blood, blood dripping from her nose. Oh, Christ—I'm sorry, I've set you off again."

This time Colin did offer his sleeve, and she took it. Then he held her against his shoulder as she sobbed.

"I'll shut up—this is freaking you out. God, what was I thinking, telling you this awful stuff?"

He stroked her hair and gave her a gentle kiss on top of her head.

"It's okay," he said, "my stupid lips are sealed. Okay? I'm sorry."

"Mmmph," Norma said. She was shaking her head.

"What?"

Colin held her away from his shoulder, "What did you say?"

"I said," Norma said in a small voice, "no. You have to finish, I want to know what happened. After that. To Brian."

"No way," Colin said. "Look at you, you're shivering all over."

It was true. She was shivering all over.

"I'm taking you inside, okay?"

And he did. He got the comforter from her bed and wrapped her in it, cloak and all. Sat her in the comfy chair and started up the fire. Tenderly, he unstrapped her red high heels and rubbed one little foot and then the other between his big warm hands and tucked them under the comforter, too.

Norma did a bit more sobbing, sobbed herself, essentially, to sleep. Colin stayed with her. Sitting on the floor. Eventually he fell asleep, too, his big worried head resting on her curled-up feet.

In the morning, of course, he found Brian's painting, and the truth came tumbling out. Fate just loves complications, don'tcha know.

CHAPTER 19

olin woke up first. Norma woke up when the aroma of "wake up and smell the scent of fresh-brewed coffee" wafted in. She opened her eyes. The fire had been stoked up again nice and toasty. She unwrapped herself from comforter and cloak. Stood up, looked down, surveyed the damage. One stocking had come loose and fallen around her ankle. The Versace looked pretty good wrinkled, probably by design. She ran a finger under the rim of her lower lashes, came away with a smear of mascara. Yup, nice morning-after pair of raccoon eyes. Her hair. She felt it. Like an unbundling roll of hay.

Norma let loose the other stocking, kicked them both off, and padded into the kitchen.

" 'Morning," she said.

Colin was kneeling, trying to scoop a raw egg from the floor back into half its shell.

"Sorry," he said. "Mathematician, not chef."

"You're sweet to try," Norma said. "And the coffee smells good. Let me clean that up."

Colin stood and wiped his hands on a dishrag.

Norma got a paper towel and bent to clean up the egg.

Colin started grinning.

"You'd better not," she said, "be grinning at me."

"No," he said, "of course not—you're a vision of loveliness, absolutely. The fuzzy hair quite suits you."

"There's more eggs," Norma said. "The next one could be for you."

They looked at each other and smiled.

"Thank you, Colin," she said. "For staying."

"That's the first time you said it," he said.

She looked at him.

"My name."

He came across the room and took her face in his hands. He rubbed his thumbs under her eyes and then smoothed back her hair.

"There," he said. "Beautiful as ever."

Norma felt a pang of guilt. What was she doing to this man?

He gave her a chaste little kiss on the lips and dropped his hands.

"Peat," he said. "You're running low. I'll be manly and fetch some, and you can be womanly here in the kitchen, okay?"

Norma nodded.

He left the kitchen. Great. She hadn't noticed before. Colin had such a nice butt.

Norma tried to think. Reception was bad. Wiggly lines, no logic was going through her head. Caffeine first. Then she'd worry about food and this new guy in her life.

She got out two cups, sugar, and the cream. Set them all on a tray, got two spoons and the pot of black coffee. She lifted the tray and carried it from the kitchen to the living room. She placed the tray on the coffee table. Then she saw her stockings on the floor. Right. That was classy. She scooped them up, then gathered her cloak from the back of the chair. That was when she realized the comforter was gone.

There was no time to trace through the scenario. Colin, ever sweet, picking up the comforter. Folding it, taking it into her bedroom to put it away. No time to figure out how it had happened, just the result. Colin was standing in the doorway, Brian's painting in his hands.

"This is a good one," he said. "I hadn't seen it before. Skara Brae, right? Back in its past? These must be what? Neolithic spooks? Quite a departure from his landscapes, wouldn't you say?"

"Oh, Colin," Norma said. She put a hand to her mouth. "I'm so sorry, I—"

"That's the second time you said my name. Funny, this time it doesn't sound so good."

"Oh," Norma said. "I—"

"You know what? I believe I'm overqualified. Alberta's pig could add this up, don't you think? You. Brian. Colin the chump."

"Oh, no," Norma said. "I—"

"What? You going to start crying again?"

He was right on the money with that one. She sank down on the chair, put her head on her arm, and let loose a big wracking sob. Brian was right. She was sick. She was cruel. Just let her get around anything in pants and she would play them. She was a horrible person. Heartless, selfish, and a fool. But what was this? Colin was there. On his knees. Holding her. Stroking her. She looked up, her eyes dripping—way beyond raccoon now.

"I'm sorry," he said, "I'm such a bastard. Forgive me, please."

"No," Norma said, "God, don't be so nice—please, please forgive *me*."

A big string of snot ran out of her nose.

"Oh, God," she said, "I'm so—so wretched." She buried her head again. "Please, just leave, go away—please."

"Not as long as I have another sleeve to offer."

Norma looked up. His leaf-green eyes were filled with tears.

"It's almost clean," he said.

"I didn't mean," she said, wiping at her face, "to do the anvil thing. Really. Not to you. I—I really like you. You're cute, you're kind, you're funny—"

"I kiss well?"

Norma had to laugh. A sobbing pitiful thing. Then she took a big shuddering breath. She let it out, watching his face. She reached her hand to him, wiped away his single tear, and gave a little stroke to his mustache.

"Very, very well," Norma said sadly. "And you have a nice butt."

This got a little look of hope from Colin, but then it faded.

"But I'm not Brian, right?" He pulled back from her and then slumped in the other chair. "I'm not Brian fucking Burroughs."

Norma shook her head.

"So you're really her," he said. "The woman. The tourist. The reason Brian broke up with Fiona."

"I'm afraid so," Norma said meekly. "I'm afraid so."

"And you couldn't have just told me?"

"I—I was ashamed."

"Ashamed? Why? So you had a summer fling—so what? Brian's a grown man. I'm sure he knew what he was doing. What's the big deal?"

"But we didn't," Norma said.

"Didn't what?"

"We didn't, uh—fling."

"But—" Colin looked at her. "Now, I'm confused. If you didn't, uh—fling, then why did Brian leave Fiona?"

"I'm not sure," Norma said. "I didn't even know he did until just a few days ago."

"Then where, if you don't mind my asking, does the shame come in?"

Norma squeezed her eyes shut. She would tell him. The whole sordid mess.

"I, uh—flinged—I flung, oh hell, Colin, I fucked another guy. In front of Brian—who I think had started to love me, though I didn't know it—I swear. I fucked a Texan while Brian watched, up against the Comet Stone."

Norma opened her eyes again and looked Colin right in the face.

"That," she said, "was where the shame came in."

Colin looked at her a moment, then leaned over and poured coffee into each of the cups.

"I think we're going to need this," he said. "Because you're going to have to tell someone now, okay? And I think it's me. Everything. From the beginning."

∽

It took two pots of coffee, because Norma did go back to the beginning. All the way back to Trey Bliss. Somewhere in there they fixed breakfast and Norma changed into jeans and a sweater and brushed out her hair. She finished up outside as they walked along the cliffside.

"I once had a nice talk here," Norma said, "with a sheep."

"Did she give good advice?"

"Yes, she did, really. It was here that I forgave myself. For what had happened, for what I'd done. And I figured out why I had come back."

"Well, that's fairly obvious," Colin said. He had his hands in the pockets of his pants and was looking out across the bay.

"It is?" Norma said.

"You love him, right? You want him. You can't very well get him all the way back in the States."

"But that's just it," Norma said. "Damn it. I don't want to *get* him. I blew it. Forever. I've come to terms with that. All I wanted—all I *want*—is for him to understand. For him to know I'm not a terrible person. The megalith whore. He's in love with Fiona, okay? What he felt for me—well, I don't *know* what he felt for me. But it's over."

"You really believe that? Really?"

Norma looked at him. "Yes, I do."

"Well," Colin said, "it's a bunch of crap." He snorted. "Chick reasoning."

Norma put her hands on her hips. "*Chick* reasoning?"

"That's right," Colin said, then he grinned. "Ewe logic. Deduction of does."

Norma punched him.

"Fine," he said, putting up his hands in defense, "fine, go on with your fantasy, then."

"What? What do you mean?"

"Look," Colin said, "if I were smart, I'd agree with you. You're right, uh-huh, yes, yes, you haven't a snowball's chance with the man. Then I'd comfort you and, with my charming butt, win you for myself. But it's because of *that* that I know that you do."

"And this is man logic?" Norma said. "I'm totally confused. Because of what? Know that I do what? What are you talking about?"

Colin took her in his arms and gave her one of his long involved kisses. He ended with a flourish, then held her away from him at arm's length.

"Because of that. All right? I know every horrid little thing about you. I know about Trey Bliss's button, for chrissake, and *I'm* still smitten. You're *better* than Betty Boop, you're hot, you're glorious, you're—you're so *you*. I know why that idiot Burroughs went to Edinburgh, you silly twit. He went to *find* you, don't you see that?"

Norma looked at him, her mouth half open.

"To find me?" she said. "You really think so?"

"Two minutes after you ran from him up on Quoyer, the bugger was probably kicking himself. Did he know where you were staying?"

Norma shook her head.

"Even what town you were in?"

"No," Norma said. "I don't think . . . Oh, man. You think he was trying to—"

"Duh?" Colin smiled.

"No." She shook her head fiercely. "No. You didn't see his face. You didn't see what Russell and I—"

"For a left-brain person, I have a pretty vivid imagination," Colin said. He looked at her and lifted one brow.

Norma covered her face with her hands and groaned, "Oh, God."

Colin gently pulled them down. "It's okay," he said. "You forgave yourself—don't you think that Brian could, too?"

"I don't know," Norma said, and sighed. "I really don't know. That's what's so silly about all of this. I hardly even know the man. Is it crazy? I mean, to fall in love—so hard in love, in like, one second?"

Colin looked at her, leaf eyes glistening again.

"Happens all the time," he said. Then he put his hand to

her lips. "Don't say it—just makes it worse. How I feel isn't the issue here. The problem is Mr. Burroughs."

"Do you—" Norma hesitated. "—do *you* know him? I mean now. Last night we—well, you never quite—"

"Finished the saga?"

Norma nodded.

"Right. Okay, let's see." Colin rubbed his chin. "I was telling you about his Gothic phase. The Betty Corrigall as Madonna—oh, lord. Betty Corrigall. I get it now. The water-works, I mean. Betty Corrigall was your common denomina-tor."

"Yeah," Norma said. "Well put, mathboy."

They had started walking again. The sun had already started its afternoon meander.

"Okay, so Brian's Gothic phase. That was pretty much the end. He was doing all the weird paintings and he started skip-ping school, spending more and more time on Hoy."

"Like, at the crofting farm?"

"Right, yes, I hadn't mentioned that. The sexton, by then, he and his wife had lost control of Brian. Everyone had. Not that anyone had ever *had* control." Colin smiled. "He was one weird dude. Anyway, sometime around then, it was before my family left for Glasgow, Brian ran away."

"You mean, from Kirkwall? He went back to the farm?"

"No. He left Orkney. Just like his mother. He up and dis-appeared."

"So—but, he came back, right?"

"He came back—twenty years later."

"Twenty years? Are you talking about when he—when he showed up two years ago?"

"Aye. That's why it caused the big stir. When he first came back nobody knew his identity. He went quietly back to the croft on Hoy. The place had stood empty all those years. He fixed it up, into his studio, you see, and just started showing up, this island, that, with his easel and his ponytail, painting the historic places. The women all went gaga. Like a competition. Who would be the one to win the mysterious, sexy stranger?"

Norma let out a sigh. "So Brian worked his way through every willing female on the islands?"

"Oh, no," Colin said. "The women were willing, all right—but Brian, he's not—remember about the priesthood? Brian is no playboy—not by a long shot. Brian painted and ignored them—drove them crazy, he did. They were just about to conclude that he must be gay and then Fiona entered the fray. The contest was over. Hands down. Fiona bagged him. And there was no question then about Brian's sexual preference. Things were hot and heavy between those two—I mean, really torrid—"

"Okay," Norma said, "I get the picture."

Colin looked at her. "Sorry. Right. It was around then— after Fiona—that everyone realized who he really was. And then the shit really hit the ferry wheel."

"You mean with Fiona's family?"

"Hers and quite a few others. Things change, but some things stay the same. People's prejudices are one of them. To some on the islands Brian will always be the Italian bastard's bastard."

"It's just—just so unfair."

"And," Colin said, "to answer your question, aye, I know him now."

"You do?"

"I know him fairly well. Him *and* Fiona. The summer after Brian showed up again, I showed up again, too. I came to spend a few weeks with my favorite aunt."

Norma smiled. "Marion?"

"Not that I don't love Annie, of course, but—"

Norma held up her hand. "No need to explain. You know, Marion, last night, she—well, she figured it all out."

"She would have, yeah, that's like her. Though it was Annie, that summer, told me about Brian. Not who he was, just the gossip. The big hot topic, right? The minute I saw him, I knew. I thought it was funny, you know, mysterious stranger, my ass. He was down on the docks painting, Stromness, one of his touristy things. So I just sidled up to him. 'Hello, Brian,' I says, 'long time no see.' And he smiled, not skipping a beat, ' 'Lo, Colin, how ya been?' Something like that. I didn't let on, to the clueless, I mean. I did tell Marion—and she'd already twigged. Can't slip much past Marion. I went to see him, too, that summer. Out at his studio on Hoy. We drank a lot of ale, did a lot of talking. Like twenty years hadn't even been."

Colin stopped.

"I hate to even say this, but—"

"What?" Norma asked.

"I still found the guy magnificent, you know? If I were a woman, I'd fucking fall for him, too."

Norma laughed. Then she hugged him. "You're wonderful, Colin."

But then he was looking at her all serious, like he was going to kiss her again. Norma pulled away.

"You've got to stop doing that," she said. "I'm confused enough as it is."

"Okay," he said. But he looked pretty pleased with himself. "Back to Burroughs—the bastard—shit, I didn't mean it like that."

"Well, speaking of that," Norma said, "did you—in all the talking—did he ever talk about his mother?"

"No, not really. That subject was pretty painful for him. It's why he left the Islands, though—I think. To go search for her. He said something once—we were mighty drunk, gone out again to the Dwarfie Stone. It was cryptic, and more to himself than to the drunken sod next to him. He said something about going searching the world when all he ever needed was to find Orkney again."

"Where the endless ocean opens," said Norma.

"That's the place," Colin said. "Brian's true love and his torment."

"His torment?"

"Orkney rejected him. Like his mother. Brian carries that pain with him, always. I think that's why— No, I shouldn't say that."

"What?"

"Why he was attracted to Fiona."

"Look," Norma said, "I've met her, remember? I think we know why he's attracted to Fiona."

"Fiona is—"

"The hottest woman in all of Orkney? The Princess of Stronsay? Miss Cambridge fucking Bryn Mawr?"

"Calm down, lassie," Colin said, laughing. "Aye, she's all of that and more. But, remember, I've met her, too. I've seen 'em together. All her looks made it easy, sure, but I think Brian, deep down, is in love with her blood."

"What do you mean?"

"That Brian is in love with the subtext of her, her genetics. Fiona, to Brian, *is* Orkney. That's what he loves, the poor git, not Fiona."

Norma thought about this, then she said, "Wow."

"Welp," Colin said as he kicked up some dirt, "that's completely blown it."

"What?"

"Any chance I might have had with you. You're just going to jump on your scooter and drive straight to him, right? Leave poor Colin in the dust?"

They had come up to her cottage. The motorbike was there beside Marion's van.

For a moment Norma actually considered doing just that. Then she shook her head slowly and her eyes filled with tears.

"Oh, lord, woman," Colin said, taking her by the shoulders, "please, don't start crying again. I—Christ, I told you all this to make you happy. Trust me, I'm not bull*shitting* you here."

Norma laughed and wiped her eyes. "Only a Scotsman would say bullshitting like that." She gave a big sigh. "Oh, Colin, you did make me happy. Happier than I've been since—well, you've lifted my anvil, okay? I think I'm—well, I'd be halfway in love with you, at least, if I weren't already so screwed up. I'm crying because—because I have hope again. But it's a fragile thing, this hope. I can't go charging up to Brian. Even if it's all, you know, true, what you said—I—I don't even know what to think about it all—not yet."

"Right," Colin said. "You need time. I get it. I understand. Just don't go using that chick reasoning again."

Norma looked off into the distance. The sky was just getting the first hints of orange. "Do you suppose it's chick reasoning to think that Brian might be better off marrying Fiona, even Fiona's subtext, than having me show up in his life again?"

"I think it's chick reasoning to not let him have the chance to find out."

"But I can't—I can't just show up—ta-dah!"

"Okay, then, I'll help you."

"Colin, I would never—I couldn't ask you—"

"Why not? I'd be perfect."

"Have you—seen him? You know, recently?"

"Not since last Christmas. But that's how we are, Brian and me. We're mates. Always pick up right where we left off.

I could do it casual, you know, hint around, see what's what—or just, blammo, tell him direct. Your choice. Or, we could do the jealousy bit—you showing up on my arm at some function—" He looked at her. "Nah, all right, scratch that. At any rate, you'll get your time, because it's going to be at least two weeks before I could do it. Maybe three." He smiled. "I've got to go back to Glasgow tomorrow. I'm selling my house, got to tend to that and some other business."

"You really did it? Quit your teaching position?"

"Aye. Had to, really. She who will remain nameless has tenure. Couldn't bear to see her face every day."

"I'm really sorry."

"It's not so bad. All of us Orcadians always yearn to come home."

"So, that's what you'll do? Move back here?"

He nodded. "I'm looking into teaching at a Kirkwall public school."

"You think you'll be happy?"

"I think so. The only thing is I'll miss my little girl."

Norma felt bad. She'd forgotten that he'd even had one.

"Is the offer of the picture still good?"

Colin beamed and got out his wallet.

"Oh," Norma said, "she's so pretty. She has your wonderful eyes."

"So," sighed Colin, "do you."

CHAPTER 20

And so two weeks later the terrific plan was carried through and everything worked out splendidly. Not.

What really happened involved a lot of Highland Park and one rather horrible visit.

Norma had a couple of euphoric days and then plunged into nervous despair. Drinking helped. There was also lots of pacing. Her emotions were worse than a roller coaster, she was on warp drive through a wormhole of molasses. Four days of this and she called Colin in Glasgow.

"Colin!"

"What?"

"Colin, what if they get married!"

"Well, screw him, then Brian is an idiot."

"No—I mean, what if they get married, you know, this week!"

Long-distance chuckling.

"It's not funny!"

"Yes, it is, luv. We're looking at months here, if not longer. Fiona's probably just now picking out the colors of the bows for the church pews. She'll have nothing but the fanciest wedding on the island. Trust me."

That got her through another two days. But by the weekend Norma was warping again. Three in the morning, Saturday night, she found herself on her motorbike heading for Skara Brae. It was colder. She had brought the comforter, the sheepskin, and an extra sweater. She also brought her little glow-in-the-dark travel alarm.

The stone bed brought her peace. She slept soundly, bundled in her Neolithic crib, and woke to the little *buzz-buzz* way before Bono showed up. Sunday was okay. A little drinking, lots of DVDs. She'd seen them before, but she was laying low these days. As few "mystery woman" trips to Stromness as possible.

Monday night found her once more at Skara Brae. This time it was cold and it started to rain. Norma shifted her bedding bundle to the tunnel and lay there protected by four-thousand-year-old recycling. She thought about Brian, about Colin, about the fact that she was losing her mind. Wasn't romance great? In the darkness of the morning the *buzz-buzz* woke her. She was covered in a thin layer of sparkling frost, highlighted by the blue glow of her travel alarm. She had a magic-fairy moment before her sense kicked in.

"I've got to stop doing this," Norma said.

∞

December rolled in, and with it one of those forewarned winter storms. Norma got a call from Colin, who said he would be gone till the middle of the month. His ex-wife was taking care of her ailing mother, so he was taking care of his daughter. Then Marion called.

"Are you doing all right?" she asked, with her usual Marion concern.

"I'm fine," Norma said.

"Anytime, I'd love to have you come stay with me."

"Another big storm like that, and I'll probably take you up."

"Please do, I'm serious."

"Marion?"

"Yes, dear?"

"Colin—he's wonderful. He's been such a help. Did he—did he say anything?"

"He said just enough and not a word more. I'm so glad you two became friends."

"Did he tell you about our—our plan?"

"Yes, he did, and I think it's totally daft." She laughed. "I'm behind you one hundred percent."

"I think I am going a little crazy, actually. I go back and forth, you know, wondering if I'm doing the right thing."

"I always say follow your heart."

"I don't want to hurt anybody."

"Love and pain, my dear, like bannocks and butter."

Norma laughed. "Maybe I should needlepoint that on a sampler."

Marion chuckled. There was a little hesitation, then she said, "About Colin . . ."

"Yes?"

"I think you'd want to know."

"Okay."

"Colin's in love with you."

"Oh, God, Marion, I—"

"No, dear—it's not a bad thing. Not at all. It's just that—well, these last two weeks, he's been seeing a lot of Ainsley—"

"Ainsley?"

"His ex-wife—the mother of his child."

"Oh," Norma said, then, "oh—*ohh!* He never said—I mean, he hardly mentioned—you mean he's—there's like—"

"Yes," Marion said. "There's like. She's never remarried, you see."

Norma felt a little sting. "Whoa," she said. "I think I'm—I think I'm jealous. Jesus. Does that make me—does it make me just a total—"

"Human?" said Marion. "Yes, I'm afraid it does. I also think Colin would be delighted."

"Oh, Marion, I—I thank you. Okay? I don't know what's going to happen, you know—with all this. With Colin—with Brian."

"Love has a way of sorting itself out, dear. I've learned that in my life, if nothing else. And now for the bad news, I'm afraid."

Uh-oh.

"I wanted to give you a little heads-up."

Norma's head went up.

"It's Helen Spence. About you and Brian. She's all but strung a banner across the middle of town."

"Oh, jeez," Norma said. "Oh, crap."

"I'm sorry."

"So *everyone* knows? Who I am? That I'm here?"

"I believe a few herdsmen up on North Ronaldsay are still in ignorance."

"Even—Brian?"

"That," Marion said, "I'm not sure of. Nobody sees Brian these days. I would bet that he doesn't, but I'm afraid, dear, it's just a matter of time."

∞

A matter of time. Norma clicked her phone shut. Time for a good mope, is what it was. A good mope and about half a bottle of whiskey. Then she looked at her phone and decided instead that it was time to launch Plan B. She'd call Colin, get moral support, and then go see Brian herself. If he knew, fine. If he didn't know, fine and dandy. Plan B was being honest and face-to-face; then she'd let fate decide.

Colin wasn't there, so Norma left a message. She took a shower and then spent an hour trying to decide what to wear. She ended up in blue jeans, black running shoes, and a black wool sweater. She went light on the makeup. A little blusher—you had to have blusher—two strokes of mascara per eye, and neutral lip gloss. Then another thirty minutes practicing in the mirror, trying to come up with her first words. Four dozen lame variations later, she decided on "Hello, Brian." Then she did her hair. First simple. Just parted down the middle. Too Cher. Then brushed it back behind her ears with no part. Then the part on the side routine. Christ. Inspiration. She leaned completely over and brushed the whole lot of it into a top-notch ponytail loosely gathered with a black elastic band. She'd do a soft bun at the top and wispy tendrils all over. Gibson girl. Perfect. She'd started looking for bobby pins when she heard the approach of a car.

Maybe Marion? Bless her heart. But no. Norma looked out her window and saw the little red sport job.

She felt all the blood drain to her knees as she watched Fiona Rousay get out of the car. Fiona didn't look happy. She looked beautiful, of course. She was wearing a bright red business suit. Her hair up in a grand blond swirl. Lots of makeup. Stiletto heels. Full bitch-slappin' armor.

Norma gulped, then tried to catch her breath. For this, she wasn't ready. She considered a full retreat. There was no back door, but the window in her bedroom was quite large. No, that was silly. She could do this. She caught her breath, put both hands out to steady herself on the air. Then she caught some self-esteem. Then even a little bit of attitude. She ran to the kitchen and filled her kettle with water, threw it on the stove, and lit the burner.

Fiona rapped loudly on the door. *What was she using—a stick?*

Norma cleared her throat.

"Come in," she called out in her most dulcet of tones.

Fiona opened the door.

Norma walked into the living room twirling a tea bag by the string.

"Oh, hello, Fiona. How are you?" She gave her fountain of hair a little shake. "I just put on water for a cuppa. Care to join me?"

Fiona's eyes were like two lapis lazuli laser beams of pure hatred. "Did you really think you could pull it off," she said, "your little charade?"

"I'm not playing any games, Fiona."

"Penelope Smythe?"

Norma smiled. "Helen Spence *is* a shark, I see."

"And *you* are a bitch."

"No," Norma answered back calmly, "I am not."

"You fucked my fiancé."

Whoa, the sweet and lovely gloves were definitely off.

"I don't know what Helen Spence told you—"

"What *Brian* told me!" Fiona said. Two spots appeared on her cheeks the exact bright red of her suit. *"Brian!"*

And then Fiona burst into tears.

Norma's attitude crumbled. "Fiona," she said, going to her. "Fiona, it's not true."

Fiona backed away. "Of course it's true," she sobbed. "He left me, he left me for *you.*"

Norma stopped, her dander resurrected. She didn't like the implication behind that *"you."*

"What?" Norma snapped out. "The Puffin Lady's no match for the Princess of Stronsay?"

Fiona looked at her with big wet blue eyes and gave a pitiful nod.

Norma had to laugh. It was more like a bark. One Bette Davis–like "Ha!"

"I hate you," Fiona said. "You've destroyed Brian and you think it's ever so funny. You're a bitch *and* you're cruel."

Norma looked at her, amazed, then the whistle on the kettle began to blow. She turned on her heel and walked toward the kitchen.

"Where are you going?" Fiona said.

"To make us some tea."

"I'm—I'm not going to drink tea with you!"

Norma turned and put her hands on her hips. "Yes, you are. We're going to drink tea and have a nice civilized conversation together. Then you're going to explain to me what on God's green earth you are talking about."

When Norma brought in the tea tray, Fiona had just about composed herself. She was sitting stiffly in one of the chairs, a decided pout on her shapely lower lip.

Norma served. "Sugar?"

Fiona shook her head.

"Milk? Lemon?"

Fiona pointed to the lemon.

"Cake?"

Fiona just glared.

Norma cut a big slab and daintily placed it on a plate. "Now," she said. "Let's get one thing straight. I didn't fuck your fiancé."

Fiona looked at her and blinked.

"Why," Norma said, "do you think I did?"

Ah, tea—the great bridger of gaps. Fiona took one sip and then told her.

"He—He came to me, the day before he left." She looked down to her lap. "He *said* he'd been unfaithful. He told me he'd met a woman," she looked up accusingly, "and that he thought he loved her."

Norma bravely kept herself from whooping. "Did he say it was me?"

"No," said Fiona. "I had absolutely no idea. I was in complete shock. I asked him who—I begged him to tell me—but he said that it didn't matter now, that he'd hurt the woman terribly and she was gone. He said then that he was going to look for her. That he didn't think he'd find her but that he was going to try. Then he—he told me—that he *thought* he had loved *me,* but how—how could it be true, when he could so easily—well—make a mess of things."

Fiona lifted her cup, but her hands were trembling and she put the cup back into its saucer without drinking.

"And then he was gone. He left the island. He *left* me. I wanted to die, can you understand that?"

Norma nodded. The urge to whoop faded.

"I thought about doing it. About killing myself. I thought about doing it on that damn grave. Maybe he'd love me if I were dead, like Betty Corrigall."

"But you didn't," Norma said gently. "You went to him, right? Brought him home? You're getting married, Fiona, doesn't that tell you anything?"

Fiona looked at her with the blue lasers again. "Yes, we're finally engaged," she said. "*I* proposed. I defied my family and said I would marry him. You know what he said?"

Norma shook her head.

"He said, 'Sure, why not?' Isn't that the most romantic thing? 'Sure, why not?' " And again Fiona began to cry.

"Look . . ." Norma said. She was starting to feel pretty bad. "Brian and I were never—" She tried again. "—unfaithful in this context. He didn't mean sex—"

Fiona glared and wiped at her eyes. "You're lying. I know you're lying. Helen Spence showed me the painting. She couldn't wait to show me the painting. You *do* know that's the last *decent* painting he's done in months? If I can call it that—God, I wanted to die all over again."

"What are you talking about? What painting?"

"*Quoyer Viewpoint*. You and Brian doing a vile little shadow play against the Comet Stone. Ring a bell? What kind of context was *that*?"

Then Fiona hit her. She reached across the tea set and slapped Norma right across the face. And it hurt. Norma reached her fingers to her nose and came away with blood.

Norma was speechless. This femme fatale stuff wasn't what it was cracked up to be.

Fiona went on, her voice low and threatening. "I *don't* know what exactly happened between you and Brian," she said, "but I *do* know that you are a bad person and you've brought out the darkness in him. I've come here today to ask—to beg you—to leave him alone."

Norma picked up a napkin and wiped the blood from her face.

"Does Brian," she said, with what she hoped was dignity, "know I'm here?"

"Brian never leaves Hoy. He drinks and he paints. Awful, dark paintings. Rubbish. Sick rubbish. That's why you have to leave. Leave Orkney before . . ." She fixed Norma with her red-rimmed eyes. "If Brian finds out you are here, you'll destroy him completely."

"Fiona . . ." Norma took a deep breath. "I haven't lied to you and I'm not going to start now. Despite Helen Spence and her tittle-tattle, Brian and I did not have sex. What happened between Brian and me was not dark and it was not vile. It was brief and it was innocent and it was real."

She stopped. Was she really saying this? She was having herself a rollicking post–bitch slap epiphany. She went for it, both barrels blazing.

"And—And given half a chance" she said, "what Brian and I have *could* become something—something wonderful. You have completely misjudged me—and you know what? You've totally misjudged Brian. All this talk about darkness. Destruction, for Pete's sake. It's crazy. If Brian is depressed it's—it's because he has become engaged to a shallow, self-centered girl who wouldn't know art if it bit her on the ass."

Norma stood up and went into her bedroom. She came out holding Brian's *Skara Brae*.

"This," she said, "might be dark, but it certainly isn't awful. To call it rubbish—my God, Fiona, this is brilliant, and if you loved Brian for who he really is, you would know that. You had me going there, for a little bit. Poor Fiona, she loves him so. Well, you know what? Crap. You are so full of crap. You know who's bad for Brian? You, Fiona, *you*. So, beg all you want, but I'm not leaving Orkney, and by—by Odin, goddamnit, I will see *whom*ever I fucking want."

Fiona's face had gone livid. She stood, and without saying a word, stalked out the front door.

Norma put down Brian's painting and mentally dusted her hands. *Ha,* she thought. *Ha-ha!* Then she grinned. *By Odin. Nice touch.*

Norma watched Fiona stalk to the car, her hands balled up into fists. But she didn't get in. Instead she reached into the passenger seat and plucked out a large square brown paper parcel. Fiona gripped it and then stalked back up to the cottage. As she walked she stripped the brown paper into long savage shreds.

Norma met her at the door, and Fiona thrust the object in her face.

"*Here,*" Fiona said, "*here's* your brilliance."

Norma looked. It was a painting.

"*Here's* your something wonderful. Take it! Go on, go hang it on your wall."

Norma took the canvas.

"That," Fiona said, "is what your precious love has inspired. I went there today. To Hoy. To confront him after what—what Helen Spence said. He wasn't even there. Just the painting, the horrible painting of *you* and empty bottles of ale."

Norma vaguely heard Fiona stalk back to her car and slam the door as she stood there with Brian's painting in her hands.

Her cell phone was ringing. She turned around and walked numbly across the room. Placing the painting on the comfy chair, she picked up the phone.

"Hello?"

"Norma? Colin here. Got your message—did you do it? Did you go see Brian?"

Norma shook her head.

"Hello?" Colin said. "Are you there?"

"Yes," Norma said. "I'm here."

"Oh, lord. It went badly?"

"Yes, it went badly—no, no it didn't—I didn't— Oh, Colin, hold on." Norma closed her eyes and put the phone to her chest. Two big tears squeezed out. Without looking she reached out and turned the canvas to its backside. Then she put the phone back to her ear. "Colin?"

"I'm here, luv."

"I haven't gone to see him. I was ready, I was going to, but then—but then Fiona showed up."

"Fiona? Oh, bloody hell. She came to the cottage?"

"Oh, yeah. It was—it was just awful."

"I wish I was there," Colin said. "I wish I could hold you, poor darling."

"No," Norma said. "No one should hold me. I feel so—so unclean."

"Christ, what did the girl do to you?"

"You mean besides hit me?"

"She *hit* you?"

"Quite a wallop for a princess."

"Did you hit her back?"

"No, I—I think I'm going to be sick."

Norma dropped the phone and made a dash for the kitchen. She stood over the sink, gasping for air. She turned on the faucet and splashed icy water on her face. That was better. She turned, saw the bottle of whiskey on the table, grabbed it and a big clean glass from the cupboard.

Back in the living room, Colin's tinny little voice on the phone was saying, "Norma? Norma? You're scaring me."

Norma picked up the phone. "I'm okay, I'm okay," she said. She uncorked the bottle and poured herself a few fingers' worth.

"I think I hear Highland Park," Colin said.

"You got that right," said Norma. She took a sip. A big one. Then another.

"You gonna tell me?"

"We had a little Venus talk," Norma said, "you know, girl-to-girl. I found myself trying to assure a very distraught Fiona that Brian and I didn't, uh—fling. She remained unconvinced. After drawing blood she put forth the suggestion that I leave Orkney. I countered with the suggestion that she was a twit unworthy of Brian and swore by Odin that she should basically go fuck herself."

"Well, good for you," Colin said, "she had no right—"

"No," Norma said. She took another drink. "She did. She had every right. We had a little showdown at the end. A duel with paintings, and I'm afraid—I'm afraid Fiona won."

"What are you talking about?"

"Brian's dark side. Apparently ol' Norma here really brings it out." She drank the rest of her whiskey and then poured another few fingers. Like a hand's worth. "Brian's holed up there. On Hoy. He's drinking. He's in a bad way. Fiona thinks it's my fault. She thinks I've destroyed him."

"That's absurd," Colin said. "A load of crap. The girl is jealous, Norma, she's put a head trip on you."

Norma was downing more whiskey. She was starting to feel it finally.

"That's what I thought, Colin, I told her as much. I gave a grand speech about love and a lecture on art. Then she showed me—"

Norma looked at the painting. The back of it. She could see three smudges in ocher. Brian's fingerprints.

"What?" The little silver cell phone was asking her something.

Cell phone in one hand, whiskey in the other, Norma drank some more, then put the phone back to her ear.

"Fiona. Her ammo. She'd brought me a painting Brian had done. I've got it. Right here. I can smell it."

Norma took a big slug, gave a whiskey shudder, then reached out and flipped the painting over.

"Oh, shit," she said, "oh, shit, it's as bad as—" Norma dropped the phone and the glass and buried her face in her hands. She was too unhappy to cry. She just let out one long moan.

"Norma? Norma!" The tinny voice was yelling from the floor.

She picked up the phone.

"Luv, I want you to stop the drinking."

Norma looked at her glass. It hadn't spilled. It had landed upright and still had an inch of drink. She finished it off, said, "Okay," then hurled the glass into the fireplace. It shattered.

"Jesus," Colin said. "What was that?"

"Let me," Norma said, "describe the lovely painting to you."

"I'm starting to really worry—"

"It's the Ring—you know, the Ring of Brodgar. It's in the past, you know, 'cause—'cause all sixty stones are there. Sixty-one, I should say, 'cause there's one, a big flat one in the middle. That's the one I'm strapped to. Naked. With chains. And Betty is there—Corrigall, not Boop. I can tell it's her 'cause of the rope. Betty's like, helping a big dark-haired Druid guy. You can't see his face too good because there's this robe thing, see? But I'd say the odds are favoring Brian. And Russell, bless him, he's there, too. Off in the distance, a naked giant with a fiddle and cowboy boots and a hard-on big as Texas."

"Norma—"

"No, no—we're just gettin' to the good part now. There's like a big sacrifice going down. Mr. Burroughs—with a big stone knife, no less—has just opened me up. Yup, stem to stern, big ol' gash with lots of nice red blood."

"Norma, please—"

"And here's the kicker, right? The pièce de résistance? He's not pulled out my heart, mind you, but a blood-drenched puffin!" Norma laughed. "A puffin! Can you beat that? With long bloody trails of my heart's goddamn blood."

"Christ," Colin said. "Norma, listen to me—"

"More man logic?" Norma laughed again. A horrible hollow sound. She took a big drink, this time gulping straight from the bottle. "Here's to following your heart, right? Right? Even if it's a bloody puffin. Oh, God. It's over, Colin. Before it ever started. I should listen to Fiona. She's a wise little princess. I should leave. I should leave Orkney. Get on an airplane tonight."

"Norma. You're hurt. You're drunk. You've been assaulted, for chrissake. You should call Marion. Go to her place. She'll take care of you, okay? Till I can get there. Till we can think this though. But mercy, woman, put the bloody whiskey down."

Norma didn't. She put the phone down instead. She clicked the phone shut and took another big slug from the bottle.

Oh, yeah. She was feeling it good now.

She looked at her hair in the painting. Long dark coils of hair spread across the stone. She looked at Betty Corrigall. Long dark coils of hair. She looked at the tea set still on the coffee table. Next to the sliced cake was the nice sharp knife. Norma picked up the knife and with her other hand grabbed up her topknot.

One, two, three saws of the knife and it was done.

The phone was ringing. Norma stared stupidly and drunk, and then let fall from her hand her long dark coils of severed hair.

She picked up the phone again.

"Colin?"

"Norma, please. Listen to me. I want you to call Marion. Don't drive now, for God's sake. She'll come pick you up."

The room had started to turn.

"You are so shweet," Norma said. "So shweet to me. Why don't I juslove you?"

"All right. I'll call Marion. You just stop drinking. I'll call Marion and then call you back."

"No, no—I'll do it—I'll call her—I'm okay."

"You don't sound okay. Not at all."

Norma reached for the bottle of whiskey, but couldn't quite lift herself from the chair.

"I'm okay—the bloody whishkey's waay over there."

"You'll call Marion?"

"Yesh, as shoon as we hang up."

"Promise me?"

"I promish."

"Nothing drastic?"

Too late for that promise. Norma's head dropped to the back of the chair.

"I'm going to go now, Colin."

"Call Marion."

"I will. 'Bye, Colin, you're a shweetie. You're a luv."

Norma pushed the off button with her thumb. What was Marion's number? Three-two-two? Three-two-four?

It was 322, actually, but it was a moot point. By then Norma Dale had passed out.

CHAPTER 21

When she came to, it was dark. And cold. The air smelled of booze and oil paint.

She sat up. Her neck was stiff, her head stuffed with Styrofoam.

There was the painting.

And her hair.

"Oh," Norma said, "God."

She stood. Oh, man. The clock on the mantel showed nine-fifteen.

Well, she thought, *that's not so bad*—then she paused—*if it isn't tomorrow.* She walked toward the hallway, her running shoes crunching across the broken glass, and went into the kitchen. There was some coffee in the pot, left from the morning. She poured herself a cup and put it in the microwave.

She saw her reflection then, in the door of the microwave. Her little sawed-off topknot. She pulled the band from what was left of her hair. Now she looked like a hedgehog.

Norma walked wearily to the shower. She took a hot one. Let the steamy water pound on her neck and shoulders. She shampooed. Short hair felt really, really weird. She came out half human. Wrapped herself in a cold towel (it had slipped off the warmer) and went back to the kitchen for her stale, tepid coffee.

Her thoughts turned like a kaleidoscope—one that was broken. All the glass chips and spangles fallen to one side.

Norma sliced a hunk of bread and a wedge of cheddar cheese. She wrapped them in a napkin, got a bottle of water, and went into the bedroom. She needed comfort clothes, but something warm. Perfect. She'd bought it at the Camden street market. A floor-length hippie dress with long bell sleeves, lined with silk—soft crushed velvet, midnight blue. She slipped it on and then a pair of long wool socks, her running shoes, and her cloak. Gathering up her comforter and sheepskin, she got her hobo bundle from the kitchen and, without looking at the painting, left the cottage.

Scarlett had Tara, right? Well, she had Skara Brae.

∞

Norma had never come so early, but Skara Brae was as dark and deserted as before. It was mild tonight, almost warm under a blanket of clouds. The half-moon glowed dully from behind. She parked her scooter behind the Tourist Center sign and took her bundles to the site. She dropped down into Building 1, the routine familiar now, and comforting.

Norma made up her bed, but she was far from sleepy, the caffeine just hitting her system. She climbed out of the hole with her bread and cheese and water. That was it. A little picnic on the beach.

The tide was low. The sound of the sea, nice. She found a

smooth patch of sand and sat down. She munched her bread and cheese and watched the waters of the bay come in, the waters of the bay go out.

Life.

Right. Life.

Norma thought about the people of so long ago. She envied them. How simple it all must have been. Norma took off her cloak. She stood, kicked off her shoes and socks, and walked barefoot across the sand.

To be primitive. Primal. Prehistoric. Norma looked up. To worship the moon. To fear it as a god. To fear the sea. To fear the darkness.

She smiled. She loved the darkness. She loved where it took her mind.

"I'm just another element," she said. "Out here I'm free."

Norma loosened the gathered ties at her neck and let her dress ripple to her feet. She stepped, naked, to the sea, her arms held up to the blanketed moon, the cold tide lapping at her feet.

Now, *this* was primal. She laughed. She did a little swirling dance along the foamy scallops of the water. Dancing in, dancing out, with the tide of the bay whirling down the edge of the shore. She stopped, dizzy, breathing hard. *I'm crazy,* she thought, then—*and freezing my ass off.*

∞

That was when she heard it. A distinctive *clink.* Like glass on metal.

Norma whirled around. All was blackness behind her. All shadows upon shadows. Then she saw. On the seawall. A darker blackness up against the stars. A human shadow. Crouched there. Watching her.

Her heart gave a big panicky thud. Where the hell was her dress? There it was. She ran to it—a pile of seaweed. She whirled around again. The shadow was gone.

Norma wanted to scream, but no sound came out. Her cloak—she could see the lump of it up the beach. She ran. Oh, man, she really felt primal now. What had she been thinking? She reached the lump. Thank God, it was really her cloak. She threw it around her shoulders, then huddled there. Could she make a break for her scooter? She searched the darkness. No movement, no sounds. She pulled the hood of her cloak up over her head, stuck her bare feet, sockless, inside her shoes, and, without tying them, walked quickly across the sand to where the beach met the grassy slope of the seawall.

There, lying on its side at her feet, was Brian's bicycle.

Norma stared at it stupidly, not making the connection. What was Brian's bicycle doing on Skara Brae? Strapped on the back fender was his paint box and easel. Nearby, his knapsack, spilling from it half a dozen bottles of beer. Norma picked up one of the bottles. On the label was a handsome bearded fellow wearing a helmet with big black wings. SKULLSPLITTER was boldly declared in red.

Then she heard a voice and turned. It was coming from the beach.

"Seeeeeeeelkieeeeeee," the voice was crying. "Seeeeeeelki-eeeeeee!"

Norma could see him. A shadow against the white, staggering along toward the ocean. Brian Burroughs. Here. Not twenty yards away from her. Her adrenaline had already had its surge in fear. Now all her heart could do was give a pitiful little flutter. What *was* the man doing?

He had walked to the edge of the water, and Norma watched with growing alarm as he kept on walking. A wave came surging in and splashed against his legs. He went deeper.

He was bending as if to plunge right into the sea. Norma dropped the bottle and ran.

"No!" she cried. "Stop! Don't do it!" Her voice was drowned by the sound of the crashing surf. But then, halfway to him, she stopped, panting, clutching the neck of her cloak.

Brian wasn't pulling a James Mason. He was walking from the water with his hands draped in a mass of black dripping seaweed. No, it wasn't seaweed. It was her soaking-wet, midnight-blue, crushed-velvet hippie dress.

He was speaking, like poetry, in a loud drunken voice.

"O Bonnie Man!" he shouted. "If thur's inny mercy in thee human breest, gae me back me ain selkie skin! I cinno live in da sea withoot it. I cinno bide amung me ain folk waythoot me selkie skin."

He laughed wildly and wickedly and held the dress up high. "Not a chance," he yelled, "not a bloody chance."

Then he saw her.

"Whoa," he said, lowering the dress, "what's this now?"

Norma had no idea what to do.

"Be ye an evil trow?" he said. "A finfolk? Come to eat up my fair selkie? Be ye the ghost of Ubby? Why then I'll *get* thee!"

Norma screamed. He had thrown the dress aside and was charging her. She turned and ran, cloak flying, and promptly tripped over her untied shoelaces. Brian tackled her, and they went sprawling in a heap across the sand.

"Ha-ha!" he said, triumphant. "Ha-ha!" And then, "Whoa-ho, oh my lord."

Norma wasn't sure whether to hit him or have an orgasm. He had grabbed her, turned her over, and exposed her in one fell swoop.

"Holy Mother of God," he said. "You're a woman."

Norma pulled away from him, scrambling backward, and managed to cover herself.

"Fuck," Brian said. He was on his hands and knees breathing hard. "I'm sorry. Jesus Christ. I— Are you hurt?"

Norma, her face covered by the hood, shook her head.

He sat back onto the sand with his elbows on his knees and shook his head like a big wet dog. He was wearing blue jeans and a thick, dark cable-knit sweater. He was soaked in seawater and covered with sand.

"Christ Almighty," he said, "I'm drunk. Please forgive me, I—I thought it was just me and the phantoms out here."

He looked at her, peering in the dark. "You're not, are you? A phantom? But, Jesus, woman, you're stark naked under there. What the hell are you doin'—" He stopped, then looked over his shoulder, then back again. "But, you're her, then, aren't you? You're my selkie!"

Norma was feeling a tad surreal. Luck had stuck out her big ol' foot and landed her in a big ol' puddle of fate. She wasn't ready. She wasn't at all ready for this.

Brian reached out with his hand and grabbed her ankle.

"You'll have to marry me, now, sweet selkie from the sea, I've got your skin, you know."

That did it, when he touched her. She could actually feel her broken kaleidoscope brain give a twist. The broken pieces of her soul fell lopsided into a crazy heap. The spangles and glass in a crazy new pattern. He didn't recognize her. He didn't know who she was. She would go with that. Go with a British accent.

"What," she said, "is a selkie?"

That wasn't so bad. The new voice. It came out in a higher register and softer, much softer than her own.

"A selkie," Brian said. "A *selkie*. Don't you know?"

Then his hand let go of her ankle and trailed down to her shoe.

"Right," he said, rather sadly. "A selkie wouldn't be wearin' these Nikes."

He started doing the peering thing again. Norma ducked her head and turned away.

"Can't I see your face?" he said.

Out came the strange voice again.

"I think perhaps," she said, "you've seen enough of me already." She could see just beyond the edge of her hood that he smiled. Oh, that was a good one, in this dangerous new game. Norma trembled at the sight of that crooked smile, the one long dimple.

"But I've got your skin—don't I? Your magic skin." He got, not at all steadily, to his feet. "It's right over here." Brian walked a few feet toward the water. Norma could see her hippie dress stretched out along the sand. "Oh," he said when he reached it. "Ah, well, another myth shattered." He scooped up the dress and walked back to her. "Could've sworn it was a sealskin, back when you shed it, you know, to do your little moon dance?"

"What," Norma said, struggling to her feet while trying to keep her cloak wrapped tight, "are you talking about?"

"Selkies," said Brian. "Magical shape-shifting seals from the sea. Come from the ocean, shed their skins for human form, do a little dance," he wiggled two fingers, "beneath the moon." He held up her dress by the shoulders. "If you get their skins, you can keep them. Orkney lore is full of them. Comely lasses gettin' seduced by the male selkies, fishermen takin' the female selkies for their wives. Selkies are gentle faery-folk, see—gentle and beautiful. Finfolk—what I took you for—are evil."

"I see," Norma said. The accent was on her now, like a magical sealskin. "And what then is an Ubby?"

"Oh," Brian said. "Ubby." He folded Norma's dress over one of his arms and gestured to the seawall. "For that, mysterious bein' on the beach, you'll have to share an ale with me."

"A Skullsplitter?" Norma said. "I don't think so."

"What then?" Brian said, laughing. "You really are a stranger if you don't know how fine our Skullsplitters be. Come on, then, this phantom chasin' is thirsty work."

And with that, Brian took off walking. Norma watched him for a moment, then followed. How could she not?

∞

When she got to the knapsack, Brian had propped up his bicycle and was draping her dress across the handlebars.

"This should dry it soon enough," he said. He reached in the knapsack and brought out two bottles. He had an opener and he popped off their tops. He handed one to Norma and she took it.

"To Thorfinn Hausakliffer," he said, tapping his bottle to hers, "Seventh Viking Earl of Orkney. The original Skull-splitter, for you ignorant off-lander types." Then he drank.

Norma took a sip. It was dark and malty. Pretty good, really.

Brian drank half of his in three long gulps.

"Ubby, now," he said, and wiped his mouth with the back of his hand. "Ubby wasn't faery-folk. Ubby was human. A man who lived on Orkney many years ago. Every day he'd fill his boat with stones and then row out," he pointed, "to the middle of yon Skaill Bay. Drop them overboard, he did, then row back in. Did it day after day, stone after stone, till one day he'd built himself a little islet. And there he lived, on his little hand-built islet until the time he died. Ubby's ghost, they say, haunts Skaill to this day."

Brian was standing there looking out across the bay.

"How do I know, then," Norma said, "that *you* aren't Ubby?"

"Sometimes, you know, I think I might be."

He ran one hand through his hair and gave a big sigh.

"We all do that," he said, "don't you think? Build our little islands stone by stone?" He looked at her and she ducked her head.

Brian finished off his ale and tossed his bottle with the rest.

"Do you," said Brian, "have a name?"

I should tell him, Norma thought. *Just get it over with. Because this is crazy. Just tell him who I am, we can have a good chuckle, talk things out and everything will be all right.* Then she pictured herself chained to the megalith—Brian with the blood-soaked puffin in his hands.

"You can call me," Norma said softly, "Jewel."

"Well, that's perfect, innit? For a drunken old pirate like me."

A cold gust of wind came up off the beach, billowing Norma's cloak and giving a toss to Brian's wild hair. He shuddered.

"Oh," Norma said without thinking, "you should get out of those clothes."

"I'll have you know," he said, swaying, "I am an engaged man. I shall do no such thing."

"I—I didn't mean—"

"I know what you meant, luv, I'm just havin' a bit of fun." Then he gave another big shiver. "And I'm very, very drunk—did I mention that? And I'm very wet and I'm talkin' to a very strange hallucination."

"I have a blanket," Norma said. She pointed to the large hole of Building 1. "Down there. We really should get warm."

Brian looked to where she pointed and then back to her.

"I'm for warm," he said, "let's go."

He picked up his knapsack and followed her over the edge of the pit, and there they were, the two of them together in the Neolithic nook.

Brian stripped off his clothes. She watched him in the

darkness, ridiculously unashamed of herself. She realized, too, how terribly drunk the man *was*. The last bit of trouser leg was too much for him, and she stepped forward with the comforter and caught him as he fell. A big drunken man was too much for her, and they sank to the ground, a cocoon of tangled limbs and beating hearts.

He was on top of her. He smelled of salt, of beer, of sweat, and of linseed oil. Norma drew in a big breath of him. Had he passed out? But no, his pale hand with the long fingers was groping at her breast. Then he was kissing it, his tongue making circles on her hardened nipple. Norma had herself a little minigasm, and then he did pass out. She lay there waiting for the resumption of her senses.

He did that by instinct, she thought, *and I'm having another of those moments.* The romantic highlights of her life happening without her. Like an urchin outside a bakery window with her nose pressed up to the glass. No, worse. How did she do this to herself? She was *in* the bakery, wasn't she? Snuggled up with a hot and forbidden loaf of fresh-baked man.

Norma struggled up and managed to shift Brian onto the comforter and herself back inside her cloak.

She looked at his naked back. The line of his spine, his shoulder blades. The slender muscles on his shoulders, the line of veins along his arm. Then her eyes went on down to Troubleville. Norma bit her lip and gently drew the comforter over his nakedness, but then she couldn't help herself. She reached out and swept aside the tangle of his black hair and kissed the base of his neck.

He moaned, and turned to her, black eyes half open. She pulled back into the shadows.

"Selkie," he said. "Sweet selkie, come to take care o' me."

Norma was silent.

"My mum was a selkie, did you know that?"

He closed his eyes. Norma thought he'd passed out again, but then he spoke, his voice low and sad.

"Never knew her—my selkie mum. She—She left me when I was a wee lad. Just the—the dimmest memories of her. Black hair. I remember that. Long black hair and big dark eyes."

His dark eyes opened. Glistened.

"There was an old woman—lived in a little stone shack. Gave me oatcakes and warm milk from the milking bucket. I'd sit on the little stool and she'd tell me stories. Like Truncherface the Trow in his gold-lined earthen mound. Evil Nuckelavee, all hairless with his bulging black veins and his single red flame eye. The good and powerful Mither of the Sea. Witches, ghosts—hogboons. But what I remember most was the selkies. She told me about the selkies, see, so I'd know where my mum had gone. You know, back to her seal-skin, back to the sea. That my mum loved me, but—but—"

Tears started to roll.

"Fuck," Brian said. "Cryin' like a baby. Drunk as a dog and cryin' like a wee bairn."

He struggled up onto one elbow, wiped at his eyes, and then gave his head a shake. He groped out into the darkness, and Norma realized he was reaching for his knapsack.

"Don't you think—"

"I've had enough?" he said. He found the knapsack and grabbed another bottle of ale. "Not hardly. You see, Jewel," he popped the cap, "it ain't enough till your skull actually splits and all the rot and madness spill away."

He upended the bottle.

He'd called her Jewel. Norma felt the kaleidoscope give another twist.

"But she wasn't, you know," Brian said. "My mum wasn't a selkie after all." He wiped his mouth with the hand holding the bottle. "Though I suppose *her* mother might've been."

"Your grandmother?"

"Aye," and he snorted out a laugh. "Dear ol' Gran. Who-ever the hell she was, eh? I come from a long line of abandon-ing mothers. Abandoning mothers and phantom fathers—so what does that make me?"

The Italian bastard, thought Norma.

"The Italian bastard," said Brian. "Oh, aye, that's what they call me." Then he stood up, the comforter slipped away, and he was naked with his back to her and yelling and shak-ing the bottle of ale to the cloud-shrouded sky. "Not to my face, goddamnit—not anymore!—but I swear to the saints, that's what they'll put on my tombstone—I'll be out there with Betty, out on the bog, only mine'll say, 'Here lies the Italian bastard.' "

He upended the ale again and finished it off. He made like to dash the bottle against the stone wall but then Norma was there—with the comforter to his shoulders.

"Please," she said. "Please?"

And his shoulders slumped beneath her hands and he dropped his arm.

"Holy Jesus," he said, "I'm so fuckin' drunk."

"You think maybe it might be all that ale that you're downing?"

Brian gave a laugh and then turned, full frontal, to face her.

Norma drew in her breath and took a quick step back, away from him.

He put out his hands, and she stepped back farther into the shadows.

He looked down and said, "Christ, I'm sorry," then pulled the comforter closed. "Don't—Don't be leavin' me, selkie—please—"

"I'm not leaving," Norma said. Still soft. Still British. She sank to the ground and pulled her knees up under her cloak. "This is just getting interesting."

Brian gave that cock to his head. "You mean that?" he said. "Is that why you've come, then?"

Norma nodded up at him. And why not? It was pretty much the truth.

He swayed again and sank to the ground, too—the comforter formed a soft tepee around him. Dark hair in contrast—black ringlets now against cloth.

"I *am* a bastard, if you want to know," he said. "*And* Italian. At least some of my fuckin' blood . . ." He paused for a moment, then went on. "When I was a boy, you see, I held a great many fantasies on the subject of my genetics. The women, they were selkies, but the men—that was—that was different and quite the goddamn puzzle. My father, now, I had him narrowed down to just the three. There was John, since in my dimmest memories he was the one in mummy's bed, there was Algie—no logic to that one—he just had the darkest hair, and then there was Stash. Stash was the least likely—no physical resemblance at all, but he was the one fixed my porridge when anyone did and was kind. He was the one seemed to love me. And he did, you know. Stash loved me, and when I asked him, all those years later, he told me the truth about my mother. *And* about my father." Pause. "My *famous* father, mind you—lead singer in a Mersey band. Well, almost famous, like they say. There'd been a single, made the charts, too. That's what he'd been celebratin' the night he shot too much smack in his veins."

"Oh," Norma said. "Oh, that's terrible. He died?"

Brian nodded his head and reached for the knapsack. "My dead junkie dad. You want another?"

"Sure," Norma said. She didn't, but it would be one less he could drink, right?

He popped two tops and handed one to her. When she took the bottle, he wrapped his long fingers around hers and held on.

"Are you never gonna let me see your face, Jewel?"

A tesla coil crackled up Norma's spine. "Do you," she bluffed, "really want me to?"

He let go. "Nah," he said. "If you're ugly, then, what would I do?"

Norma clinked her bottle against his. "To midnight confessions," she said, and took a swallow. *Now* she wanted it.

Brian didn't drink. He turned his head to the cold and ancient hearth and gave a sigh.

"Eleven years old when I found out," he said. "Gone home. Run home again to the little stone hut where I'd been raised by gypsies. Grown by flower children along with their mushrooms and dope. Found him there that day. Stash. Strange man, with the top of his head bald and his hair in a braid down his back. He called me 'little dude,' and gave me a big hug. He'd come back for his dope—Stash's stash. There was a lot of it, too. Wrapped up in foil and bread bags and lowered down the well. He rolled a big doobie, right there, lit 'er up and started talkin' about the good ol' days. My first high, that day. High and all those words come crushin' my eleven-year-old shoulders. I learned about my dad, my mum, my mum's dad—"

Brian took a drink then.

"My mum's dad. My grandfather. You see, that's where the Italian blood comes in. My mother's father was a prisoner of war. One of the miracles of Camp 60." He gave a snort. "I'd never really known what an Italian was, exactly. I always thought it was just part of the word bastard. Like son is part of a bitch. So Stash explained it to me. All about the war, the barriers, the little chapel, the baby on the altar. He'd learned the story from my mother, of course. From Mary. So

Stash's version was a little bit screwy. My mother—when I was around five years old, this was—did some mushrooms. She did mushrooms and went to the chapel, where they'd found her as a baby. Lit candles, rolled around on the floor awhile, then had herself a grand revelation. Her father, she concluded from her psilocybin vision, was one Domenico Chiocchetti, the Italian master painter of the chapel itself. She left the next day to go find him."

Norma's heart was pounding. Very softly, not wanting to break the spell, she said, "That's incredible."

"Incredible? Yes, incredible is exactly what that was. That drug-inspired revelation set in motion all the elements that make me who I am today." Then he dropped his head.

For a moment Norma thought he was crying again, but it was laughter. Harsh laughter—then Brian raised his head and yelled to the sky.

"A motherless fuckin' drunk who thinks he can goddamn paint!"

Then he looked into the darkness where she sat. Norma had reached out her hand.

"Sorry." His voice was quiet again. "Shit—look at you— you're tremblin' there. My little selkie is freezin'." He held out one edge of the comforter, careful to keep the rest of him covered. "I promise," he said, "I'm way too drunk—I'm of-ferin' for warmth and nothin' else."

Norma pulled her hood forward and down as low as it would go and then scooted over next to him. He wrapped her in the comforter—his strong arm around her, his warmth and his scent—his Brianness. The trembling wasn't going away—not by a long shot.

"That's nice then, innit?"

Her head was against his chest and she could hear the beating of his heart. She nodded.

With his other hand he took another swallow of ale.

"So that's the awful truth then, Jewel—I've let it slip. I'm a painter. That's what started it—all my artistic ambitions. Stash left me a little kid-sized portion of his dope, then went back to where he'd come from. I started to draw. To draw, then to paint. It was my secret. I would be like my grandfather. That would show 'em. I stole supplies from the art room at school and made myself a little kid-sized studio. I'd smoke a little kid-sized reefer, then I'd do art. I was fair good, too. I stole books from the library—did kid-sized copies of the masters. Botticelli, Michelangelo, Raphael—not Rembrandt, though. Too Dutch. I liked Italians. Though when I was twelve, I discovered the Surrealists. Surrealism and saints—my formative years. Catholicism and cadmium red.

"The church let me down, though, in the end. Should've known better, of course. Takin' my paintin' to a nun. She was the art teacher. Art teacher on the outside, but nun to the core. Wasn't even that bad of a paintin'. Just one naked breast, hardly any blood—'blasphemous' was one of her more positive criticisms—and then she took me to the priest and he took me all the way to Edinburgh to see a psychiatrist. Not that I found that too discouragin'. Read enough about artists by then to know bein' considered crazy was a prerequisite to fame. And, in the city, I was able to contact Stash again. Took a lot of courage, that did. He'd given me his number and I'd kept it for years, my little graphite talisman to the past. So I called him, right there in the waitin' room while the priest was off talkin' to the doctors. Stash told me where to meet him—then I left. I was fourteen years old and a fugitive from God. I had a plan of sorts. Set in place when I was eleven and high on vintage well-weed. My mother had left Orkney—left me—in search of her father—so I would leave Orkney in search of her. Stash hadn't known where she was, but he'd known a woman who'd known another woman who had once seen her on the street, and that was good enough for me."

Brian paused and took another drink. And then he sat there, staring into the nonexistent fire. Norma had stopped trembling, finally. She couldn't have been warmer or more content. She could stay here forever, in fact. Her head on Brian's chest, listening to the rumble of his words.

"Nether Edge," he said. "That's where I found her. Poetic, innit? Nice little village just south of Sheffield. That's how far she'd gotten from Orkney. Just a little south of Sheffield. And there she'd stayed. She'd been hitchhikin', see? Hitchhikin' to Italy to find her father. Only, it hadn't quite worked out that way. She'd been picked up by a bloke—a very nice bloke, it turned out. He was nice and he was rich and he was very much taken with the black-haired hippie girl with the dilated eyes. Had a wife already, but that wasn't much of a problem. Two years later they were married, in a fancy house, with his-and-her Jaguars."

Brian stopped again.

"I sound pretty damn bitter, don't I?"

"It must have been awful," Norma said quietly.

"Awful for both of us," he said. "She cried. Wouldn't stop cryin'. She told me how, her life, you know, how crazy it had been. How she'd, when Jeremy died—that was his name, my dad—and when he'd died she'd just never come down. Not doin' heroin, not much anyway, but hashish and mushrooms—all the time—just kept herself high all the time."

"Even after—I mean, wasn't she—"

"Pregnant? Maybe that's my problem, eh?"

Norma pulled away from him then. She had to or she was going to burst into tears. She reached for her bottle of Skullsplitter. Brian dropped his arm and she took a drink, not looking at him.

"She told me something. There in Nether Edge. She told me that after she'd left Orkney she sometimes didn't know if she'd ever really had a child at all. It was very strange. That's what I had become to her—a bad flashback—an uncertain memory lost in the haze."

"Oh," Norma said. She turned. "She can't have—she—"

Brian's head was bowed, his black hair hanging down.

"No. She never said that, exactly. My mother—my poor mum—she had all those years of guilt built up inside her. When I showed up like that, just out of the blue. . . . She'd never told him, see. The husband. About me—about any of it. He was her clean slate—and I couldn't begrudge her that. I *wouldn't* begrudge her that nice, clean slate. The comfort—the stability—the sanity."

He wiped his eyes.

"Did you ask her—did you talk about—Italy?"

There was a moment of silence.

"Italy," Brian said finally, "never really came up. There *was* the big surprise of me showin' up on her doorstep to deal with. Then the tears. Then the story—her story—we never really got to mine." He shook his head. "She served me tea. We had a nice tea, mother and son, with Fortnum and Mason biscuits. She started lookin' at the clock then, my mum. Just quick little looks. Nervous-like. I was fourteen, but I knew what those little looks meant."

Brian rolled the bottle of ale between his hands.

"I asked her, finally—I said, 'You don't want him to know, do ya?' That got to her pretty bad. So she cried again. I held her and she cried. She said she would—she *would* tell him—but I told her no. Told her it was okay, that I understood, and that I loved her. So that was that. I—I let her abide among her ain folk waythoot her selkie skin."

Norma *was* crying now. Silently, behind her hood.

"You left?" she managed to say. "You never—that was it, then?"

"I left. I never. That was it, then."

She let loose a big sniff.

"Pathetic, aye," he said. "That I am."

Norma turned away again and wiped at her eyes.

"You know, little selkie," Brian said, "I've never told that story to another livin' soul."

It took all the strength Norma had not to just turn back around and leap on the man. Tell him who she was. Hold him close, heal him—love him. Make everything all right again.

"But then," he said, "do selkies even have souls?"

Norma took a deep breath. She couldn't do this anymore. Not anymore. She wiped at her eyes again and her nose. He was silent. Norma slowly let out the breath. Then she said, in her own voice, "I have a soul, Brian." She pushed the hood of her cloak back from her face and turned around.

Brian had keeled over to one side.

Well—well, hell's bells. Norma let out a little snort of frustration. *Jesus. Look at him there.* His eyes were closed, mouth half opened, black tangle of hair in his face, high cheekbones wet with tears, and Skullsplitter was spilling from the bottle in little glubs of rot and madness. She'd never seen anything more beautiful.

Norma reached over to take the bottle. He held on—his eyes fluttering open.

"No you don't, selkie," he said, "you got your own."

Norma froze. Now he would see her—*now,* without hearing her great line.

But he didn't. He didn't look up—he just smiled with that one heartrending dimple, shifted over, and lay his big head in her lap.

Norma stayed frozen. Then with one hand she pulled the hood back over her head. With the other she stroked a long coiled strand of hair from Brian's face.

He sighed.

They stayed like that for a moment. No sound but Brian's gentle breathing and the surging of the Skaill Bay tide.

Norma wasn't sure if he was conscious.

Quietly, back to British again, she said, "Did you ever find him? Your grandfather?"

"He wasn't my grandfather."

"He—He wasn't your grandfather?"

"Nope," Brian said with his eyes still closed. "I found him, though. The great Domenico Chiocchetti. I went all the way to Italy and I found him. My mother gave me 377 pounds that day. Her grocery money, I suppose. She thought—well, I told her, actually—that I was goin' back to Kirkwall. I told her I had a lovin' adopted family there and not to worry. Then I left. I went to the Nether Edge train station and bought a ticket to London. After that it was kind of tricky. Stash had given me the name of some caravan people and sent along some goodwill dope. They would have taken me without the dope—they all thought smuggling a runaway boy across Europe was a grand lark. We only had two borders to cross and we were in Moena in four days."

"Moena?"

"That's all I knew about Chiocchetti. His hometown, Moena, Italy. He was quite well known, though, and easy to find. So I showed up, once again on a doorstep, and presented my pitiful self."

"How—What did he—"

"He was very kind," Brian said. "Very kind. And he wasn't my grandfather, but he knew who was."

"He knew?"

"He was fairly certain."

"An artist?"

"No," Brian said. "A cook. From Milano. A chef. His name was Demetrio Gianella. Twenty-three years old. In the latter days of the war—there were some of the prisoners they trusted. Demetrio, it seems, cooked up some Italian delicacies for the premiere of one of the plays the camps were allowed to put on. He was brought over after that, then, to Mainland, to cook for one of the Kirkwall families. Spent weeks there. And somewhere, somehow, he met my grandmother. She apparently saw more in him than his culinary skills. Chiocchetti hadn't a clue to who she was. She wasn't from the Kirkwall family, he knew that, but somehow a romance had started. Despite the danger, or perhaps because of it, the affair had turned serious. Chiocchetti knew of all this, you see, because Demetrio had come to him. He'd come to him in despair. Demetrio knew that things were getting way out of hand. And he also knew that it was up to him to put a stop to things. He had a plan. He would be transferred to another camp—a camp of workers. Isolated on the barriers, he could resist temptation and wait out the war. Only then could he return to Orkney as a free man and 'pursue his love with honor.' That's a direct quote. 'Pursue his love with honor.' "

Brian had opened his eyes. He stared straight ahead and they glistened in the darkness. "So Chiocchetti agreed to help him and the transfer was made."

"This doesn't have a good ending, does it?" said Norma.

"Demetrio was killed two weeks later. Crushed under several tons of concrete."

"My God."

"Chiocchetti never knew about the baby. And until the day I arrived in Moena, he had never told Demetrio's secret to anyone. He wept when he saw me. Even at fourteen, apparently, I was Demetrio's image."

"Wow."

"Aye," said Brian. "Wow. And I had finally found a home. I stayed in Italy for the next four years."

"With Chiocchetti?"

"No, actually, with my great-grandmother. Chiocchetti took me to her. She lived in Milano, close to Moena, they're both in Northern Italy. Grandmother Gianella was ninety-seven years old. Sharp as a tack, too. Had been a widow for fifty years. Demetrio had been her only child. When she saw me, she wept, too. We all did. There was lots of weeping and a great deal of happiness. I stayed with that wonderful old woman, cared for her, until the end. She was one hundred and one years old when she died in my arms."

Norma gave another big sniff.

"I was eighteen, self-schooled, an illegal—but Chiocchetti was my guardian angel. He pulled strings and got a British passport for me—arranged for Gianella's small legacy to pass legally into my hands, and, over the years, encouraged me to pursue my paintin'. I loved Italy, still do—but the Orcadian in me—my unknown genes—had started a siren call."

"You came back?" Norma's brain had gone back to kaleidoscope mode. She knew he hadn't come back, and the lie slipped from her lips with uncomfortable ease.

"No. Went to London first—later to Edinburgh."

Brian stopped talking and closed his eyes again.

Norma watched him for a moment, then his eyelids fluttered and he spoke.

"Skullsplitter finally workin', I think, but I've come to the end of my tale." He yawned. "The interestin' part, anyway. There was art school, an unhappy commercial stint, then—" Brian gave another yawn. He dropped the bottle from his hand, snuggled his arms into the comforter, and went still. Norma was thinking he had passed out, and then he said, "I know who you are."

Norma took in a breath. Here it was then. He *had* heard her.

"You're my muse, aren't ya?" His voice went lower as he drifted off. "My beautiful—selkie—muse."

Norma let the breath out slowly. She stroked one finger along his dark brow. He smiled.

"Feel's good," he said sleepily. Sweetly.

Norma kept stroking him. Her Brian. Right in her arms. She knew now. She knew his truth. When morning came, he would know hers. She could do it. She could tell him the truth. Show him the truth in the light. It was right and it was perfect. She was his beautiful selkie muse.

Brian stirred.

"I love you," he said, "Fiona."

Norma sat there for a while. Crushed under three nasty syllables. Then she edged herself out from under him, reached for his knapsack, and placed his head carefully on it. She tucked him into the comforter and placed the sheepskin on top of that. She didn't kiss him. She climbed from the hole, put on her blue velvet hippie dress—stiff and horrible—and drove home.

CHAPTER 22

Norma woke to pounding. She first thought it was her head, then focus came and she realized it was the door.

"Norma?" she heard. "Norma? Are you all right?"

It was Colin.

She climbed out of bed, still wearing the blue velvet selkie skin, and walked unsteadily into the front room.

Pound pound.

"Norma—please!"

This time it was Marion. Great.

"I'm okay," she said. Her voice was sadly feeble.

She opened the door.

Colin and Marion, their faces as worried as shar-pei dogs, both gave out cries of relief.

"Thank God," was Colin's.

"Norma—we were so—I'm so glad you're all right!" was Marion's.

Then they both rushed forward to hug her.

Norma let them, but felt guilty and irritated at the same time.

"Jeez," she said, "I'm fine. Can't a girl tie one on in self-pity anymore? Colin, what are you doing here?"

"Have you looked at your messages?" he said. "I tried calling you fifteen times."

"I passed out," Norma said. "Okay?"

"Norma," Marion said gently, "Colin called me last night. You hadn't phoned back, so of course we were worried."

"Well, I'm sorry I worried you," Norma said. "I apologize. But I'm fine. I didn't need the Fifth Cavalry, for Pete's sake." Then she felt doubly bad, so she smiled. "Some coffee would be nice, though."

"I'll make it," Colin said. He glanced at Marion, then went toward the kitchen.

Marion was looking at Norma's salt-soaked hippie dress, her chopped-off hair.

"Dear," she said, even more gently, "what happened last night?"

"Nothing," Norma answered too quickly. "Nothing happened. Well, everything happened. Fiona came for tea—I'm sure Colin told you. I got a new Burroughs for my collection."

Norma looked. The painting was facedown on the comfy chair. God—could she ethically burn the thing?

"We mean later." This from Colin in the doorway. "After I phoned you."

Norma looked from one to the other.

"I came here last night," said Marion. "Around eleven. Your motorbike was gone. The door ajar—glass on the floor—and your hair . . ."

Norma reached up and touched it where it used to be. Colin looked like he was about to cry.

"I didn't promise," she said to him. "About the drastic thing."

"We don't mean to pry, dear. . . ."

Yes they did. They meant to pry. Norma felt a rise of anger, then it faded back into guilt. They meant to pry because they cared about her. Great crime.

"I . . ."

They waited.

"I . . ." Norma was waiting for her brain to give a nice comfortable twist into place. She wanted to see the proper angles and colors again. She didn't expect a picture—anything clear—but simple abstracts would have been nice. Anything but the jumble of dimmed shards and scratchy pain. "I don't know if I can—you know, tell you guys."

"Norma, we—" Colin said.

"No." Norma lifted her hand. "I know. I know. And really it helps—I'm glad you came. That you care."

"Did you see him?" said Marion. Norma wondered just how gentle the woman could go.

"Aunt Marion," Colin said, "maybe we shouldn't—"

The kettle whistled.

"I saw him," Norma said. "I saw him, but he didn't see me, okay? That's all I—all I can really say. It's resolved, though. I have my answers. Brian and—" She heard him say it again, *I love you, Fiona.* "Brian is—I—I have decided to leave well enough alone."

Norma felt her jaw quiver. She wasn't fooling anybody, least of all herself. Nothing was resolved. She was a total wreck and an utter idiot. Her puffin heart was excised and stomped on good. The tears started to roll.

"Oh, crap," said Colin. "I'll— Let me talk to him—"

"No!" Norma hadn't meant to yell. She put a hand to her face and took a breath. "He doesn't know I'm here—I

don't *want* him to know, do you understand? I—I want—I want . . ."

Marion had stepped forward. And she did have one more level of gentleness in her.

"What do you want?" she said.

Norma wiped at her face and forced out an unconvincing smile.

"Some caffeine," she said. "Then a— Oh, God, Marion, do you know a good hairdresser?"

CHAPTER 23

Norma was at the bottom of Hellihole Road, laughing inwardly at the irony. She was not on her motorbike and she was not wearing her cloak. Neither Penelope Smythe nor the mysterious Jewel were to be seen on the flagstone streets of Stromness again. This was all part of her new plan. But she wondered what plan she was on now. Plan C? D? Maybe just Plan Hellihole. Yes, that would do fine.

She went up the steps to the Stromness Public Library. Founded 1905. She went inside, inhaled universal library smell. You could go into a library on planet Zelp in the Crab nebula and still smell that smell. A wrinkled man looked up with a smile from behind the information desk.

Norma pointed.

"Archives," she said in the universal library whisper.

The man nodded.

Norma went up the stairs. The archives room was cozy and crammed top to bottom with *The Orcadian*. There had been a buttload, as Russell would say, of Thursdays since 1798. Norma spotted Alberta Sinclair in a cluster of dusty beige computers. Alberta looked up and gave a little fluttery wave.

Norma went over. They were alone, so Alberta spoke in a notch above library whisper.

"I'm so glad you came," she said. "When Marion told me, I was just thrilled."

"Well—"

"I had no idea—a professional genealogist!"

"No," Norma said, "I worked for professionals—I was a researcher, but never had the accreditation—"

"All the same," Alberta said, "I'm just so tickled by your offer."

"Well, I do have thumbs," Norma said.

Alberta looked at her blankly, then chirped, "I've gotten past the Rs finally. See?" She pointed to her computer screen. "Scambester, Scollay, Shearer, and here are my Freddie's Sinclairs."

"Well, what can I do?" Norma said. "Just anything is fine. You're doing *me* the favor, really. I love it—the cottage, I mean—but I was starting to get, well—cottage fever, I guess you could say. Can't wait to get my hand in—back to the ol' archivist game."

Alberta smiled sweetly.

Norma was lying through her teeth.

"All right, then." Alberta patted the chair next to her. "I've got you all set up here. Let's just go over the basics, shall we? And then I'll set you onto the Scambester line."

Norma sat down. Not that she wasn't here to help. She would archive till it hurt. She was lying, sure, but she wasn't going to risk bad karma to boot.

Two weeks, she figured. Two weeks and she'd have Orkney ancestry pretty much under her belt. Her plan—Plan Hellihole—was simple, really. Lay low. Keep her fingers crossed. Find out who Brian Burroughs's grandmother was.

Norma hadn't leveled with Marion. Or Colin. They were both mighty suspicious, too. Suspicious, but trusting, like the good people they were. She had asked of them two things. Of Colin, to go to Kirkwall and trade in her motorbike for a car. He'd done that. Gotten a good deal on a little battered blue Golf. Of Marion, to get her volunteered to help Alberta without any questions—and here she was.

She had leveled, however, with Helen Spence.

Helen had been slyly surprised to see Norma show her face at the gallery.

"Hello, Penelope," she'd smirked, "lovely to see you again. Love the hair."

"Which do you prefer?" Norma had asked her outright. "Sinking your teeth into the bloody gossip—or Brian Burroughs turning you a profit again?"

Helen's shark eyes had opened wide.

"Because that's your choice. I've spoken with Fiona. Neither one of us want to see Brian hurt by this rampant speculation and innuendo. Let the hot gossip cool, Helen— let it die a natural death—and Brian, with Fiona's help, will start painting commercially again."

Helen had studied her a moment.

"And you get?" she had asked.

"My privacy back."

"Which is worth more than Brian?"

Chomp.

"It's your choice, Helen," Norma had said. Then she'd walked out of the gallery.

∞

Two weeks later, and she did have Orkney's ancestry pretty much under her belt. They had filled in most of the Swansons, and the Taits were next up on the tree. Norma, by then, had free run of the place. She had set up a hidden file dealing with the population of World War Two–era Orkney. She had exactly two clues on which to base her research. One, Brian's grandmother was a female, and two, she was probably living in Kirkwall at the time of Mary's conception. Norma figured the age range could have been anywhere from sixteen all the way to forty, and she couldn't rule out married women. But common sense told her that Demetrio's heart had been won by a young, single Orcadian—and Norma's sense of romance had added beauty. That still left her with hundreds of likely candidates. She had created spreadsheets and categories and charts, and eventually narrowed the possibilities down to seventy-three. There, she was stuck. Common and romantic sense could carry you only so far. Now it was up to the genealogist's old standbys—persistence and blind luck. Norma began perusing decades-old yellowing copies of *The Orcadian*.

Research had been consuming her thoughts with the interesting "what" while at the same time distracting her from the uncomfortable "why." But, usually late at night, the questions would dance about untidily in her head. Yes, yes, she was digging for the truth for Brian. For the little boy running wild on Hoy—for the artist, for the man searching for the other half of his soul. But beyond the easy answer lay the toughie. When she found out—if she found out—how would she use it? This valuable information. This nugget. When she looked herself sternly in the mirror, she was forced to acknowledge undecided eyes. Green flecks of self-interest in the noble brown.

One Friday found Norma alone in the upstairs archive. She sat on the edge of a nicely dilapidated sofa with the January through March 1945 issues of *The Orcadian* in their black binder in front of her on the nicely dilapidated reading table. She had been through late 1945, 1946, all the way through

1950, and had found no mention, not a hint, of the foundling baby or her subsequent adoption. But here in black and white was proof of poor Demetrio Gianella. Not his name, of course. Just a sad little mention of the death on the Churchill Barriers of an Italian from Camp 60.

He had been killed in March. March nineteenth. Norma counted on her fingers. That was it, then. Precisely nine months before the baby was born.

"Hard at work?"

Norma jumped. It was Colin. She had the presence of mind not to slam the binder closed in guilt.

"Sorry, luv," he said, "didn't mean to startle you."

"It's all right." She laughed, ha-ha. "I was—I was—Alberta has me—it's those pesky Taits, you know—you're all over the place."

Colin smiled. But he looked over her shoulder, his eyes moving back and forth across the type. Then he looked at Norma.

"I've seen that," he said.

"What?"

"The article."

She slammed the binder closed in guilt.

"It's all right, Norma, really. And it's no great surprise."

She looked at him. "How?" she said.

"Well, I know you still love him, silly goose, that much is obvious."

"I *mean* how did you see the article?"

"Oh," Colin said. "Sorry. Brian's studio. In a drawer. A Xerox. I never mentioned it to him. It seemed—well, I figured if he wanted me to know . . ."

"His name was Demetrio. Brian's grandfather. He was from Milan. Demetrio Gianella."

"You're good. This research stuff."

"I'm not that good," Norma said, "believe me." She

sighed. "I'm—I've been trying to find his grandmother, if you must know. Dead ends. Everywhere dead ends."

"You want a break?" Colin smiled his charming smile. "That's why I've come, really—you know what today is, don'tcha?"

"Umm." Actually, she didn't.

"It's December twenty-second."

"And?"

"December twenty-second. Winter Solstice. You know—Winter Solstice?"

"Shortest day of the year?"

"Very good. In just," he looked at his watch, "four hours and, uh, twenty-seven minutes, Orkney, after having only six feeble hours of the palest of suns, will be plunged into official cold winter darkness, marked with ancient and mysterious efficiency in the stone-chambered hallway of our beloved Maeshowe."

Maeshowe. Then she twigged. Of course, she'd even been there. Maeshowe. The Neolithic tomb under the big mound in the heart of Neolithic Orkney. Norma remembered the guide that day, proudly pointing out how the ancients had in-geniously constructed the building so the last rays of the win-ter sun setting behind the mountains of Hoy would be cast down the long hallway of Maeshowe, bathing the stone-stacked interior in golden light. There'd been pictures even. There was a Webcam hooked to the Internet. Solstice on Orkney. A pretty big deal.

"Maeshowe," Norma said. "Of course."

"So," Colin said, "you want to go?"

"To Maeshowe? To the chamber? I mean, isn't it—do they let you in?"

"What we do—well, what we used to do, anyway," Colin said, "is to go out there, watch the sun go down, then, well, we'd build a bonfire, outside the ring, of course, and have a big party. In my day we'd boogie all night—now, I suppose the young folks will have a rave or some such thing. But I'd bet they'd still let us old hipsters in. What do you say?"

Norma realized that raving at the Maeshowe Solstice sounded very fun indeed.

"I say, let's boogie."

"Right on."

"Far out."

They both burst into laughter.

"Anyway," Norma said, "I thought you said you were hard-core punk."

"No, what I said was soft-core punk. If we couldn't get the Pistols, we'd take what we could get."

"I see," said Norma.

"Two acoustic guitars and a bagpipe, usually."

"Even that sounds—it sounds lovely, Colin. Really."

"Great, then. Sunset is three-seventeen. I'll pick you up around two. I'll bring us a Solstice picnic—hot soup, bannocks, big thermos of Highland Park toddies."

"It's a date," Norma said.

They looked at each other, but all Colin said was, "Dress warmly, luv."

∞

Norma was dressing warmly. Black jeans, a creamy wool sweater. She felt happy, and realized Colin did that for her. She walked to the mirror. Her hedgehog shag had grown out a bit and been repaired by Anne's hairdresser into a rather fetching layered bob. She picked up her mascara and did some lashes. A little blusher. Lip gloss. A light dash of perfume. Then she gave herself a soul-searching look.

"I should let him go," she said quietly. Then repeated it. "I should let Brian go."

And this grandmother thing. She faced it. Her motive. Unworthy. Selfish. Underhanded. She wanted to give Brian what Fiona couldn't. She wanted to give Brian his place in Orkney. She wanted to answer his siren call. That was her to a T. A siren. She wasn't his good selkie. She was one of the finfolk, wasn't she? From the dark side and wanting to lure him in. Leave well enough alone. Hell.

Norma put the bottle of perfume on her dresser. She walked to the front room and then out her blue front door.

The light was downright eerie. The sun like a sickly splotch low in the pale gray sky—not enough cadmium yellow mixed with too much titanium white. She went to the little lean-to storage shed behind the cottage. She'd stuck it here. Brian's painting. The bad one. Wrapped up in her blue velvet selkie skin behind a mud-caked pair of galoshes. It was her cloak she'd come for. Jewel's cloak. She'd hung the cloak on the splintered handle of a hoe.

"I can be Jewel without him," she said. Without Brian. Or the dream of Brian. That was all she had, really. Not a man. Not love. The expectation.

"And I'm not lowering them," she said fiercely. "Not this time. I'm going beyond expectations, damn it."

Norma shook out the cloak and swirled it in a grand arc around her shoulders.

∞

"Well, I'll be biffled," said Colin.

They were looking at a crowd of at least five hundred people. People scattered across the semicircle of a peat field just to the south of the circular bank and ditch of Maeshowe itself. Maeshowe, from where they stood, was a big gray bump in the distance.

"It's grown," he said.

"Look." Norma pointed. There was a wooden platform with a band setting up.

"My God, they've got a generator. Electricity! It really is a rave. Think we can score some X?"

Norma thumped him.

Two Druids walked in front of them. The man had little papier-mâché antlers on his head.

"Glad I wore my cloak," Norma said.

In fact, the Druid theme was quite prevalent. As well as an assortment of elves, chain-mail types, and rather Gothy-looking fairies.

Colin looked down at his plain green sweater and blue jeans.

"Gee," he said.

"You look just fine," said Norma. "Handsome even. That green makes your eyes look like emeralds."

Colin twinkled them at her.

She twinkled back.

"Let's find a place to put this blanket," he said.

The blanket was a nice black and green tartan. He'd brought along a huge basket, stuffed with goodies, he'd assured her.

They found a place, spread the blanket, and settled in with two cups of hot chocolate just as the band struck up its first chords.

It took them a minute, but then they placed the tune. "Sunrise, Sunset," from the musical *Fiddler on the Roof.*

"You wouldn't think it would translate that well to techno," Norma yelled.

Colin answered with head bangs and a grin.

By the time the sun had slipped in golden-red glory behind the ridge of the Cuilags, Colin and Norma were dancing wildly with the best of them in the midst of the throng.

Twenty minutes later they lay gasping for breath on their blanket.

"I didn't think—" Norma panted. "—you could—sweat so much—when it was this—cold."

"I think—I need," answered Colin, "a—defibrillator—quick."

Norma was laughing.

"It's not fair, you know," Colin said. "No one would share their ecstasy."

"I think it was their youth they needed to share."

Colin rolled onto his side facing her. "No mere youth could match your beauty right now."

"Right," Norma said. "This isn't sweat, it's glow."

"I wish I could kiss you."

Norma didn't look at him.

Colin sat up. He started to busy himself with the picnic basket. "I've got some water in here somewhere."

"I think I wish you could, too."

Still with his back turned, he said, "Too many verbs."

"Verbs?"

"There was an extra verb in there. When you get down to one verb, I'll make love to ya so hard your head'll be spinning."

Norma smiled and sat up. "Where do you think they keep the WC around here?"

Colin grinned. "Well, that's a good question. In the old days we'd just go out yonder and water the peat. They must have some kind of portable loo, though. You want me to—"

"No," Norma said. She got to her feet. "I'll just follow the next urgent-looking fairy."

"Aye," Colin said, "and while you're gone I'll lay out the bannocks and stew."

Norma wandered off into the crowd. The band was taking a break, but she could still hear music. Singing, even the distant wail of a bagpipe. She soon spotted the row of porta-loos and, after not too long a line, relieved herself. Then, of course, she realized she hadn't marked their spot too well. She was on the other side of the bonfire, she knew, and Mae-showe was on their left, right? Man, it had gotten dark quick. Norma picked her way through the crowd. The band started up again. Thundering out a strange dirgelike thing. What was that? An electric lute?

And then she saw them.

Brian and Fiona.

Norma stopped dead.

They were about five feet away from her. On a big patch-work quilt. Bottle of wine. Two glasses. Brian had his arm around Fiona. She had her head on his shoulder. As Norma watched, Brian leaned down and kissed Fiona on the mouth. A deep kiss. With tongue. Fiona's shapely slender fingers went up through his wild dark tangle of hair.

Norma kept watching. The clinch grew even more com-plicated. Brian's fingers crept up Fiona's slender and shapely back. Beneath her jacket, beneath her sweater.

Still Norma watched. The kiss ended. Another one began. Fiona's other hand was now moving slowly up Brian's be-jeaned thigh.

Maybe they'll do it, Norma thought. Right there in front of her and the ravers and the brand-new goddamn winter. Maybe then she'd stop giving a shit. The lead singer sang out in a long and painful scream. Norma joined him. It felt good. Screaming at Brian and Fiona not five feet away.

The clinch continued unabated.

Norma turned around. There was a red-bearded Druid standing there, a big silly grin on his face.

"Isn't it beautiful, man?" he yelled.

"Yes," Norma yelled back, "fucking beautiful."

When she found Colin, she had composed herself. She took the earthenware bowl of lamb stew. It was delicious. Sweet turnips, carrots, and plump whole mushrooms swimming in just the right amount of fat.

"This is delicious!" she yelled, just as the band went silent.

Colin was watching her. "Norma, what happened?"

She put the bowl down. "You can tell? Just like that?"

"You should see your face. All the light has gone out."

"There isn't any light," she said. "Maeshowe sucked it all away, remember?"

Colin waited.

Norma jumped on him. Pushed him to the ground and planted a big wet kiss beneath his mustache.

Everyone around them burst into applause.

"That's right," somebody yelled. "Go for it, lassie!" There were wolf cries and whistles.

Colin kissed her back for a minute and then abruptly pushed her away.

"Just who are ya kissing?" he said roughly. "What happened out there?"

Norma sat up. "I'm sorry," she said. "I was—honestly, I was kissing you, Colin. But not—it was wrong. I'm so fucked-up. I—I saw them. Brian and Fiona. They're here. Together—very, very together. It was—it made me sick. Sick at myself—sick at the whole goddamn world."

"You want some whiskey?" he said sadly. "It's hot. Got butter in it."

Poor Colin. The Solstice picnic was ruined.

"I just want to go home," Norma said.

Even the ravers around them on X were all bummed; everyone, of course, but Fate. Fate licked her index finger and made a snarky little score mark in the air.

CHAPTER 24

Norma was having herself one of those long dark nights of the soul. Now she knew exactly what that phrase meant. Her soul felt like pulled taffy, sticky and stretched to the limits. And, of course, it was the longest fucking night of the year.

She lay in her narrow bed for hours. Hours and hours, while thirty minutes went by. She turned the clock facedown. This wasn't working. It was either drink herself into a stupor or . . . she looked at Brian's painting of Skara Brae.

No. That was a stupid idea.

On the other hand, Skara Brae never gave her a hangover. And, God knew, Brian wouldn't be there. Things were probably just starting to hop at the rave. Or Brian and Fiona had already hopped themselves home—gone to Fiona's bed or Brian's bed, or maybe they just pulled over by the side of the road and did it right there.

Maybe she could just get some bamboo splinters and stick them under her fingernails.

She got up. Put on her jeans and two button-up sweaters, wool socks, and running shoes. She looked at her remaining comforter. She'd already sacrificed the one *and* her North Ronaldsay sheepskin. Norma wondered for the first time what Brian had done with them. Probably left them there. Bono was probably curled up in them right now. Probably at the rave with *his* girlfriend.

Norma snatched the comforter from the bed. She stalked into the front room and put on her cloak. She saw the half-empty bottle of Highland Park. Or was it half full? She snatched that up, too. That was the ticket. Drunk as a skunk *and* Skara Brae.

∞

Somehow, driving the blue Golf out there wasn't very satisfying. Norma pulled into the parking lot and killed the engine. She got out of the car, got her blanket, the bottle, and slammed the door closed. Then she stood there. She listened to the ocean. Took a deep breath.

It was totally, totally dark. No moon. The stars as thick as glitter poured by children on some vast celestial glob of black Elmer's glue.

Norma sighed out a deep breath. There was peace here. No, more than that—serenity—that's what one found on Skara Brae. This land, this space, had been there, done that, four thousand years ago. If Skara Brae didn't care, why the hell should she?

She walked toward the site. Toward her hole. She stumbled. She looked. She'd just tripped on something dark. She walked carefully to Building 1.

Norma sat on the edge for a moment. The hole was black as a pool of tar. Blacker. She waited, hoped that her pupils could go wider. A cold wind blew in from the bay. She pulled up her hood. But the wind was colder than the black was blacker, and she slipped over the side clutching her blanket and booze. She could just make out the stone dresser, the stone beds. Dim rectangles of not so black. She walked to the bigger bed.

The bed was already made.

Norma stared. She had to get down close to really believe her eyes. The crib of stone had been filled with some kind of dried—she could smell it—heather. The bed had been filled to heaping with dried heather.

"Jewel," a voice said behind her. "I knew you'd come."

Norma turned. Confused. It was Brian's low, sexy, gravelly voice, no mistaking that. For one long dreadful moment Norma was thinking Fiona was there, too. A dim shape rose from the direction of the tunnel. One shadowy shape against the not-so-black stones. Brian's shape, and he was alone.

"I've been comin' here, I'll have you know," Brian said, "every night for seventeen days. I've been sleeping in the tunnel on the bedding in which you left me all rolled. Brought my sleepin' bag finally, 'cause it's just gettin' too damn cold. But I knew my selkie would come back. I knew it."

Norma tried to say something. Tried to speak in her soft Jewel voice, but she couldn't get past the big lump in her throat.

"And I'm sober," he went on. "Sober as a Presbyterian, I swear. I owe that, among many things, to you."

"Me?" She got that much out.

"Oh, yeah, you. Do you know that night how goddamn drunk I was? When I woke up—when I came to, more's the truth—I thought I was dead. You know, lyin' there in a hole—cold as the grave, covered with frost, and wrapped in a shroud? Most of my brain cells were just gone, but the few

I had left—four, five, maybe a half dozen—they started sparkin', trying to piece it together—and the image that arose was you, Jewel. My selkie—naked on the beach, sure—there's an image a man can't forget—but mostly, it was you, listenin'. There I was, a ramblin' drunken old pirate, crazy out of his head, and you listened. My heart said then, she wasn't real, fool. She was conjured outta Skullsplitter ale and misery. But what was left of my brain pointed out, then where did the blanket come from? That sweet-smellin' sheepskin? I sat up, saw that army of dead soldiers lying scattered on this sacred ground—and that was it, the turnin' point. I had sunk to the bottom—do you understand that? And you pulled me up from the depths—I was saved by my beautiful muse."

Norma's heart was thumping in deep, scary beats. She thought she might faint—but then how could she tell if blackness was welling up or not? This was absolutely nuts. Brian here. Telling her this. It was absolutely nuts. She fell over.

When she came to, Brian was holding her. Saying her name. But it wasn't her name, was it? She was Norma. Norma Lynn Dale. She had to tell him. Didn't she? She had to end the charade.

"Are you all right?" he was asking. "Tell me you're all right."

"I'm all right," she said. Accent British as a fucking Yorkshire pudding.

"Are you sure? Maybe I should take you—"

"No," Norma said. "No, I'm fine. I—I just wasn't—I wasn't expecting to—"

"Christ." He held her close. His cheek resting on her hair. Norma realized he'd taken her hood down. But he couldn't see her, could he? Not in the blackness. "I'm an idiot, even sober," he said. "I've scared you half to death."

Norma let herself feel. Feel Brian all around her. Then

she could smell him, too. He smelled of Brian and of Fiona's perfume. Then she felt the bottle of whiskey still clutched in her hand. She lifted it.

"I think I should maybe drink a little of this," she said softly. "Isn't that what they do for the vapors?"

"What is that?" Brian said. He ran his hand down Norma's arm and then to the bottle in her hand. "That feels an awful lot like Highland Park."

Norma couldn't answer. *Do that,* she was thinking, *run your hand down my arm again.*

"My muse has mighty fine taste in whiskey." He took the bottle from her, unplugged the cork, then offered it back.

Norma took the bottle and drank.

"Are you from Manchester?"

Norma almost spit the whiskey back out. Instead, she swallowed, took a deep breath. Could she do it? Outright lie? It was a brief skirmish between the truth and all that darkness—darkness kinda won out.

"Near there," she said. That's all she said for a moment, then, "Why do you call me that? Your muse."

" 'Cause you are," Brian said. Then those wonderful stroking fingers stroked along her hair. "I paint, remember? I hate to say artist—I have very large doubts about that—but like a hack can say he writes, I say I paint. And even the most unworthy of painters, I learned a fortnight ago, gets a muse. You found me at a very low point in my life. *The* low point—which you probably figured out from all my whinin' and self-pity. I've been—to put it graciously—all fucked-up. Way, way fucked-up, for going on four months now. Shit. Truthfully, since I was a boy. So anyway, there I was, makin' an honest effort to drink myself to death—then something magical happened."

He kissed her softly on the top of her head and then said, "I saw a selkie dancin', dancin' in the waves under the moon."

He shifted her then. Turned her around and faced him. Her pupils were as wide as they were going to get, and all she could see were the glints off Brian's.

"Look, Jewel," he said. His hands were on her shoulders. "I know you're a human bein'. Someone real. You have a life somewhere. No doubt a lover, maybe a whole damn family, but I—I have to thank you for—for at the very least just listenin'. Listenin' to a sad man rant at the world, rant at himself. You comforted a stranger. That alone makes you an emissary of the gods, you know. That alone. But you did something more for me, something that puts you on up in the category of muse. You inspired me. Just your image. That cloak, you, a faceless woman—like the quintessential woman—underneath. Here. Here in Skara Brae. That's why I kept comin' back. Kept hopin' you'd come again. I want to paint you, Jewel. Can I paint you, do you think?"

"Paint me?"

"Paint you."

"Now? Here, I mean?"

"Now. Right here."

Norma looked around. "It's, you know—"

Brian laughed. "It seems daft," he said. "But— Well, no offense, but it seems you're no stranger to daftness."

"But," Norma said, "it's totally black."

"Not totally." Brian let go of her shoulders and stood up. "There's the stars. You see—bear with me here—I did a paintin'. A year ago to the day. Did you know it's the Solstice? The Winter Solstice?"

Yes, she knew.

"I came out here last year. Did a paintin' in the dark. It was of Skara Brae—the people of Skara Brae, long ago, do you see?"

Yes, she saw.

"It was the best thing I'd ever done. The *only* good thing

I've ever done. I loved that paintin' and I hated it. I hated it because—because I wasn't true to it."

Brian was moving about across the circle of the room. She could just make out the shadows. He was setting up a shadow easel, shadow canvas, shadow paints.

"That's been a lot of my problem. Not bein' true."

Norma heard *that*. She took another slug of whiskey. This was getting downright weird.

"And, of course, truth has that fractal nature. You know fractals? If you're not true to the big stuff, then all the little stuff just—you know, it all goes to shit." He stopped moving and looked at her across the dark. "Let me ask you something."

"Okay."

"Why did you come here? I mean before. In the middle of the night. Why was your blanket and sheepskin down here?"

"I was . . ." Norma paused, but the answer was easy. "I came here for the serenity. I—The real me, the human being, I'm—well, I'm graciously fucked-up, too. I had made a really bad error in judgment—no, that's not true. I had done something, not on purpose, but the result, well, it was bad. I couldn't sleep—I had, you know, the midnight thinks. So I came here. This place—it's like all the lives lived out here, the generations, four thousand years old, they cleansed the space. They allowed, I don't know, I guess they allowed perspective. I could find peace with what I'd done. I could sleep here, that's all. Here I could sleep."

"Exactly." Brian had squatted down a few feet away from her. "Perspective. Exactly. See, you're my muse, all right. Can I paint you, Jewel? Can I paint you in the dark light of truth?"

He'd hit that nail pretty much on the head.

Norma smiled, though he couldn't see her.

"How can I say no?"

"That's wonderful." He paused. "Now comes the embarrassin' part."

Oh, lord.

"I'd like you to be like you were before. How I saw you on the beach."

He meant naked. *Yikes.*

"I see you that way in the paintin'. On the bed, there, like it was in the past—they filled them with heather, see. Long ago. So I did that. Been haulin' a burlap bagful here, every night—then cleanin' up before that god-awful singin' boy comes in the mornin'."

"Bono."

Brian laughed. "Right, Bono."

"Okay."

"Okay?"

"But not—I mean, I get to keep the cloak on, right?"

"Aye," Brian said. "Of course. The cloak, the hood, on the bed, with just a glimpse of the line of your body. The line of one breast, along your belly, along your thigh. Just that—reflected in the starlight, see?"

Her belly. Norma's body had quivered as he had said the word.

"Look," he said. "Look up behind you at the sky."

Norma looked. The great glittering streak of the galaxy was just above the edge of their private horizon.

"See the line of the Milky Way? Like the line of a woman, innit?"

"Perspective," Norma said.

"Exactly."

"Okay, I get it. I'll do it. But you gotta turn around," she said. "I know it's dark, but—"

Brian turned.

Norma put the whiskey bottle down. She stood up. Unbuttoned her top sweater, then the one underneath, and let them slip from her arms to the ground. She hadn't bothered to put on a bra. She kicked off her shoes and unzipped her pants, letting them drop, and then stepped out of them. Then the panties. She was shaking. Not from the cold, either.

"Can I keep on my socks?"

"Aye."

Good. Maybe with her socks on she wouldn't do a meltdown into a big ol' puddle of desire. Socks—the eternal buffer against the erotic.

Norma put up her hood, then went over to the stone bed. She sat down. The heather was surprisingly firm. Firm and wonderfully fragrant. She lay a little on her side. Like the woman in the Milky Way. She pulled back one edge of the cloak along her body. Another quiver. She took a deep breath and let it out slowly.

"Like this?"

Brian turned back. "Christ," he said.

He just stood there a moment not saying anything else. Then Norma heard him let out a long breath, too. Then he spoke.

"Perfect. Thank you. Now, don't move."

The shadow painter went to his easel. Norma could hear the *scratch scratch* of charcoal against canvas.

"Are you freezin'?"

"Not unbearably."

"Don't move."

They were silent for a while. This was unbelievably sexy. Torture, delicious torture. Norma felt a grand connection to a long, long line of unclothed artists' models back through time. She started to tremble. Tremble hard. She gripped the cold edge of her stone bed, wrenching her mind from where it was headed and back to the cold edge of now. The question popped into her thoughts and out of her mouth before she could stop it.

"Can I ask *you* something?"

"Anything," Brian said.

Okay. That had stopped the trembling. Now she had to ask it.

"Before—last time—up there—you said you were an engaged man."

"Did I?"

"Yes, you did."

"Well, I suppose it's true."

"I didn't think engagement could be a supposition."

Brian didn't answer right away. Norma got a whiff of linseed oil.

"There is a woman," he said finally. "Thinks she wants to marry me." Pause. "And I think . . ." Another pause. "All right, I'll tell you what I think. Because you, selkie, are the only one in the world to whom I can." Then came a really long pause. "It's only these few weeks that I've known it myself—or, I don't—hell, maybe I've known it for months."

He went silent again and Norma heard the sounds of paint on canvas. *Swish swish, daub daub. Daub daub.* Pause. *Daub, swish, swish daub.*

"I do love her."

Despite her best intentions the word "crap" came into Norma's head.

"She's beautiful."

Double crap.

"She's smart, talented—"

Has a great left hook.

"She's sweet—"

Enough already.

"Has a wonderful sense of humor. She even cooks."

Okay. That did it. Triple fucking crap.

"But . . ."

Swish, daub, swish, daub.

"Sometimes I find myself almost hatin' her. It's a twisted kind of hate and it took me a long time and a lot of ale and a talk with a selkie to really figure it all out. It's a hatred of myself, see—of who I am—or I suppose I should say, who I'm not."

Norma heard him let out a sigh.

"You know all the things I was tellin' you, about my past and all, have been quite an issue between us. Not on her part. God, the woman is a saint. She's stood up for me to her friends, her family—everyone in the Islands, it seems. No, it's me. It's *me*. I'm the problem. I somehow—it's like I look down on her for lovin' me. Like that Groucho Marx thing—how he wouldn't belong to any club that would have him for a member? Only it's not funny. Not a bit damn funny. To despise the lady you love because she loves you? How fucked is that, would you say?"

Pretty fucked.

"And then . . ." Pause. "Then there was this other woman."

Here we go.

"I guess—truthfully—the other woman came first. Things between Fiona and me, that's her name—Fiona, well, on the surface, things were fine. Then this—this situation came out of nowhere. A chance meetin'. She was just a tourist out on a day trip to Hoy. A tourist—goofy—you know, the way Americans are . . ."

Boy, did she know.

"She was pretty, though." Another sigh. "More than pretty. She was damned attractive. I mean that literally and not just the physical, either. I was *attracted* to her. Drawn. It was strange. I'm a grown man, and I've been attracted to plenty of women. But something happened between that woman and me that windswept day out on Hoy. Something dangerous."

Daub, daub, daub.

Norma was trying to keep the tears in. She'd asked for this, hadn't she? Now she should take it.

"We didn't have sex, was the odd part. God knows the urge was certainly in me. There was a moment—" He stopped. "We men are just basically beasts, you know. Beasts with shirts on. There was a moment out there when I just wanted to throw her to the peat and—well, I'll spare you the details, but something overcame me concernin' that woman and it's never really gone away. Hell, I didn't even see her after that more'n a total of maybe—maybe an hour." Pause. "Though the last five minutes or so were pretty intense, I'll tell you that." He snorted. "I was such a goddamn fool. I told Fiona. I had to. The truth was killin' me. Tearin' my heart in two, like some fuckin' sentiment on a cheap Valentine card."

He went silent. He was still painting. Norma could see movement. No daubs, no swishes, though. Maybe he was doing the stars.

Another couple of minutes and then the movement stopped.

"I'm through."

"Really?" Norma said.

"Yeah. I'm through."

"Can I see it?"

"I can't even see it," Brian said. "Not until the winter sun decides to show his face tomorrow. I think it's good, though. Like the other one."

Brian had squatted down again. Norma heard him open the paint box. There was the sound of liquid, then the smell of turpentine.

"It's funny," he said. "The other one was sold. To a Span-ish guy, my agent told me. He paid cash. Didn't leave his name. My paintin', my one good paintin', and it's in Madrid, or Barcelona, or God knows where."

"The Spanish guy," Norma said, "he must have seen— you know, the beauty of the thing."

"Maybe so."

Brian stood up and faced in her direction.

"Can I," Norma said, "move now?"

He didn't answer. She could see the white of a cloth on which he was drying his hands.

Then he said, his voice gone all low, "Don't."

He took a step closer.

"Don't?"

"No, luv—don't. I'm not through seein' you—I don't think I'll ever be through seein' you like that."

Whu-oh.

"And, while I'm bein' truthful, here, selkie—seein' ain't the half of it, either." He took another step. "You know that beast I was mentionin'? Truthfully, little selkie—I find myself havin' a tussle with that beast right now."

Norma kept perfectly still. In the darkness she saw Brian's hands go up to his face and then back through his hair.

"Mother of God," he said. "Mother of fuckin' God. What am I doin'? Have I totally lost my mind? *This* is what I've spent four fuckin' months tryin' to drown from my god-damn stupid head! *This* is what I tried to tell Fiona—do you understand? I *asked* her how I could love her when I wanted so badly to make love to another woman, when I was so fuckin' *possessed* with another woman. But, *no,* she went on lovin' me, didn't she? She *forgave* me, for God's sake, stood by my madness, my drinkin', my self-fuckin'-indulgent despair— Fiona was in my arms, not two hours ago. Two *hours* ago and now look at me. With you. Doin' this with you. Possessed? I'm a fuckin' slut."

Brian dropped his hands and took one more step. Then he

reached out and Norma moved. She moved damn quick—back against the stone wall. And here was the kaleidoscope again. Twisting through her brain in broken shards and crazy patterns. She clutched the cloak closed, her breath—what little she had—starting to come in sharp useless jags.

But Brian hadn't been reaching for her. He'd been reaching for the bottle of whiskey. She heard the cork pop, could see the glint of the glass as he lifted it to his lips. He drank, then sank to the ground, his back against the stone bed.

"I'm sorry," he said. "Really sorry. I'm an asshole sober as well as drunk. And you get to be everything, don't you? Jesus Christ. My selkie, my confessor, my muse—and now the object of my fucked-up desires. I'm just a fuckin' bastard is what I am." He took another drink. "A fuckin' bastard. And you, Jewel, you're magic—you're perfect—and I wanted to put my hands on you. How dare I even think to put my hands on you?"

"Do it," Norma said.

She touched his hair. His black tangle of wild hair.

"Put your hands on me—please. Before I die."

Brian turned and looked at her through the darkness. She looked back. The tesla coil sizzled and arced between them. Norma pulled open her cloak. Brian blew out one sharp breath and dropped the bottle on the ground. He got to his knees and reached out his pale painter's hands and touched her. Long fingers on each breast—first gently, and then he seized her and pulled her to him. He kissed one breast and then the other, and then his tongue was making circles on her hardened nipple.

"Jesus," he whispered then and his head rose—looking, searching in the darkness. "I—I thought I'd dreamed it—but I've done that before, haven't I? I've tasted you, Jewel."

He rose to the bed and found her face with his hands. Stroked her eyes, along her cheeks . . .

"Let me taste your lips now," he said.

They kissed. Sweet first, then hungry. Hungry, wet, and deep.

She groaned. She couldn't help herself. She groaned.

Brian kissed down her neck and to her breasts again and then kissed on down her belly—oh, yeah—and still farther. And he murmured while he kissed, low and sexy and gravelly—something about her other lips, and then—bingo. The kaleidoscope burst into a perfect rose-window glory of light. And she no longer fucking cared. She *was* Jewel. Just for this time, this space, this place with *him*.

"Make love to me, Brian," she whispered desperately. "Make love to me."

They both started tugging on his pants. Off they came, then he pulled off his jacket and thick sweater.

She reached for him. *His* skin. Brian's unattainable skin. She kissed his chest, then licked him, then licked up to his neck and his ear.

"Ah, *Christ*," Brian said fiercely. He pushed her down on the bed of heather and kissed her on the mouth again.

"You feel that?" he said hoarsely. "I could push it through the fuckin' stone."

She reached down and guided him to a much better place.

They both groaned as he entered her, and then they made love—furious and thorough love. The climax was vocal for both of them. Clear enough to wake the Neolithic dead.

CHAPTER 25

"My ass is freezin'," Brian said.

She giggled.

He rose, then gathered her up naked in his arms.

He kissed her. On the nose.

"Oops, I missed," he said. Then he carried her to the tunnel.

She crawled through first. She could feel the silk of his sleeping bag. On top of it was the soft woolly strands of her sheepskin. She lay down, then Brian lay down with her and covered them both with the comforter. They held each other in the darkness, trembling together, from cold, from excitement, from the danger.

Brian rubbed her up and down. She rubbed him. The rubbing turned to strokes, then he kissed her again. She could feel his hard-on return against her leg.

"Do you think it's against the rules to fuck your muse?" he said.

"I think it's practically required."

Brian buried his head between her breasts and let out a long sigh.

"Christ almighty," he said. "The release. From everything. I've never felt so good in all my life."

"Me, too," she said. Her hand was entwined in his hair.

"Let's just stay in here forever," he said.

"Okay."

"Bono can bring us food."

They both started to giggle, and then the alarm went off.

Buzz-buzz.

Suddenly she was Norma again.

Buzz-buzz.

Brian was laughing. "You left that here," he said. "Damn handy, too."

Brian was rummaging through the blanket with his hand.

"Don't!" said Norma. But it was too late.

Within one long agonizing second, like watching a slow-motion gunfight in a neowestern, Brian had found Norma's little glow-in-the-dark travel clock and casually flipped it open.

Who would have thought one little blue light could be so, so, so horribly huge?

For a brief moment of respite they were both blinded, then Fate, the bitch, stepped in.

Brian looked at her. He still had the leftover curve of his smile. That faded as recognition dawned.

"Oh, no," he said, *"not you."*

The words hung between them, then dropped, like laundry into the dirt.

Norma slapped him.

Brian jerked back, put his hand to where she'd hit him. He looked absolutely bewildered.

Norma couldn't take it. She struggled from the comforter, half crawling down the tunnel, away from the light.

She tried to run, hit her head—*smack*—on the hard stone ceiling. She dropped to her knees, crawling—then she was out, stark naked in the stark black night, in the stark new black winter cold. She was in Building 4. Now what? Hearing Brian coming down the tunnel after her, she ran, her arms out in the blackness until she collided with a wall. She climbed, naked toes between stones, and hurled herself up onto the sharp cold grass. Then she crawl-walked as fast as she could until she felt the stone rim of Building 1. She dropped down. God, she was freezing. She felt along the ground until she found her clothes, struggled into her pants, her shoes— her two sweaters were hopelessly knotted.

Hearing Brian coming down over the side, she made a break for the wall. She'd scrambled halfway up, then Brian grabbed hold of her ankle.

"No you don't, goddamnit. Not this time."

Norma struggled, but he pulled her off the wall.

"Let me go!"

"I won't."

Brian had her by the shoulders and he shook her. He shook her hard. Then he made a noise like a wounded animal. A terrible strangled cry. He shuddered horribly—he was naked, freezing, angry, and in pain—all because of her, she realized.

"Oh, God, Brian—God, please—"

"You said my name before—" His fingers dug into her skin. "—*didn't you?*" He shook her again. "While we made love. While we made *love*, Norma, god*damn* it. How could you do this to me?"

"Me?" Norma yelled at him. "Me? How could you do this to Fiona?"

Brian let go of her shoulders with a push, turned, and wrapped his arms around himself.

That worked. *Just twist in the knife, bitch.* Norma wanted to die.

"Brian—"

But he just stood there shuddering, naked.

"Brian—please, put your clothes on. You're freezing."

She groped through the dark to the stone bed, found his clothes, and picked up her cloak. She went to him and put the cloak around his shoulders.

"We need to go in the tunnel," she said. "Okay? We need to get warm."

They went back. The little clock still glowed its blue betrayal.

Brian dressed himself while Norma untangled her sweaters and put them on. He tossed her the cloak and put the sleeping bag around his shoulders.

They sat there, ragged breath, shivering—miserable.

Norma didn't want to look at his face, but it was difficult to avoid. He had tears on his cheeks. He looked up at her.

"You're bleedin'," he said.

She felt at her hairline. Yes, she was.

"When did you come back?"

"I never really left," Norma said.

"And you've been, what—stalkin' me?"

She looked at him. "All I wanted," she said, "all I ever wanted, was for you to understand. I admit that I—I loved you. I guess I've loved you from the first moment I saw you glaring at me at Betty Corrigall's grave. But I didn't come back for that. I had no hope of that after—after what I'd done."

"You mean when you fucked the cowboy?" Brian put one hand to his face and covered his eyes. "Shit."

"Right," Norma said. "That's what I did. I fucked the

cowboy. But you thought I'd done it on purpose. In front of you on purpose—and I hadn't. I had no earthly idea you were up there. I had no earthly idea you had any feelings for me. I'm not a whore-bitch from Hell, okay? And I'm not a stalker. I'm just a—a goofy American tourist, that's all. I—"

"Oh, God," Brian said, still with his eyes covered. "I said that, didn't I? I said you were goofy."

"You said I was pretty, too."

He dropped his hand and looked at her.

"I said you were more than pretty—and you are, Norma Dale. Jesus, I never thought I'd see your face again. I was haunted by your face, don't you see? How could you not know how I felt?"

"Your words—your words up on Quoyer Viewpoint— they were, like, branded onto me. I knew *then*—but I couldn't go to you. I'd ruined whatever it was that we had. It was such an unspoken fragile thing, and I ruined it. And there was— well, then I knew about Fiona, Brian."

"Fiona. Right." Anger flared again in his eyes. "And did you enjoy *that* in this little game you've been playin'? Me barin' my heart to ya, *Jewel*?"

"Don't call me that. Please."

"But you said I could, didn't you? *Didn't you?*"

"Jewel was the name my father had chosen for me. On the day I was born. He told me on his deathbed. Jewel is who— who I was meant—meant—" The tears welled up and started to flow. "I'm so sorry," Norma sobbed out, "I wasn't lying, not really lying. I didn't plan on this, any of it."

"Didn't you follow me that night, then? Knowin' I was drunk and at your mercy? Do your little moon dance for the poor unsuspectin' sod?"

"No!" Norma wiped at her eyes. "No, no, no! *I* was drunk that night. Me! My plan was—my *plan* was—" she took a shuddery breath. "Earlier that day, I'd—I'd decided I was going out to see you. On Hoy. I was going to tell you everything—finally—everything. I was dressed to go. Colin had called—"

"Colin? Colin Tait?"

"Yes, Colin. He's my friend. I have friends. I have a life, okay?"

Brian held up his hands.

"So Colin was the one who'd convinced me. That you would understand, you know? That you wouldn't hate me. Then Fiona came."

"Came where?"

"To my crofting cottage. It's close to here. I rent from Anne Skathamore."

"Colin's aunt?"

"That's right," Norma said. "I know Marion, too."

"So you're tellin' me that Fiona knew who you were? She's known all along that you're here?"

"Not all along. I think Helen Spence told her."

"Christ," Brian said, "do the whole fuckin' Islands know?"

"A few herdsmen up on North Ronaldsay are still in ignorance."

Brian stared.

"That's what Marion said when I asked her the same question. Jesus, Brian, I didn't want *anyone* to know—there was nothing *to* know, for God's sake. That shark you call your agent put zero and two together and came up with three, okay? You started it, by the way—putting those little revenge shadows in your *Viewpoint* painting. Helen Spence assumed *we* were the shadows, then she couldn't keep her trap shut, and Fiona came out and plugged me on the jaw, okay?"

Brian's dark eyes had grown wide. "She hit you?"

"During tea. It's a girl thing, really." Norma tried to laugh, but nothing came out. "She loves you. Fiona loves you. She shouldn't be blamed for any of this. She tried to tell me.

She *did* tell me—and I—I changed my mind about seeing you."

"I don't understand. Then why did you follow me here?"

Norma put her hands to her head in frustration. "I didn't! I did not follow you. *Not.* Did *not,* okay?"

"You're sayin' it was coincidence? Chance? I don't believe that."

"It wasn't chance, exactly," Norma said. "It was—oh, I don't know—the interweaving of fate. Like tonight. Do you think I followed you here tonight? If I was so intent on stalking you, why haven't I come out here every night for seventeen days? Why tonight?"

Brian blinked. He was getting that bewildered look again.

"I came here tonight, as a matter of fact, to get *away* from you. You and your precious Fiona, okay? I was there at Maeshowe. With Colin. We were having a wonderful time. Colin is a great guy, by the way. I was having fun with my *friend,* okay? And I went to take a piss, and who did I see but you and Fiona, okay? Your tongue was halfway down her throat, and her hands were practically—" Norma stopped. She had started to yell. She started up again quietly. "As you had every right—being engaged and all—but it put a certain damper on *my* evening, and Colin took me home. I couldn't sleep, so I came out here—to be alone, like I've done many times—*many* times—including the night you happened to choose to get stinking drunk and chase down innocent selkies on the beach—okay?"

"Are you sleeping with Colin Tait?"

Norma glared.

"All right, I'm sorry," Brian said, putting up his hands again. "I believe you." He rubbed his face with his hands, then ran his fingers back through his hair. "God, I think I must be goin' mad."

"Me, too," said Norma.

"I'll be back," he said abruptly, threw off the sleeping bag, and crawled from the tunnel.

He came back with the bottle of whiskey. Taking his handkerchief from his pocket, he pulled out the stopper with his teeth and spit it to the ground. He poured whiskey on the handkerchief and scooted across the little space between them.

"Let me tend to that," he said.

Norma winced as the whiskey made contact with her scalp wound.

"Sorry," he said, and then, "You've cut off your beautiful hair."

Norma nodded.

He dabbed silently for a moment. "You're goin' to have a little scar there, I think."

"Great," Norma said. "Something to remember the evening by."

Brian put one long finger under her chin and tilted up her face to his.

"Don't be tellin' me that—that you won't remember."

He leaned in and kissed her. It was the sweet kind. And afterward they did the eyes-to-eyes thing. Searching.

"Ah, my little selkie," he said. "I should have known."

"I should have told."

"Why?" he said. "Why didn't you?"

Norma started to speak, but Brian put his hand to her lips.

"No," he said, "I don't care. I just care that it *is* you, do you hear me?"

He kissed her again. Then he reached over and shut the travel clock.

He smoothed out the sleeping bag and spread the sheepskin on it once again.

Norma lay down with him. In his arms. And he drew the comforter over them.

They lay in the dark, neither speaking. They just held on and listened to each other breathe until finally came peaceful sleep.

∞

Norma woke up with the new winter sun scratching at her eyelids. The light was feeble but persuasive. She stirred and stretched and remembered where she was. She opened her eyes.

Brian was there on one elbow, watching her.

He smiled.

Norma said, "Bono!"

"Relax. Tomorrow is Christmas eve. The place is closed."

"Well, that's a relief." She rubbed at her eyes, coming away with mascara on her fingers. "Oh, lord," she said. "How bad do I look?"

"Well, there's that unsightly gash, and your face is a mess, but at least you haven't got puffin shit on you."

"God."

Brian chuckled.

Then she looked at him. "Your painting!"

He grinned.

"You've seen it already, haven't you?"

"Well, it's my bloody paintin', innit?"

Norma sat up and pushed the comforter away. She crawled out of the tunnel. The painting was on the easel.

She stood there.

Brian came up behind her. "Well, what do you think?"

"I think its beautiful. It's perfect. I can't believe you did this in the dark."

She turned around and looked up at his face.

"Don't do that 'I'm just a painter' crap, anymore, okay? You are a fucking artist. It's brilliant."

"You like it, then." He grinned at her. "Maybe I can get another Spaniard interested, eh?"

Norma dropped her eyes.

"Hey, what'd I say?"

He cupped his hand under her chin to lift it, but Norma pushed away. She walked back to the tunnel and got her cloak, put it on, and wrapped it around her.

"What is it?"

A seagull gave a lonely cry from overhead.

Norma felt sick. A great big chunk of truth had just presented itself.

"Norma?"

"I was the Spaniard."

"What?"

"I bought your painting of Scara Brae."

"You did?"

"Helen Spence lied about it. I lied about it, too, I guess. Pretending to be—I was so stupid, Brian. I was—I went to the gallery because I thought I could learn more about you there. I saw the painting and I—I had to have it. Not just because *you'd* done it—not because Helen Spence was so obviously blind to its value—I had to have it simply because it was so damn good." She looked at him. "It was the painting that brought me here to Skara Brae. I came at night—because you had been here at night. It was the first thread."

"In our interweaving fate," he finished for her. "I think that's bloody wonderful."

"But it's not," Norma said, her voice choking on the words. "It's bloody awful."

He came toward her, but she held up her hand.

"The truth, Brian. The truth is bloody awful. We can't be doing this."

He laughed. "Don't be goin' daft on me, woman. We *are* doing this."

"Well, not anymore. We have to stop. It's all wrong."

Brian came to her anyway and grabbed her. He had stopped laughing. "What are you talking about? You've come back to me—it's like a miracle. We've finally found each other. Our fates are interwoven, Norma—that's the bloody truth."

She let him kiss her, and kissed back. She held his face in her hands and kissed him for all she was worth.

He was holding her. Stroking her hair. "That's right, that's better," he was saying in her ear. "You're mine now. That's all that matters."

"Brian," Norma said, "Brian, I have to tell you."

"No, you don't."

"Yes, I *do*." She pulled away. "It's the painting. It's— Brian, when you were painting last night, who were you talking about?"

Brian looked at her.

"Fiona. You were talking about Fiona. How you loved her, why you loved her—"

"Ah, crap," Brian spat out. "I was talkin' about Fiona because you asked me. Remember that? And, if you remember, I ended up talkin' about *you*. Then I was doing more than that, if you remember, I was doing more than talkin'—"

"Brian, please," Norma said, "hear me out."

"You're killin' me."

"Look, it's killing me, too—to say this. But I have to. I've known it—I've known it and I've hated knowing it, ever since that moment when— Oh, fuck." Norma put her hands to her face.

Brian stood there helpless.

Norma struggled for control, but the tears came anyway.

"When what?" he finally said.

"When—When Fiona showed me the painting."

"What paintin'?"

"It was the day she came to see me at the crofting cottage," Norma said. Her nose was running. She didn't care. She wiped it with the back of her hand. "She was really angry. She thought—well, you'd told her you'd been unfaithful. I tried to tell her that we hadn't, then she started begging me to leave you alone, telling me how bad I was—that I was a bad person, that I would—would destroy you."

Brian made a sound of disgust, started to reach for her, but Norma held up her hand.

"No—let me finish. I got mad, too. When she said that. I got plenty mad. She started in on your painting—your drinking—said what I inspired in you was trash. Dark and trash. I got up then and went and got *Skara Brae.* I showed it to her—yelled at her, told her she was full of shit—"

"Well, she was." Brian's voice was angry.

"No," Norma said, shaking her head. "She wasn't. She— She had brought another painting with her. One you had done—one of me."

Brian's face changed. "Christ," he said. "That fuckin' thing." He pushed his hair from his face. "I knew—well, I thought it was her who took it, but . . .." Then his eyes widened and he looked at her. "Norma, Jesus, Norma, I— that's not—you can't be thinkin'—I was crazy, I was fuckin' drunk—"

"I know," Norma said. "I know. But it was the truth. That's what you paint, Brian—you paint the truth and we can't get around that. That day—that awful day—Fiona gave me that painting and *I* got crazy drunk, too—okay? I drank and I cried and I felt that stone knife in your hand, Brian— cutting out my heart."

"Fuckin' Christ—"

"No, let me finish," Norma said. She didn't look at him.

"That's why I came here that night. Why I came to Skara Brae. I came to release myself—from you. That's what my dance was about. Naked—in the dark. I was ending it, okay? Trying to end the damn thing. Then Fate stepped in. God, she hates me. Fate hates me. Or she loves me—she can't get enough of me, anyway. And I tried to dodge Fate by becoming Jewel. I got myself all tangled up in that—that stupid charade. I almost told you that night who I was. I really did. But then I saw myself chained to that rock—and you with the knife—"

Brian stepped close and took her hands. "Norma, listen to me. Please. There's no bloody truth to that paintin.' The truth is what's between us—what's between us here and now. Can't you feel it? I know you feel it. That's not bad—it's *not* bad—I'll never believe that, do you hear me?"

Norma looked at him and smiled. A very sad smile.

"I feel it," she said. "I'll always feel it. I'll always remember the feel of heather on my back and you inside me. That wasn't wrong. That wasn't bad. But it's all we can have, Brian. It's all Fate is going to allow."

She paused to take a breath.

"Colin told me once that what you loved about Fiona was her—her subtext. That was how he put it. Fiona, to you, *is* Orkney. I think he was right. You said it yourself. How you hate the Brian that is reflected in her. What you hate is the wall. The wall that divides you from Orkney. That belonging—what you've never had—what you have always sought—is the truth that you paint. I can see that truth now. We both need to face it. Fiona is on the other side of the wall, in the light—I'm over here with you, in the darkness. We'll never get around that. Do you understand?"

Brian looked at her.

"I didn't hear a word past the part about the heather on your back and me inside you. In fact, I think a little more of that and you'll just shut up with all this psychobabble bullshit." He moved to embrace her, but she put up her hands again.

"Brian, no."

"I see," he said. "That's it, then? I just let my selkie go back to the sea? Norma, I fuckin' *love* you. But it's more than that—don't *you* understand?" He pointed to the painting on the easel. "That's you there. *You.* You inspired me to *see* in the darkness. I thought I was goin' mad, last night. What I was feelin'—what I felt for *you,* Norma Dale—when I didn't even fuckin' *know* it, was you. Do ya need more proof than that? More truth than that? Fuck Fate. I need you, luv, I need you in my life, and there's no way in bloody hell that I'll ever let you leave my life again. Do you hear me? Do you understand that?"

So Norma let him hold her. She let him kiss her. She let him hold her and kiss her, and she felt his big sigh of relief when he looked at her and smiled. She traced one finger down his long lone dimple and sighed herself.

"I need a shower," she said. "And coffee. And some eggs and beans on toast."

"That sounds great—"

"Alone," Norma said. "Okay?"

Brian frowned. "Did I not get through to you?"

"We can talk about it more, okay? But not now. My head hurts, everything—it's just—"

Brian touched her bump. "That's a pretty big goose egg you got there. But you're not—Norma, if you're planning on running away—"

"I'm not."

"You won't do that to me—"

"I just want to take a shower."

"All right, then." He kissed her on the lips. "I know where you live, now, you know. I want your phone number, too. I'm not going to lose you. I'm serious. Not again." He went to his paint box and picked up a piece of charcoal.

She gave him the number. Then she gathered up her blankets, her sheepskin, and her bottle of Highland Park whiskey, and went home.

∽

But Norma was, in fact, planning to run away.

CHAPTER 26

Norma had her shower. Her coffee. Her eggs and toast. (She'd been lying about the beans, too.) Then she sat in her comfy chair, in her robe, staring into the ashes of her cold stone hearth.

She'd meant it. Every word. She just hadn't told him the entire truth why. She felt numb about it all. Probably because she'd just cut out her own damn heart.

Norma heard a knock at the door.

Crap. She couldn't face him so soon.

"Norma?"

It was Colin, thank the gods.

"Come in," she said. Then loud enough to be heard, "Come in!"

Colin came in. He had a tiny Christmas tree, with silver tinsel and tiny twinkling lights. There was a tiny gold puffin on top.

"How you feeling?"

Norma got up. She smiled, went to him, and kissed him on the cheek. "You are the sweetest man," she said.

He handed her the tree. "Merry Christ— Jesus, what happened to your head?"

"I bumped into some reality last night. You want some coffee?"

"Uh, sure."

Norma took the little tree into the kitchen and he followed her. She put the tree on the table, poured him a cup, and gave herself a warm-up.

"So, what happened to your head?"

Norma smiled. "It's a long story," she said.

"Well, then we'd better sit down."

Norma picked up her tree again and went back to her comfy chair. Colin followed.

She put the tree on the coffee table and watched the lights twinkle for a minute.

"You know the day Fiona came over and I got so drunk and later I went out?"

"And you saw Brian, but he didn't see you."

"Right. Well, the reason he didn't see me was because I was wearing my cloak, for one thing, my cloak with the hood, and the other thing was because he was blind drunk."

"That's our Brian."

"And my hair, of course. I'd just cut off my hair. We were out on Skara Brae."

"Skara Brae? The two of you? How the hell—"

"It was fate, the interweaving of fate," Norma said. She took a sip of her coffee. "We started drinking Skullsplitters—"

"Oh, my goodness."

"And talking. Actually, Brian did most of the talking. About his mother, his father, his grandfather, all the mystery years—all of it. He told me everything. And I just sat there listening, with my hood pulled up and not letting on who I was."

"Aye," Colin said, "I'm beginning to see this, now—

and the next morning was when you decided to take up genealogy again."

"That's right," Norma said. "I fooled myself into thinking it was for Brian, but it was for me—all for me. I wanted to find his grandmother. Fill in that last little bit of the puzzle—be the one to give Brian his heritage, his place in the big Orkney tree—"

"Norma, you're talking like that was a bad thing."

"My motive—"

"You love the bloke, there's your motive. Simple as that."

"Well, it doesn't matter, anyway." Norma had to dab at the corner of her eye. "I didn't find her. And last night—"

"I think you should just go see the man, Norma. Get it over with. He's going to find out soon enough, and—"

"He knows I'm here, Colin. Last night, I went out again. I saw him and—"

"Don't tell me Fiona did that to you!"

Norma laughed, then waved her hand. "No, no. It was nothing like that. I went to Skara Brae again and Brian was there. Alone."

"Now I'm flummoxed. Totally."

"Okay, I know—I kinda left out some stuff, from before. See, the first time out on Skara Brae—well, Brian was drunk, really drunk, and he thought I was a selkie."

"A selkie?"

"Before I knew Brian was there—I was kinda doing a dance thing, on the beach, under the moon—without my clothes."

Colin lifted his brows.

"Brian chased me—thinking I was a selkie, see—and all I could find was my cloak, and then he tackled me, so we had this—kinda atmosphere between us. He kinda ended up—he was really wasted, see, and he thought I was . . ."

"Yes?"

"Magical." Norma felt her face grow red.

Colin's eyes were twinkling like the tiny lights on the tree. "I've always thought so."

"Well, anyway—it turned out, I found out last night, that he'd been going out to Skara Brae every night. For all this time. He wanted to paint me, see?"

"On the beach? Doing the moon dance?"

"No." Norma took another sip of coffee. "Okay, I left out another part. See, I'd been—you know Brian's painting— the one I have in my room?"

"*Skara Brae.* How could I forget?"

"Right. Sorry. So, one night, I couldn't sleep—this was the night before I met you, actually. I went out there. To Skara Brae. I took my sheepskin and my comforter and I slept in one of the stone beds."

Colin was shaking his head.

"What?" Norma said.

"I'm just—speechless, I guess. Aye, speechless. Please, go on."

"So it became kind of a habit, really. Sleeping at Skara Brae. That's what I was going to do the night of the moon dance. But I didn't stay. Not that night. I just wrapped Brian up, so he wouldn't freeze, and I left him there."

"In the stone bed?"

"Well, we were just on the ground, in Building 1."

"I really ought to turn you in to the heritage police."

Norma smiled. "So, I hadn't gone back in all this time, but Brian had—"

"Every night."

"Yes, every night for seventeen days."

"Because he wanted to paint you."

"Actually, he wanted to paint Jewel."

The brows went up again.

"I told him my name was Jewel."

"Like what your father wanted to name you."

"You remembered that?"

"Mind like a steel trap." Colin tapped his head and grinned.

"So anyway, that's what happened. He had his easel all set up and he'd filled the bed with heather and he painted me."

"And he still had no idea who you were?"

"Well, I was kinda doing a British accent thing. And it was pitch-black, Colin. That was what was so weird. Brian painted this *masterpiece* with no light, I mean nothing but the stars."

"And then what happened?"

Norma went to take another sip of her coffee, but there was none left.

"Or do I already know?"

She looked at him sheepishly and nodded.

"I'd been—I'd asked him about Fiona—you know, subtle-like, and he just spilled his guts. It was so weird, the way he just opened up to me. I was like—well, he called me his muse. Somehow, you know, the anonymity, I guess, he just poured out his heart. And then he was talking about me—me, Norma, me—how he'd met me on Hoy and broken up with Fiona, and then he was suddenly—well, he was there, next to me, and it got—got—"

Colin put his cup on the table. "Stop," he said. He looked pretty miserable. "I don't think I want to hear this part."

Norma let out a big breath. "I couldn't tell you anyway. Not that. It was so—so—"

"You're telling me." He put his hands to his ears. "La la la la la—"

Norma laughed. "Okay, okay."

Colin put his hands back down. "Did he know it was you?"

"No. Not till—afterward. It was horrible, Colin. How he found out. I had this stupid fucking alarm clock. It went off and Brian opened it. There was this awful blue light and, just like that, blam—I was exposed."

"What did he— Oh, Christ, the bastard hit you?"

"No—no, no—I did this to myself. I was running away."

"You ran away?"

"Yeah, the big chicken, right? Only he caught me this time. We had—well, there were words exchanged, then we—we calmed down and, well, it was kinda nice after that. Weird, but nice. I told him. You know, everything."

Colin looked at her for a moment.

"So, then," he said. "As for me, I'm pea green with jealousy, but for you—are we looking at a happy ending here?"

Norma's eyes teared up. She lifted her hand, palm outward, then out squeaked a sad little, "No." She wiped at her eyes and took a couple of sad little hiccup breaths.

"Crap, then, darlin'. You want to talk about it—or you just want my nice clean shoulder to cry on?"

"Maybe a little of both," Norma said. "Oh, Colin. It was good, really good. Brian was—well, he was wonderful, and his painting—we went out together to look at it in the new morning light. He was so happy, then I started—I started—"

"What did you start?"

"I told him that it wasn't going to work between us."

"Why on earth did you tell him that?"

"Because it won't. I know it won't. Fiona is right. She's right, damn it. I'll destroy him. The painting—the horrible painting that Fiona brought me—that's the truth of the thing. The truth of me and Brian. There's a darkness to us—to me!

God, Colin, *we made love—like strangers—in total blackness. Do you understand?* I lost myself in him. I *lost* myself!"

"Norma, you're not making sense."

Colin went to her, took her in his arms. She clutched at him.

"You told Brian this?"

Norma nodded over his shoulder.

"Silly woman."

"I'm *not* silly! Brian wouldn't believe me, either. He thinks we—he thinks we can—"

Colin was patting her back. "He thinks you can be together like a grown man and a grown woman without all this darkness nonsense?"

Norma pushed Colin away. "I hate you both," she said.

"Norma," Colin said patiently, and sat back on his heels, "does the term 'emotional roller coaster' mean anything to you?"

"I'm not hysterical," Norma screamed. Then she smiled. "There's a reason I know this to be true. I didn't tell Brian—not the whole truth—but I'll tell you."

"I'm listening."

"When Brian saw me—after the light came on—when he saw me and he saw who I was, do you know what he said?"

"No, Norma, what did Brian say?"

"He said, 'Oh, no, *not you*.' "

Colin blinked. Then he remembered. "Trey Bliss."

Norma nodded. "Do you understand? Brian was speaking the truth. In those four little words—the truth. See, Brian knows the truth—he can't see it now, but he *knows* that I'm the darkness in him. In that moment of light, out it came. He *knows*. That's why he had to cut out my heart. He was cutting out the darkness. And if he stays with me—if he stays blind to the truth—I'll destroy him. Just like Fiona said. The bloody puffin heart, Colin. Do you see? I'll never—I'll never get around those words. Do you understand now? Those horrible, horrible words."

Colin just looked at her a moment. Then he patted her on the knee.

"So, what are you gonna do, then, luv?"

Norma sighed. "I don't know exactly," she said. "I'll have to leave Orkney, of course."

"Of course."

"Maybe go somewhere warm." She gave half a laugh. "Maybe Spain."

"Spain sounds nice."

She reached over with one finger and touched the tiny golden puffin on the top of the tiny tree.

"You know what I'd like to do, though?"

"What?"

"Maybe go to the Shetlands—"

"Oh, aye, the Shetlands are real sunny this time of year."

Norma thumped him. "I mean in the spring. To see the puffins, you know, more'n twelve of them? That's what this trip was all about in the first place—I wanted to see a whole buttload of puffins."

"And to find yourself."

She looked at him. "Well, for a while there," she said, "I thought I had. Now I'm—I guess I'm just . . ."

"Lost in the dark?"

Colin reached up to Norma's face with his thumb and wiped first under one eye and then the other.

"I came here to ask you something," he said.

"What?"

"Marion's having the gang over for dinner tomorrow evening. We're having roast goose, plum pudding, Christmas crackers with funny hats—the works. Do you think you could come with me?"

"Oh, Colin."

"You weren't planning on running away tonight, were you? Take the red-eye to Madrid?"

"I'll come," Norma said. "I shouldn't just curl up in a ball and die, right?"

∞

Later that night, Brian called.

"I love you," was the first thing he said, his voice all gravelly.

Norma reconsidered the curling up in a ball idea, then said,"Hi."

"I've been thinking about this," he said.

Yeah, you and me both.

"I want to do it right. You know, pursue my love with honor?"

He waited.

"Okay."

"I want more than anything to come see you tonight—"

"Brian—"

"To touch your skin—"

"Brian—"

"But, I want to do things right." Pause. "That's why I'm going to see Fiona first. I'm going to tell her. Tomorrow. And break it off."

"On Christmas Eve?"

"Shit. I hadn't—no, it's gotta be, I can't put it off."

"Brian, maybe you should give it a few days. Really. Besides, I think we need—some space, you know? To be sure this is right."

"Don't start with that, luv. It's not workin' for me. I know it's right. You know it's right, too."

Okay.

"Norma?"

"Good night, Brian."

"First, tell me you love me."

"I do," Norma said, "I do love you."

Norma shut her phone, went to her narrow bed, and cried herself to sleep.

CHAPTER 27

Norma sat, wearing her stupid paper crown, feeling not the least bit of cheer. She was faking it pretty well. At least she hoped so.

Marion had taken her aside at the start of the evening and assured her that nobody knew what was going on. Norma then pointed out that Marion obviously knew—and then Marion assured her that Colin had given her only the briefest of outlines, and then she handed Norma an eggnog laced liberally with rum.

The rum wasn't helping. Neither was Colin, with his obvious condescension.

"Stop pretending that you're not humoring me," she had hissed at him when they were alone in the kitchen slicing up the plum pudding.

"All right, Norma," he said.

"Stop it," she hissed again.

He hadn't stopped, of course, and everyone else was so bloody full of Christmas fucking spirit. Norma wondered if she should just pack up tomorrow and leave on the first southbound ferry. To hell with the whole bloody island.

Everyone was looking at her expectantly.

What?

"Read your joke, Norma," said Bryce. He was wearing a green bow tie that had flashing red holly berries. "You're the last one."

"Oh, right," said Norma. "Heh." She unfurled the little wad of pink paper in her hand.

" 'What do you get if you cross a kangaroo with an octopus, a sheep, and a zebra?' "

Everyone at the table said, "What?"

"A striped, woolly jumper with eight sleeves."

Everyone roared with laughter.

Norma didn't get it. Then she did—right, jumper—kangaroo, but it was too late. The laughter had died down. She felt her chin begin to quiver.

Colin took her elbow, "Hey, luv, how about helping me with more nog?"

Norma got up from the table but took her red cloth napkin with her. By the time they reached the kitchen she was in full tears.

"I'm sorry, Colin," she said.

"Don't be," he said. "That was a pretty bad joke."

Norma smiled and wiped at her face with the napkin.

"You're gonna get through this, you know."

"I'm going to leave," Norma said, "without seeing Brian again. I've decided."

Colin took her arm. Roughly.

"Colin!"

He was actually angry. He started to speak, but Alberta's gray head suddenly poked into the doorway.

"Norma?" she said sweetly.

Norma looked around and Colin let go of her arm.

"Do you think I could speak with you a minute?"

"Sure," Norma said. She looked at Colin, and he gave a little shrug.

Norma left the kitchen, and Alberta took her down the hall and into Marion's bedroom.

"I wanted to speak to you privately," Alberta said. She patted the bed. "Sit down."

Norma did.

"First, I want to apologize."

Norma looked at her in surprise. "Whatever for?"

"Well," said Alberta. "I snooped."

Norma got a sinking feeling. Alberta had found the file.

"I found your file."

"Alberta," Norma said, "I'm the one who should apologize. I came to you under false pretenses. I—"

"Nonsense," said Alberta. "You have been a tremendous help. I am only bringing this up because—well, here."

There was a carpetbag by the bed. Alberta opened it and brought out a little black-and-white photo. She put it on Marion's chenille bedspread.

Norma studied it. It was a bit out of focus. Two girls—teenagers—were standing arm in arm in front of a building. Norma recognized it as Saint Magnus Cathedral, in Kirkwall. The girls wore white blouses, calf-length skirts, and white bobby socks rolled down to their ankles. One was a smiling blonde, her hair in a shoulder-length page boy, and the other . . . Norma studied the picture, then looked up at Alberta.

"This is you?" Norma said.

Alberta nodded. "I was nineteen. That photograph was taken in the summer of 1943."

"You were so pretty—" Norma realized her gaffe. "I mean—"

" 'Were' is appropriate," Alberta said. "For heaven's sake, I'm eighty years old."

"And this other girl?" Then Norma looked up again, suddenly understanding.

Alberta was looking her straight in the eyes. She nodded. "She was Brian Burroughs's grandmother."

Norma looked at the picture again. A chill went up her spine. She could see it. Brian. The shape of his face, and, oh God—the girl had his one long dimple.

"You knew her?" A stupid question.

Alberta smiled. "Her name was Irma. Irma Grace Duncan."

"And you've known?"

"Yes, I have known all these years."

Alberta sat down in a cushioned chair across from Marion's bed. She folded her hands.

"I thought I would take the knowledge with me to the grave. But now it is time, I think, for the truth."

Norma looked at Alberta in amazement, then down at the picture again.

"Irma came to the Islands in 1942. She was sixteen years old. She was from Coventry. Her family—her mother, father, two sisters—had all been killed in the horrendous bombing that occurred early in the war. She had a brother, in the RAF, but he, too, was killed."

"That's terrible."

"Irma had distant cousins in Kirkwall with whom she came to stay. My father and I lived four houses down on the opposite side of the street. My own mother had died when I was quite young, and Irma became the sister I never had."

Alberta's little blue eyes were glistening with tears. She gave a little sigh and went on.

"We saw Demetrio, for the first time, just a few months after that picture was taken. Demetrio Gianella. I can still hear her say that name in her little singsong voice as she danced around the room. 'Demetrio Gianella. Demetrio Gianella.' They were so pretty together—oh, dear."

Alberta paused for a moment with her eyes closed, then opened them.

"Irma lived in a house with a big surrounding backyard wall. Her guardians were two old women—her distant cousins, like I said. Irma, she was slight, but she was a bit of a tomboy and liked to climb the wall and sit in a vine-covered alcove formed from two big stones that had given way—at the very top, at the intersection of three stone walls. From this perch, which was quite hidden, she could see what was going on in the street beyond and in three different yards of the houses behind hers. I would climb up there with her some days, though I was kind of prissy myself and it would take a lot of coaxing on her part."

Norma smiled.

"So on that one day we saw Demetrio down below. He was very—what is it the young people say?—Demetrio was 'hunky.' He was so unusual for Orkney, of course, with his olive skin and his thick black hair. But it was not just that. He was simply a beautiful man. I will never forget that day. He was down in the yard catty-corner to where Irma lived and he had brought out four ladder-back chairs. He came striding out of the house with both of his arms strung with noodles. They were long and flat and a wonderful golden yellow. Like he had cut off the hair of Rapunzel, Irma said. We just giggled and giggled with our hands over our mouths. Then he strung the noodles on the backs of the chairs—to dry, of course, but we thought at the time we were witnessing some exotic ritual. We did not know he was from the camps. Not until later. He had on white pants and a white shirt, with a long white apron tied around his waist. The sleeves were rolled up and we could see the muscles of his arms."

Alberta put her hand to her bosom.

"Oh, dear," she said. "Forgive me, Freddie, but I must have been a little in love with him myself."

She gave another little sigh. "That first day, everything was so innocent. Irma—oh, she was bold! She plucked some small black berries from the vine on the wall, and every time his back was turned she would pitch one down so it bounced off the top of his head. *Pop!* He would stop and look up to the sky, all puzzled, shake his head, then go about arranging his noodles again. Then *pop!*

"Finally, she popped one too many times. He did not look up that time but stood there, and when she raised another berry, he whirled around, pointed his finger right at us, and said, 'Aha!'

"I thought I would die, but Irma went ahead and threw the berry and it landed square between his eyes."

Norma was laughing, and Alberta laughed, too.

"My goodness," she said. "It's been so long—oh, poor Irma. Poor, poor Irma. Anyway, he came over, shaking his fist—speaking out a long string of Italian curses—and then he saw her. I was pretty, but—well, you see there in the picture. He looked at Irma with his dark, dark eyes, and held up his hands like he was beseeching her. *'Tormentatrice bella,'* he said. Beautiful tormentor."

"Oh, jeez," Norma said, "that is so romantic."

"Yes, it was. The two of them—at that moment—just linked."

"Did he speak any English?"

"A little—but it was no matter. They needed very few words.

"I had no idea, at first, what was happening between them. But later Irma confessed everything and swore me to secrecy. Actually, she didn't confess everything. My goodness, at that time I hardly knew what intercourse was. Just the fact that she was kissing him was shock enough for me. I was caught up in the romance and daring of it all. As for consequences, well, we lived with too many consequences. So much hatred, so much death, destruction, fear—were the Nazis going to parachute right into our very front yards? I wish I had been wiser—I wish I could have warned her—but such is life, such is life."

Alberta picked up the picture.

"One day Irma came to me, completely distraught and yet blissfully happy. Demetrio that day had sworn his love, but then he told her that they had to stop seeing each other. He would come no more to Kirkwall. She begged him, but he was firm. After the war, when he had his honor back, he would return and court her—court her properly, he said. She deserved no less. Then—well, you know this part, do you not? I found *The Orcadian* open to the article."

Norma nodded.

"Two weeks later, he was dead. It was horrible. Just a horrible tragedy, but that was just the beginning. It was a month before Irma could find out the truth she dreaded to learn. She was frantic, absolutely frantic, and yet she dared not give herself away. She and I—we bicycled out to the little graveyard, finally. When she saw his name on the little wooden cross, she screamed and threw herself on the grave. I had no comfort to give her. I just stood there helpless as she tore at her hair and beat at the cold black sods of peat. She lay there finally, exhausted and voiceless, and I went to her. She looked up at me and whispered, 'I would join him, you know, but I'm carrying Demetrio's baby.' "

"My God, Alberta," Norma said.

"She was proud. Determined. She said they were married in the eyes of God. And they were. I've never doubted for a minute that they were."

"And no one ever knew?"

"We kept it secret. We were foolish girls, thinking that we could. No one knew. Not until the end, and by then it was too late. My father was a physician. The old-fashioned kind. With a heart. I made Irma promise that when the time came, she would go to him. But, in the end, I think she was just so afraid they would take the baby from her. I am not sure, you see—I have never known exactly what happened the night that Irma had Demetrio's baby. The night she died."

"She died?"

Alberta nodded.

"She came to the house. My home. It was midnight. She had taken her cousins' ancient old automobile, God knows where she got the petrol. What had gone through her mind, the decisions she had made, all the wrong decisions. Well, I came rushing down the stairs. My father was already at the door. Irma was in his arms—her skirt just soaked in blood. I ran to her—'Where's the baby—the baby?' "

Alberta closed her eyes. Her voice had become once again nineteen.

"I thought she was already dead, but then she looked up at my father, then at me, and Irma's last words were, 'She is with Mary and Jesus.' "

Norma reached out, took Alberta's hand, and squeezed it. Alberta looked at her, her face crinkled in memory and pain.

"I told my father what had happened. Everything. He never spoke a word of blame. We thought—we thought she meant the baby had died, too. That she had miscarried. Irma was soaking wet and covered in mud. We thought she had de-livered the baby in a field, and buried it there. It was dreadful."

Alberta was crying now. Norma, too. Norma squeezed her hand again, then noticed Marion standing at the door with a box of tissues.

"Alberta told me this afternoon," Marion said, passing the box around. "She wasn't sure if she should tell you."

"I'm glad you did," Norma said. "Did you tell her about Brian?"

Alberta nodded.

"Good. I mean—I can tell him this, right? You want him to know?"

"Yes, I want him to know," said Alberta. "He has the right. He's always had the right, and I've just come to understand that. And it's nothing to be ashamed of, is it? It's a beautiful story. A beautiful story of love."

This set off another round of tears and blowing of noses. But Alberta composed herself again and told the rest of the story.

"We—It was a long while before my father and I understood. There were rumors, later, of course—about the baby in the chapel. Everyone knew, but it was never talked about. One day my father drove me out to Lamb Holm. One of the workers had fallen ill, and the camp doctor was away. We knew the truth the minute we saw that beautiful Madonna and Child. The baby was with Mary and Jesus, Irma had said. The meaning was clear. My father had arranged things about Irma. Her cause of death was listed as severe trauma as a result of an automobile accident. There were no questions, no one made the connections, and the mystery of the chapel baby endured. There is a marker in the Kirkwall cemetery for Irma, but that was not her final resting place. Father had her cremated, and we took the ashes out, secretly, and spread them on Demetrio's grave."

They were all silent for a minute, all three of them dabbing at their eyes. Then Alberta said quietly in a singsong voice, "Demetrio Gianella, Demetrio Gianella." Then she gave one last sigh. "I am glad I told you. It feels right."

"It's odd," Norma said. "After all this. Brian's grandmother was from Coventry and his grandfather from Milan. He has no Orkney heritage at all."

"Oh, no," Alberta piped up. "There you're wrong. Irma was born in Coventry, but—here, let me show you." She reached into her carpetbag and pulled out a sheaf of papers. "I printed these out just yesterday." She spread them out with her papery hands across the bed.

Seven sheets, pieced together, forming a huge branching family tree.

"You see," Alberta said. "Irma's grandfather, there," she pointed, "went to Scotland in 1887. Her father—here—moved to Coventry in 1915. But before that . . ." She moved her hand up the branches of the tree. "See, Irma was descended from a very ancient line of Orcadians. I can trace the family all the way back to Norway, itself, to 425 A.D."

```
            Heytir Gorrsson
             born Abt 0425
          Of, Raumsdal, Norway
```

"Wow."

"And look at this," said Marion. She was tracing her finger down the line of descendants. "Six fifty. Heytir's grandson was Sveide the 'Sea King' Sviadrasson."

"That's right," said Alberta. "Irma Duncan and her grandson are both descended from a line of Norse Viking kings."

"Oh, my God," Norma said. She was staring at the listing six names down.

```
       Thorfinn I Rollo (Brico)
   "Hausakliffer" ("Skull-Splitter")
             Einarsson
           born about 0890
       Orkney Islands, Scotland
```

```
died after 0977
buried Burial Mound, Hoxa,
Ronaldsay, Scotland
```

She pointed.

"Is that—is that the guy on the beer?"

Marion laughed. "Yes, he is, dear," she said. "Orkney is covered with his famous descendants. Even our own Saint Magnus—am I right, Bertie?"

"Yes." Alberta was nodding. "Magnus is not on this chart, though. See, Irma's connection—and Mr. Burroughs's, of course, is through Thorfinn's youngest daughter." She pointed. "We don't even have her name, as you can see, but she was married into this Orkney branch here. The branch barely survived, but they managed to keep going, until finally there was only Irma's family—all killed in the war. And these distant cousins, both of whom, as you can see, remained unmarried."

"And now there is only Brian," Norma said.

"Yes, indeed," said Marion. "Connecting Europe through his genes all the way from the crown of Norway to the boot of Italy."

There was a knock on the door.

"It's Freddie and me," said Colin from the other side. "Can we break up this hen party?"

∞

On the drive home neither Norma nor Colin spoke for the first mile. Then Colin finally did.

"I know you expect me to apologize for grabbing your arm like that," he said, "but I ain't gonna do it."

"Colin—"

"Being in love with a woman who's in love with another man isn't what you'd call a bed of roses."

"Colin—"

"No. Let me say what I've got to say. Being Brian's champion and your best pal is beginning to suck. Big-time. And now with your damn foolery—Norma, you've *got* him, you've won the man's heart. Your goddamn fates have interwoven, woman—I can't stand by and let you just chuck it all down the damn privy hole—"

"Colin!"

He looked at her.

"Something happened tonight."

"Something to do with that hen party?"

"Alberta knew. She's known for sixty years. And tonight she told me. Colin, I've found out who Brian's grandmother was! Isn't it wonderful?"

He considered this for a moment. "Is it?" he said. "Is it wonderful?"

"I think so," Norma said. "I—I'd love to tell you, you know. I'm bursting to scream it from the rooftops. But, you understand, don't you?"

"You want Brian to know first."

"Yes."

"Norma, please tell me you've come to your senses."

"Colin," Norma put her hand on his, "you have to trust me, okay? I see everything quite clearly now."

Colin looked at her again. "Why doesn't that reassure me?"

And he had every reason to worry.

CHAPTER 28

Norma spent Christmas morning making arrange-
ments. Then she turned off her cell phone and put it
in with the rest of her luggage. She looked around the little
cottage for the last time, then closed the blue door behind
her. The key, she had slipped into Anne's purse the night before.

She was down to Plan Z, and since it *was* the very last
plan, it had appropriately occurred to her in one great blind-
ing flash of insight as she sat on the pink chenille bedspread in
Marion's bedroom.

Norma drove her battered Golf across Mainland and
reached Kirkwall by midday. The streets were deserted. Everything was closed. Everyone was home enjoying Christmas
Day with their loved ones. She sat in her car outside Fiona's
flat and ate her simple lunch of bread and cheese. Fiona's red
sports car was parked right in front of her, two wheels on the
curb.

Norma waited until she felt good and Zenlike, then got

her shoulder bag, got out of the car, and went to Fiona's door.

She knocked, but there was no answer.

She knocked again.

She knocked a third time, and this time said, "Fiona, it's Norma Dale."

She heard footsteps.

The door opened, and Fiona was in front of her in all of her fury.

"Fuck you," Fiona said. "Fuck you."

Fiona was a mess. Her hair uncombed. Red, red eyes. She had on mismatched pajamas and a tatty bathrobe. Her clenched fist held a wad of overused tissues. She almost wasn't beautiful.

"Fuck you," Fiona repeated, just in case the first two hadn't been clear.

"Fiona, I need to talk to you," Norma said. "Please. It's important."

Fiona just stood there.

"I'm leaving Orkney," Norma said. "For good."

That got her. Fiona stepped back from the door. She was wary, but interested.

Norma stepped in. The room was furnished tastefully, modern things. Flat tailored couches, smooth chairs with smooth holes in odd places. White paper lamps like so many skillfully sculpted hornet nests.

Norma took in a breath. *Ah, jeez.* She could smell him. Brian. How long ago had he left? Oh, well. She wanted to get this over with. She put her shoulder bag on a tasteful white plastic cube.

Fiona shut the door.

"First let me say, Fiona, that I think you were right. About me. About Brian. It's hard for me. You can imagine how hard, to admit this. Second, I want to be honest. I have no re-grets about what happened. Brian and I—"

Fiona went for her. Claws out, teeth bared, full glory of a woman scorned.

Norma managed to grab Fiona's wrists. Zen went right out the window.

"Listen, you stupid bitch," Norma yelled, "I'm leaving him! *Comprende?* I'm outta here and Brian can be yours on a silver platter if you'll just take the plug outta your ass and *listen*!"

Fiona jerked her hands away. She glared and said, "Maybe I don't fucking want him anymore."

"Oh, you want him," Norma said. "We both know that, and I've got what you need to get him back."

"What are you talking about?"

Norma went to her shoulder bag. She opened it and got the roll of Alberta's printouts.

"This," Norma said. "Brian's Orkney roots. His grand-mother's name all the way back 1,579 years to Heytir Gorrs-son sitting on some ice throne in Norway. Do you get it? Do you know what this means?"

Fiona stepped forward, red-rimmed lapis lazulis wide.

"Let me see."

Norma handed her the papers. "The last sheet there, handwritten, it's the story of his grandmother. Her name was Irma, by the way, Irma Grace Duncan."

"Duncan?" Fiona said. "The Duncans of Sandwick?"

"No—the Duncans of Coventry. But don't worry. Brian's got plenty of Orkney cred. Plenty. More than you, most likely."

Fiona was scanning the papers, one by one. The deep blue of her eyes glittered.

"Thorfinn Einarsson? Oh, my God, he's—"

"Yes," Norma said, "Brian is a Skullsplitter. Happy?"

Fiona's glittery eyes focused on Norma again. "This is incredible," she said. "I don't understand. Why are you giving this to me of all people?"

Norma had promised herself she wouldn't cry. Fat lot of good that did. Two big ol' tears dribbled down her cheeks.

"Promise me one thing," Norma said. "After he gets through this, let him paint, okay? Let him paint the true stuff."

Then Norma retrieved her shoulder bag and walked out the door.

∞

The drive to Hoy was the hardest. Being so close. Norma stood next to Betty Corrigall's grave for the longest time. She almost called him. Twice she went to the car to dig out her cell phone. Twice she tramped back to the grave. She knew that if she heard his voice she would never be able to go. So she finally got the envelope out of her pocket. She'd put it in a plastic bag—not very romantic, no, but just in case he didn't come here right away. She pictured him there—just to torture herself one last little bit—opening the envelope, getting out the folded card, and reading the two inadequate words of good-bye.

The plastic bag was a good idea, too. Four days it took him. It rained every one, and for the record, he didn't take it very well.

CHAPTER 29

Norma never made it to Spain. She went to France. She went to Portugal. She went to Switzerland. She even went to Cyprus for a while.

She was fucking miserable.

She kept waiting for the great release. For the amazing karma to kick in after the really swell thing she'd done. Nada. She felt hollow and stupid and utterly, utterly alone. Somewhere around Istanbul, she convinced herself that she had still done the right thing. That the right thing was *supposed* to feel so lousy—otherwise doing the right thing would be easy. And we'd all be living in a utopian paradise.

Spring came in like a North Ronaldsay lamb, and Norma's fancy turned north. She decided to go to the Shetland Islands and do the puffin thing.

No stopover in Orkney, though. No sirree Bob.

(Though she'd had a brief but wrenching Brian-soaked fantasy at the British Airways counter.)

The Shetlands were pretty spectacular. Norma tried to

appreciate it, but with her equilibrium somewhere between blah and kill-me-now, it was increasingly difficult.

The puffin season was definitely in full swing, however, and Norma dutifully booked passage on a puffin tour. The largest colonies could be found on either Fair Isle or Foula. Norma picked the latter because it most matched her mood.

So, four months after leaving Orkney (and, oh yeah, Brian) Norma found herself 12,000 feet above sea level on a breathtaking cliff overlooking the blue churning North Atlantic. Unfortunately, even 100,000 clowns of the sea failed to bring her cheer. Fifty thousand mating pairs of Tammie Nories and one sullen, single Norma.

"I screwed up, Daddy," Norma said to the wind. "I'm sorry."

She had been there for hours. All the other tourists were long gone. She suspected that the tour boat had left without her. She didn't care. Another would come along. If not, she could just dig a burrow somewhere and crawl in.

Norma heard her stomach growl. Okay, okay, fine. She'd packed a lunch. Cold kidney pie, vinegar crisps, and just for cruelty's sake she'd bought herself a Skullsplitter ale. She got the bottle from her pack and stared at the proud man with the raven's wings on his hat.

"Drinkin' my ancestor's brew are ya, woman?"

Norma smiled. That's just what Brian would have said, too. Then she twigged. He *had* said it.

Norma turned with unbelieving eyes.

Brian Burroughs was standing there on the cliffside, the sun behind his wild black toss of hair like a nimbus of righteousness.

"Oh, my God," Norma said.

Brian came to her in three strides, stripping off his backpack and Windbreaker and throwing them to the ground.

He took her face in his long pale fingers and kissed her, hard.

Norma dropped the bottle of ale and put her hands to his back, his neck, then up into his mass of hair. He kissed her again on the mouth and then kissed down her throat. He pulled off her T-shirt and then her bra, grabbed her breasts, and kissed them hungrily, one then the other. Norma grabbed his shirt with both hands and ripped—the buttons flew—and pressed herself to his skin, his beautiful, beautiful skin. Her pants were next. She tugged at his, then he just ripped off her panties and threw them to the blue Shetland sky.

Then he was in her, Brian in Norma, just where he belonged. He lay her against the ground, one arm behind her, holding her, and looked her in the eyes.

"Hear these words, Norma," he said fiercely, "hear this truth—thank the gods, thank Fate herself, that it's you." He was trembling, holding himself back. "Do you *hear* me, luv, *do you*?"

Norma was crying, nodding her head. She pulled him to her, bursting with joy.

∞

They lay naked, in each other's arms, at the top of the world. Two puffins were picking at the grass nearby, eyeing them with caution.

Brian got up on one elbow. "Your hair's grown longer," he said. "Your beautiful hair." Then he reached over to his pants and pulled something from his pocket. It was a folded card. He opened it and showed her the two inadequate words.

" 'Forgive me,' " he read. Then he looked at her. "Forgive me?"

"Oh, Brian—"

"You know I almost killed myself that day. When I found this. I'd been to Edinburgh, I'd been to London, I'd tried to call your mother—did you know that? Do you know how many Dales there *are* in your country?"

"Brian, I'm so—"

"Do you know what stopped me? I had the rope, just needed to pick out the croftin' barn—but you know what stopped me? Anger. Raw anger. And the drinkin' was no damn good anymore. I'd done that the last time, remember? Drinkin' only reminded me of you."

Norma turned her head away, but he turned it back.

"Oh, no, you have to look at me," he said. "You *hurt* me, Norma, and that's what made me angriest—that you could."

"I thought," she said, "I thought—I guess I thought that it would hurt you even more if I stayed. But—I was so wrong. I know that now. I've known it all these months, but I was too stubborn, too damn stupid to admit it to my-self."

"And in the meantime, Brian gets to go through the tor-tures of Hell."

Norma touched along the side of his face.

"I'm so sorry," she said, her voice gone all small. "Can you ever forgive—" She stopped, pulled her hand from his face to cover her eyes. "Goddamn it, Brian—I should have known, shouldn't I? I wrote those two little stupid words al-ready knowing I was wrong."

Brian pulled her hand away. Relentless.

"Fiona was the worst of it," he said. "The way you did that. Very clever of you, really. You'll be pleased to know it worked pretty well for a while. My anger drove me back to her, of course, and she was waitin' there with those lovely open arms. That yellow hair of hers, those eyes, the hot com-fort of her body . . ."

Norma took it. She deserved this.

"So, for a while there, I even did forgive what you'd done. I started fallin' for it—all that nonsense—all you'd left me with, that nonsense about dark and light. About Fiona bein' good for me and you bein' bad. 'Cause Fiona had changed—it was overwhelmin', you could say, the change. The subtle shifts in the manner of her regard—like, she took me to meet her parents, that was something, don't you think?"

"Well, she—she could, then, right?" Norma said. "With—With the truth about you coming out?"

Brian looked at her. "You see," he said, "that was the problem. The truth about me hadn't come out."

"But—But I—"

"Oh, my little selkie—that had been your intention. But Fiona kept the truth about my grand lineage all to her selfish little self."

Norma sat up. Flabbergasted. "She—she did? She *did*?"

A gust of wind made Norma shiver. Brian sat up, got his shirt, and put it around her shoulders.

"I—I don't understand. How could she not tell you?"

"She liked havin' it—the power—her knowin' and me not."

"But that's—that's so . . ."

"Dark?"

Norma looked at him. "How did you—I mean, you *know*, don't you? About Irma? About Irma and Demetrio?"

"Yes, I know all of it," Brian said. "Thanks to Alberta. Kind, little Alberta Sinclair. She came to me in March—a little over four weeks ago. She'd read about our weddin'—Fiona's and mine—and she'd come to the flat to apologize, of all things, to apologize for keepin' the secret so long."

But Norma hadn't heard anything past "weddin'."

"Oh, God, Brian—you—you married her?"

Brian's black eyes flashed. "You were playin' with the burnin' flames, girl, didn't you understand that? Yes, I married the bitch, I married her. I loved her—don't you remember tellin' me that? Her and her fine new passion."

Norma started to cry. She reached for him, then stopped. She hadn't the right, really, had she?

But Brian grabbed her. He kissed her again. Held her close and stroked her hair.

"Ah, Christ, that was cruel of me," he said, "lettin' you know like that. I wanted to hurt you, Norma, I admit it. But hurtin' you just turns back on me, doesn't it? I'm sorry, I'm so sorry."

"No, I'm sorry," Norma sobbed back, "I'm sorry."

They went on like that for a while, crying and apologizing. The puffin couple up the way started to look downright disgusted. Then Brian reached for his pants again and got out his clean white handkerchief. Dried Norma's tears, kissed both her eyelids and then the tip of her nose.

"It was a marriage under false pretenses," Brian said. "Do you understand that, my love? In the eyes of the gods, I'm married to you."

Norma smiled through her tears.

He held up his hand.

"See? No ring. I flushed it down the loo just like Trey Bliss's button."

Norma opened her mouth. "How?"

"Colin," said Brian. "I owe that man everything. He tried to tell me, right after you'd left. Tried to knock some sense into my head. I acted like an asshole—I was kinda hittin' my angry peak then—tried to twist how he loved you—anyway, I didn't listen to him. I went blindly back to Fiona. Then a few months later I got the visit from Bertie Sinclair."

"Oh, Brian," Norma said, "Alberta told you—I mean, that I knew?"

"I was just completely in shock, you know, and totally confused."

"And you thought—"

"That you'd left knowin' without tellin' me. Aye. That was pretty much the bottom of the pit."

"You must have hated me."

"No," Brian said, "that was the strange part about it. It made no sense at all for you to do that. I knew then. I knew something was not right—so, of course, the first thing I did was turn to my lovin' bride."

"Did she tell you the truth?"

"She didn't have to. I knew she knew the minute I brought the subject up. The ugliness of it hit me like a brick-bat. The woman loved me—if I can even use that term—she loved me *more* for it. Bein' descended from kings. It was like she'd been drivin' around in a Volkswagen, pretendin' to be one of the people, then, you know, suddenly got behind the wheel of a shiny new Rolls-Royce."

Norma started to laugh, then shook her head. "Oh, jeez, Brian—"

"No," he said. "It's funny. It is *now.* Then, I wanted to strangle her dead. She finally confessed how you had come to her on Christmas. She gave it her best shot, then. Tried to blame you. Tried to blame both of us. Sayin' she'd been waitin' to make sure you weren't comin' back. But I knew. I knew why she'd done it. I left her that same day. Moved back to Hoy, back to my studio. Not that I was gettin' any paintin' done. I think I must have sat there for like a solid week, turnin' slowly to a standin' stone. Then Colin came. He brought ale. And advice. And a ticket for the Shetlands."

"To the—but how did he know I'd be here?"

"Trigonometry, I think. He's real good with those spherical triangles, relations, and such. Plus, you told him, of course. That helped. And he had a lot more faith in you than I did. And connections. Like his aunt Marion's first husband, still on good terms, who works for the puffin tours booking agency. He'd had you traced, see?"

"Colin," Norma said.

"Look, see this?" Brain pointed to some faint bruising on his chin. "Colin did that, too."

"He punched you?"

"That's right. Finally got to knock some sense into me. Told me that if I didn't go find you, then he bloody well would. Then he told me about your prom night. About that twit Trey Bliss. About how my stupid fuckin' words had penetrated to the core of your pain and made you go crazy on me. Made you leave me, Norma, just when I'd found you. You won't do that again, will you? Leave me?"

Norma shook her head no.

"Promise?"

"I promise."

Then several hundred puffins took off from the cliff in a flurry of orange, black, and white. Tourists. The sound of tourists nearby.

Laughing, Brian and Norma got back into what was left of their clothes. Brian fetched his backpack.

"I brought you some things," he said.

He sat back on one heel and opened the flap of his pack. "First this."

He pulled out a rolled-up canvas, started to unroll it, and Norma's heart skipped a beat as the first stone of the Ring o' Brodgar came into view.

"This was my first official paintin' after comin' to my senses," he said, "or repaintin', I should say. See? I fixed it."

And he had. The sixty stones were still there. But Betty Corrigall was gone, as was Russell. Brian was out of his Druid suit and Norma was out of her chains. She was still naked, though, as was Brian. They sat together on the broad flat stone, whole and good, and everywhere, like in some color-ful happy Hitchcock movie that had never been filmed, were perched puffins. On all the various megaliths. On the ground. On Norma's shoulders. On Brian's head. Clean, happy, won-derful puffins, not a one of them bloody.

He grinned, showing his dimple.

"Pretty prescient, don't you think?"

"Oh, Brian—"

"And there's this."

Next from the pack came Norma's midnight-blue crushed-velvet hippie dress. It was clean again, all soft and folded and tied with a green ribbon.

"It's your selkie skin," he said. "And I give it back to you. I don't want to possess you, Norma, understand? I want to be your partner, and you be mine."

Norma took the dress.

Brian reached into the pack.

"And this."

It was a little stuffed puffin. Not her old Tammie Nories. It was new. The tag still attached to its fat orange feet.

Norma took the puffin in her hands.

∞

So that's it then. Where it ends. Not for Norma and Brian, of course. They went on for many, many years in their little crofting cottage on Hoy. And Fate . . . well, Fate sighed and then opened up that scary ancient book of hers and dipped the nib of her raven's feather deep into the ancient well of black and crusty ink.

The word she wrote in her scary scrolling script was, thank goodness, *Happily.*

Then, *Ever After.*

ABOUT THE AUTHOR

NANCY BAXTER lives in Austin, Texas. *Norma Ever After* is her first novel.

ABOUT THE TYPE

This book was set in Bembo, a
typeface based on an old-style
Roman face that was used for Cardinal
Bembo's tract *De Aetna* in 1495.
Bembo was cut by Francisco Griffo
in the early-sixteenth century. The
Lanston Monotype Machine
Company of Philadelphia brought
the well-proportioned letter forms
of Bembo to the United States in
the 1930s.